C000096539

THOSE WHO FEAR US

Anthony Estrada

Printed in the United States of America
Published in Hellertown, PA
Cover design by Christina Gaugler

ISBN 978-1-958711-96-5
Library of Congress Control Number 2023922979

For more information or to place bulk orders, contact the author or the publisher at Jennifer@BrightCommunications.net.

Bright
COMMUNICATIONS

To Dad and Mom,
who showed me every day, in every way,
how to meet fear with love.

CHAPTER ONE

Eric

I think death was the best thing Carlos could hope for and the thing he wanted the most.

Holding the tears back—along with a flood of memories in each drop—I stand here wondering if maybe death was what Carlos needed in order to see life anew.

He had a son. He had a wife. Both of whom he pushed away. Or maybe they were responsible for the separation. I don't know. I'm still trying to make sense of it myself.

But when I think of Sergeant Carlos Lopez, I think of hope. It's all I can think of for now. All I can muster in the blazing, hot sun, though I need to continue on.

Continue on. One of the greatest lessons he would leave me with.

I'm starting to get it now. I'm starting to understand why he had to go.

There was hope in him leaving.

There was hope in death.

Death—not physical—but a death of ideals, a death of code, and a death of laws. All things Carlos believed in. Things he spent his life protecting, both for the communities he served, and most importantly, for himself.

Maybe it was all self-preservation. Though, I like to think not.

Did he do it for his own edification? I don't know. Was it his ego that ended it for him? Probably. Did he find peace or is he still looking for it? I think both can be true.

Those are things I will always want to know.

There is one thing I now know to be true: Carlos Lopez showed me how to love.

And how he went out was the only way he knew how to show it.

CHAPTER TWO

Carlos

Pop. Pop. Pop.

Three cracks in the windshield and flashes of white light made me slam on the brakes of the Crown Vic.

I grabbed Jimmy's head and pushed it down to the seat, his nose punching keys into the computer. I tried to keep the car from slamming into the wall where City Terrace had just laid claim to their new territory, the loud screeching of the brakes surely waking up everyone who had contemplated still sleeping.

The bullets whizzed by. Each snap—the sound barrier broken—struck a new sense of fear inside of me. I called it in. "Suspect has an automatic rifle. Ten thirty-three! Repeat. Officers in need of help!"

Saying this now sends chills down my spine.

"Ten thirty-three, go! You're on the patch," the female dispatcher's voice called over the radio.

Jimmy's head laid in my lap as we stayed huddled over each other. "Partner, I'm flattered. But, not on a first date," Jimmy joked as we struggled to take off our seatbelts and get out of the car.

"Jimmy, we're going to get out on the driver's side door."

"Copy that, Partner."

Pop. Pop.

Each pop and puncture of the windshield was a reminder of our certain demise if we stayed in there much longer. We crawled, staying below the dashboard, until we hit the ground. It was our only chance at survival.

I feared I wasn't ever going to kiss my wife when I got home again. The thirty minutes before Eric got up, before I hit the pillow, before Sandy went off to the hospital, those were ours. All of it was about to be taken away in the flash of a muzzle.

I never was going to see my son become everything he ever wanted to be. He never understood how much I loved this job. How much I loved being a police officer. How much I loved him.

But his understanding is something I can't control. I see that now.

Once I resigned myself to the fact that I was as good as dead, I knew I had to do everything in my power to make sure when I went, this son of a bitch was going down with me.

I needed to go out on my terms. My way.

Isn't that the bitch of it? The more we seem to want to control life, the more it fights back.

I liked fighting back. Maybe it was the reason this all happened. It's too late, but I'm trying to take accountability for it now.

Accountability. Ha.

The sound of bullets was amplified by the graffiti-covered walls, each shot closing in on us. Our five department-issued Beretta 9mm 92 FS were no match for one AK-47 shooting armor-piercing 7.62 mm rounds at 670 meters a second.

Other Devil Dogs and I had seen them in Kuwait in the hands of Saddam's minions. At least we had tanks. Airstrikes. The US government. Those weapons belonged in some foreign country, in some foreign war, not in the hands of a twenty-three-year-old Mexican gangbanger in the back alleys of East Los Angeles. The only thing we had to protect us was each other.

The high beams of the gangbanger's bullet-riddled, dirt-covered white 1994 Grand Caravan made the shooter a shadowy figure, from which he unleashed death at 600 rounds a minute. All we could do was launch a volley of what might as well have been David slinging pebbles at Goliath.

David had God. We didn't. He wouldn't have survived at the intersection of Cesar Chavez and Kern that night, or any night for that matter. God wasn't coming to save us. Grocery store candles on street corners with Jesus and Mary on the front of them lit the way for some poor soul's journey home.

East LA made us all doubt the very existence of God.

Us? We were the beacon of hope.

To think this is what Cesar Chavez fought for—these tattoo-ladened, wife beater-wearing, dope-slingin', sorry excuses for

Latinos. They're not like us. Those of us who worked hard to gain respect in society. These are the ones who gave us bad names. They tried to bring Mexico to America. They're the reason why all these activists still think we get no respect in society. We all know the truth of the world. Some just make more excuses than others.

I worked to get everything I wanted. I earned my beautiful lawn and the Craftsman mower I mowed it with. I earned the right to take my kid to Little League.

They had bottles of Olde English in their hands and their kids were smoking weed at age six. I saw it every time I walked into one of those houses to serve a warrant—the kids sleeping on the floor—God, it pissed me off. They had to. It was sleep on the floor or risk not waking up from a stray bullet through their window. No decency. How could you let your family live like that?

Muzzle flashes created a yellowish-white light and gave me a glimpse of what lay beyond. The cracks were reverberating through the night air, sending any clear thoughts out the window. I could only fall back on my training.

"Drop behind the engine block, throw down covering fire, and pray!" I shouted to Jimmy.

Jimmy took one to the thigh.

Garcia couldn't move out of his car fast enough. The 7.62 ripped through his door and then his carotid artery. I wished I had been the one who was taken. Garcia's family actually loved him.

He was my brother. I had thousands of them all across the country. All of us brothers and sisters serving the blue. Serving the badge. It's a bond and a brotherhood. We stand behind all that is good. Hated the bad apples in the bunch.

We shared moments like this. We were sheepdogs watching over the herds as they slept peacefully at night. No choice but to fight in order to protect the greater good.

Jimmy patched his leg with one hand, held his gun in the other.

"Jimmy."

"A little busy, partner."

"Jimmy."

Jimmy looked over at me. With the cracks of the hundreds of bullets snapping off all around him, I would have expected him to be frazzled. But as he always did, he stayed calm, cool, and collected while he wrapped his leg with bandages from his first aid kit. The white cloth turned crimson at a pace faster than Jimmy could bandage.

I was scared. But I couldn't show it. You're not allowed to. Not here. Not now. Not ever.

"I love you, Jimmy."

"I love you too. I still ain't doing you."

I heard an empty magazine hit the asphalt. This was my chance. I took a deep breath and one last look at the abandoned Al Pastor taco stands, wondering if I'd get another chance to taste the perfect combo of spicy and sweet.

"What do you think you're doing, partner?" Jimmy shouted.

I popped out from behind the engine block. I had the mixture of deep fear and courage in my heart that I had grown accustomed to over sixteen years of policing.

The cholo struggled to reload. He saw me pointing my barrel his way. An easy kill shot. One pull of the trigger.

"Drop it!"

He fumbled the magazine in his hands. He had lost the fragile sense of power he'd held with a fully loaded mag. I felt all that anger, wherever it stemmed from, directed toward us. In all my rides with guys like him in the back of my squad car, they had one simple choice—kill or die. He wasn't going back to prison. Why should he? He wanted to go out on his terms. He refused my command. His death sentence.

"Drop it now!"

The magazine clicked into place. He looked up. I put three 9mm rounds through his chest and took away any sort of future, any misery he felt or was ever going to feel. He dropped to the asphalt, among the broken Modelo bottles and half-smoked joints left behind by teenagers headed toward the same bleak future as him.

You don't forget those things. I would see it every night for the rest of my life. Just like you don't forget watching a lifeless six-year-old floating face down in a pool who'd accidentally fallen in. He had been playing with his baby brother. I'd known at the time that each chest compression and every puff I blew into the kid's lungs were for show. Maybe there'd been some part of me clinging to hope I could save him? That one kept me awake the most.

"Suspect down!" echoed throughout the alley.

A big exhale of relief met the normal ambiance of the warm Southern California summer's air. I was suddenly aware of the traffic going by as if nothing had happened. The red-and-blue lights flashing against the alley wall. Like the world had permission to start again at 00:17.

We'd all earned the right to go home.

Jimmy limped up to the cholo, kicked the AK out of the gangbanger's lifeless hand, and kept his gun pointed at him. You never took the risk of Lazarus rising from the dead, especially when Lazarus had an assault rifle. Ian and Bishop followed right behind, guns still drawn. The power dynamic was back in its rightful place. The cholo held onto his last breaths, his eyes wide open, nothing behind them but a faint cling to whatever life he had left.

Jimmy raised up a four. All clear.

And then one single crack, stronger, louder, hit me harder than the 729 other shots fired earlier in the alley.

It was an execution.

Ian had shot the already downed man point-blank in the head. The bullet perforated his skull, along with any sense of honor I felt.

"We're the fuckin' police. Don't fuck with Fort Comanche," Ian yelled at his lifeless face. Bishop punched Ian in the shoulder. A sign of solidarity in the adrenaline.

"You're the fucking man. That's the shit I'm talking about. You fucked him up." They hugged. Bishop rolled the lifeless body over and cuffed him.

Jimmy and I stared at this cholo's lifeless body.

"You murdered him," I said.

"Come on, Lopez. This is Fort Comanche. We're in this shit together. For life. It's kill or be killed out here. Only the strongest. You know that."

Fort Comanche was the best of the best. To survive East Los Angeles as a cop, or hell, as a civilian, any weak link meant the difference between life and death. It's why any new trainee got the book thrown at them. This wasn't the academy. This was the real thing, 24/7.

There were no more paintball guns. No actors playing make-believe from a script. Just a city's worth of people who didn't want you here. Most of them wanted you dead. We had so many trainees cry. They were too soft. I couldn't stand the ones who cried. But if they could make it past the first two weeks with us, it usually meant they belonged.

Nothing can prepare a person for something like this. They don't teach this shit at the academy.

"I have to report this," I said.

The belly laughs Ian and Bishop let out seared my soul.

"Come on, Lopez. Don't get all high-and-mighty Mexican on us now. You're as white as me and Bishop. You've said it yourself—pieces of shit like this give guys like you a bad name."

"We swore an oath." I shook my head in disbelief.

A bad cop, an unjust cop, went against everything I stood for. We'd never had any problems before. Ian came to my house often. Eric loved when he did. Until Ian took over the PlayStation controller and gamed for longer than Eric did. But I didn't care what ten years of friendship meant. There was the thin blue line, and Ian had crossed it. You put the badge above all. It's black and white.

"If you report this, it's all gone. We couldn't let this fucker back on the streets. He spends three years in county and then he's back at it. Doing this again. Putting us in danger. Leaving our families behind, just like Garcia's. Is that what you want?"

"He deserved a trial."

"Trial?"

Ian and Bishop laughed again.

"I always knew you were a spic."

To every cop within fifty miles, I might as well have been holding the AK.

Brothers in blue. *Bullshit.*

CHAPTER THREE

Carlos

I did the right thing by my badge.

Though that's never been anything but cold comfort.

My captain said it would be in my best interest to find something else to do with my life. Except this is what I knew I was born to do. No one, not even Sandy, could understand that. I couldn't see my life any other way. So they sent me up to run the precinct at San Eugenio. In a public relations move, I was "promoted" to sergeant to "award a good cop for doing the right thing."

Optics. It was a jail sentence. It was a goddamn execution, 274 miles away.

Ian's scumbag defense attorney had said if he hadn't put the bullet through the cholo's head, he would have died within a minute from his other gunshot wounds. The legal ones.

"So what was the big deal?" the scumbag had said. "He did it in the name of justice."

Case closed. Ten years for manslaughter. It was a slap on the wrist for what Ian had done. For the trust he had shattered in one pull of a trigger.

Me? I got life.

Lost everything. I went to bed every night, wondering why I was even holding onto the broken shell of myself any longer.

"Hey, Sarge, your boy is on TV again."

Jimmy always knew what to say to piss me off. He loved it. We didn't look the same seven years later. Jimmy still hobbled from the 7.62 in his leg, and he had put on at least fifty. But so had I. What can I say? The only good thing in this town was the food. The Al Pastor carts near the liquor stores always gave us a small discount to look the other way on health code violations. You learn to make fair trades like that when they don't hurt anybody. And damn it, they might not have been as good as the ones in East LA, but good Al Pastor is good Al Pastor.

Jimmy and I used to be what ideal cops looked like. A marketing agency couldn't have done a better job casting a commercial. I was Mexican; he was Korean. Both of us with chiseled jaws, clean-shaven, luscious heads of hair, and ripped. Jimmy will never admit it, but I was always a little more jacked. We were able to hop fences and chase down suspects on foot with the best of them. Now, I doubt either one of us could even run a mile without having to pass out after for a week. Our hairlines receded, and spots of gray patched through our hair.

It's who we became. We were still cops. The best of them.

"Can't believe little Eric became an ambulance chaser."

Eric's liberal brain had fallen for the media because he needed the attention. *Black Lives Matter. Defund the Police. Fuck Twelve.* Eric, like most people, knew what the media told him. They don't know me. They don't know my pain. They don't care. So why should I? I know I'm supposed to, but why? When you're all alone, why care?

That's what I paid $250,000 for. For my Ivy League son to spite me.

"Don't you have work to do?"

Jimmy looked at his watch. "Ah, yes. It's six o'clock. Time to go to Jimmy Choi's House of Pain."

"Just say you need to go to the bathroom." I laughed.

"If you were my colon, you'd understand. You hear the pipes rattling, after ten minutes, call an ambulance. I'm sure Eric won't be too far behind." Jimmy waddled off like the proud Korean duck he was.

I watched as my son came on TV and spouted a claim of victimization on the steps of the Davidson Courthouse for an illegal field worker, Roberto Hinojosa, and by proxy, the entire Latino population in the US.

"This is an egregious act against the very fabric of America. When will Latinos be seen as more than just pickers, maids, gang members, and murderers?!"

Activists lined the streets, and you better believe my boy was front and center of it all. A young Jesse Jackson would have wished he had the charisma my son had. He was spewing whiny, victimizing, defensive bullshit. "Latinos of America: It's time to rise up! For us to take a stand against these acts continuously perpetuated against our people. It saddens me we've been brought to this point. A brown man who is being terrorized by a white supremacist can't stand his ground. Yet, a white man in Florida can. A white cop in Missouri can. Another white cop in Minnesota can. Where are Latinos in all of this? When will we be recognized as victims of the system? When Mr. Hinojosa is released from these errant, heinous charges, he will be a source of pride for this nation, and he *will* become a great citizen of these United States that he and so many Latinos—Latinos like my great-grandfather—fought so hard to build a future for. We will rise up."

Mexican Moses had handed down his tablets, and my vocation and I were made out to be in the forces of evil. Disgusting.

Hinojosa's upcoming trial was something of an anomaly in these parts. It actually meant something. About forty-five minutes away in Davidson, the closest thing you could call a "city,"—I use that term loosely around here—an illegal worker toiling in the strawberry fields killed a member of a white nationalist group called the White Patriots.

The group was mostly into misdemeanor crimes and otherwise kept to jerking themselves off with their white pride in online forums. They were mostly harmless back-country rednecks with nothing better to do than burn crosses and ink shitty homemade SS tattoos on their man titties.

But *this*. This became a massive story across the nation right away. Those hicks crossed a line. Was this illegal going to be sentenced to life in prison? Was he going to be deported? Some in the media said it was self-defense. Others said it was murder. Hinojosa was being charged as such.

The liberal media showed photos of Roberto Hinojosa as a family man and the epitome of the American Dream. Someone who had come from nothing, made a life for himself, and earned a house and a family. He was now a killer justified in his self-defense, at worst.

The dead guy, Don Watts, got the same sort of treatment from the conservative stations. Yes, he was part of a white supremacist group, but he was a dedicated man of the church, a loving father to four kids, and a "wonderful husband," his wife would say on camera through her chubby, Twinkie-loving mouth.

It's not that the conservative stations condoned the killing or defended Watts. It was more like a *look the other way and people can decide for themselves* approach.

Both sides of the media were disgusting in how they twisted things. People needed the truth. They needed the facts. But the media didn't care. They wanted to continue to stoke the fires that bred them ratings and loyalty to their version of "the truth."

My attention was drawn away from the TV to Theresa, whose desk faced mine. One of the finest cops I had met in my thirty-one years on the force.

"Why don't you stop being an impotent prick and pick up *your* daughter from school? It's your day. No. I can't. I told you I have to work. It is your week. Remember how you sobbed in court saying you were desperate for time with her? Cry me a river, get on a fucking canoe, paddle over to your daughter's school, and pick her up."

Theresa had graduated top of her class at the academy. She would have been put on the fast track to captain. But she'd shacked up with a bum cop who'd left her pregnant one month after their first assignment out of the academy. The prick didn't own up to it, and she'd been tossed in the garbage, just like me. She became known as *used goods*. How's that for a fair shake?

"Be polite? Sure. How's this? Stop being a degenerate fuck for two minutes and take care of your daughter. Oh good, you will? Thanks for doing the bare minimum, asshole."

Theresa was not one to ever back down from confrontation, especially when it came to her daughter. This was a conversation we were used to hearing. And honestly, you didn't want to get into it with Theresa. She was so headstrong, fighting her was a losing battle. God, I loved her.

She never complained. She did the work every single day, waiting for her chance to show she belonged. I always wished she would've recognized she didn't need anybody to tell her how good of a cop she was. I think if she'd had her chance, she would've won the Medal of Valor. Probably made chief. But that's in the past now.

Forget the past and forge ahead.

"Sarge, do yourself a favor and don't have a one-night stand with the guy who finished number two behind you at the academy."

"Well, there go my plans for Thursday night." I tried to make the best of it for all of us, and she did the same for me.

"Why does being a parent have to be so hard?"

I took a breath and pointed over to the photo on her desk. "Tell me, how do you get so big of a smile out of that kid?"

Theresa kept a photo of herself with her five-year old daughter, Bella, at Disneyland on her desk. They both had on Mickey ears, and Theresa was making a weird face where she puckered her lips and made her eyes bulge out her head. Bella was laughing so hard she couldn't keep her eyes open, her Mickey ears tilted off her head, as she wrapped her arms around her mom's head with a most affectionate hug. I loved it. A picture of parenting at its best. And Theresa was an all-time great one.

"I want to feel like what I do has meaning, Sarge. I want to make my daughter proud, and I don't feel like I'm doing that when I'm busting seventeen-year-olds for drinking tequila behind Poncho's."

"We chose this. If it was for everyone, this world would be a lot safer. But not everyone is called to be cops. We were."

"I want my chance, Sarge. I'm not going to get it here."

"You'll have your day. We all get a chance to show who we are."

"Thanks, Sarge. I'm heading out on patrol." She walked down the hall to gear up.

That's right around when the call came in.

Jimmy was waddling in, still buckling up his pants from his daily excursion. Our bathroom at Fort Comanche had been bigger than three quarters of this entire station. And rightfully so. That was the real deal. This was rent-a-cop work.

"L-T to San Eugenio. Come in, San Eugenio." HQ was always babysitting us.

"Copy you, HQ. Go for San Eugenio," Jimmy answered.

"San Eugenio, a prisoner transpo will be dropping one Roberto Hinojosa into your custody for the evening."

I glanced around my station, as if seeing it for the first time.

Our phones hadn't been switched out since the eighties. Our walls were more chipped than painted. We had three jail cells, none of them prepared to hold anything worse than some illegal stumbling home too late after a night of the San Eugenio Cocktail—a combo of heat exhaustion from working the fields and too much tequila.

This one-story building had opened in 1935 right after all the Mexicans arrived in town during the Depression. It's been touched up once since. It used to be San Eugenio's library. How they'd decided it should be a police station was beyond me. Should've stayed a library. Maybe somebody around here would've spoken English. The one saving grace is that this place made me feel like John Wayne. You know how he could sit in the same room and watch the bad guy he'd just captured? That was the one way I felt like I meant something to someone. One way I felt like a hero.

That feeling was a lot better than the one I felt a few weeks ago when I stared down the barrel of my department-issued Beretta 9mm 92FS. That night, I envisioned what the splatter pattern would look like on the beige walls of my one-bedroom house. It might make the place look a little more alive—add some color to a colorless world. More alive than my house, and more alive than this broken-down prison they called a police station.

That was the last time I felt like I had control. It was the last time I felt anything. Back then, I could control the narrative about me. I think that's what we all want—a chance to tell our story the way we see it.

The public, my brothers in blue, hell, maybe even my family might have remembered me for what I used to be. What they think I did might find itself as a footnote. Dead cops play well to the media. Maybe that would boost our image. We could be the good guys again. They get to show me as someone who served his community. They get to say how tragic it is and then three segments later, to get ratings back up, talk about how the country needs to "defund the police." What a load of bullshit. It's the media's fault where this country is right now. They divided us. They did the same stuff to me, and they did it again, with this dead White Patriot and this illegal. It's all for the ratings. Where's the honor in that?

"Negative, L-T. The Three Little Pigs could provide better security than we could," Jimmy said.

"Not a request. Straight from the top, Officer Choi. You are to hold the prisoner overnight. Transpo will arrive at zero four hundred tomorrow morning. Three black and whites will hold a perimeter around you. The no-fly zone around the precinct will keep the media out of your hair. ETA to San Eugenio, two hours."

"Copy that, L-T. Over and out." Jimmy hung up the walkie. "Once an asshole, always an asshole." I remember the look on Jimmy's face when he walked back into the bullpen. Like he had seen Kim Jong Un wearing a thong.

Theresa returned then, ready to hit what would no doubt be quiet streets.

"Hey, Theresa, before you head out, remember that immigrant dude from the news?"

"Get the kimchi out of your mouth, you constipated Korean." Theresa always liked being a part of the boys. She had to be. Being a woman, there was no other way to survive. She wouldn't get any favors.

"HQ just called, and they're sending a transpo here to drop him off for the night."

"You told them that's impossible, right? That the … "

"… Three Little Pigs could provide more security. Yes, I said it all. They're sending three black and whites to hold a perimeter. We're out of media range. No-fly zone. It's just for a few hours. Straight from the top."

"This is going to be fun." Theresa's jokes never hit harder than that one.

A high-profile murder suspect was the least of my worries. The self-righteous immigration defense attorney who I hadn't seen in five years was sure to follow.

CHAPTER FOUR

Carlos

I needed to get out of that station before the circus began. I ended up going on patrol instead of Theresa.

The rows and rows of strawberry fields had become a listless verse of eternal hell. Every day, day after day, they were there. Taunting me. In between the rows with their plaid shirt-covered backs toward a God they believed in, but who had forgotten them. The illegals worked, well, illegally. Most of them were honest. At least in some way they were making themselves useful.

My stomach got bigger with each passing year, and any sense of adventure I had left for the job was well past gone. For a lifetime of service, this was a fitting end, I suppose. What does service get you in the end? Jack shit.

I had to answer the call whether I was ready to or not.

I usually went on patrol just as the sun went down on the fields. When the honest folks went home and their kids came out. The kids were the ones who caused most of the trouble. I could maintain peace simply by driving around. Everyone understood the rules.

I knew that the White Patriots might be out to cause some trouble because of what had happened. Intimidating the immigrants made them feel useful from time to time. Mostly, the Mexicans stayed in their lane, and the whites stayed in theirs. It was a peaceful coexistence, a blurry line, sure—but the line meant something. A self-established order no one breached.

I was in no mood for illegals. I mean most days, I'm not, but with what lay ahead, I definitely wasn't having it. A group of workers, finishing up for the day, hopped in the back of a truck. It was common that a worker with a truck would take the majority of them home. All bunched up in the back. Almost like they had their own personal shuttle service. They pitched in whatever they could to pay for gas.

Though they were breaking the law, what I respected about those people above all else was how they always seemed to take care of each other. A far cry from what I had known.

They were drinking beers in the back of a Yo-Yo. That's what we called those mid-sized trucks, Toyotas that were missing the T, O, T, A, and S. Almost like it was a badge of honor and a way of identifying them.

A beer was a great reward after a hard day's work. I guess that was something both Americans and Mexicans could find common ground with. There was both humility and a feeling of infallibility. But I mean, really what was I going to do? Deport them? Like the DOJ would really make a trip out here for something like this. Especially when these guys kept the economy running. They made the system work. They kept the grocery prices down and the stockholders happy.

A little blind eye never hurt anybody.

I took a deep breath, and I turned my red and blues on. The workers scattered as I drove up. They knew the drill. If I gave more than two plays of the siren and they weren't making the effort to get out, their asses were mine.

"Hold on, amigos. You know the rules. This is the state of California. This ain't Mexico. No open containers in public. Toss the beers."

I might as well have been speaking French to them.

They should've left the library open.

"You hear me? Toss the beers."

I got out of my car and walked up to them. I pointed at their bottles and signaled to them to dump out the beers.

"*Cervezas*. Out." They looked around at each other.

"Don't look at them! Look at me. I'm the police. Pour your beers out ... *Ahora!*" I grabbed a half empty beer out of one of the illegal's hands and threw it to the ground. That made their attitudes turn *rapido*. They all poured out their beers together. Now they knew better.

"I need to see your papers or *¡Déjame!*" They all started to run to God knows where.

"*¡Cálmate!* It's all good, Lopez." I had come to hate this man's voice.

They called him *El León*—The Lion. This nickname didn't make any sense to me. At first glance, he might have looked like a misguided mama's boy. A skinny, gangly kid with shitty tattoos all over his body, a bald head, and a perpetual five o'clock shadow. Even with how ridiculous he looked, an evil lurked behind his eyes I couldn't forget. A wickedness bred in the abusive, unstable homes that some of these kids grew up in. Too far gone to find any sort of measure of good back in their lives.

His khaki pants were two sizes too big and permanently falling down. The town always knew what shade of plaid boxers he wore on any given day. He was the only real sense of terror in the streets, which meant mostly petty crime. He was a low-level thug with aspirations of an empire that could never exist in this town. His gang of thugs was a bunch of hangers-on to a small-time drug dealer of mostly really bad weed.

But it was an escape of some sort. And the people fed off of it. In an attempt to expand his "empire," he had started to get into dealing opioids. With all the back-breaking work these people were doing—the kind of shit you or I would never want to do—his product was slowly starting to creep in. Whether I liked it or not, El León was starting to make a name for himself across Davidson County.

I wasn't going to have that. Not in my town.

The few times we had him in one of our cells, it was for assault. He really could beat the hell out of someone when he wanted to. He had a viciousness that I don't think even he understood, nor wanted. Though he seemed to aspire to it.

He never traveled alone. Two or three of his thugs were always alongside him. Looking for some way to suck on this perceived power teat. He took advantage of the weak. Used them. He used these poor day laborers as mules or dealers for him. He labeled himself as a *Savior* of his people. A sorry excuse for that.

"Causing problems for us, Lopez?"

"I don't see an *us*. I see you and your wannabe tough guy butt buddies. I see these honest gentlemen here with open containers in public. I have no issue with you, León, unless you had something to do with it."

"Nah, Lopez. Just make sure you don't harass our people."

"These aren't *your* people, León. They don't belong to anybody."

El León laughed smugly. He looked me square in the eyes. "You chose the blue. But the brown was born in you. You can't turn away from it. It's who you are. You ain't better than us. That uniform don't make you shit. You're one of us, Lopez."

"I know who I am. I protect. You destroy. I help the weak. You prey on them."

León and his buddies looked at each other and laughed. They said something in Spanish that the illegals got in on too. My eyes scanned, never locked onto one spot, one individual. It's how we were trained in these situations.

"You gonna arrest all of us, Lopez?"

He started to walk toward me. My left hand shot up to hold him back. My right went to the side of my textured leather holster.

"That's close enough, León."

His hands went up, mocking me. As they did, León lifted up a piece of his plaid shirt to reveal a .38. The piece was a new addition. His two friends covered their belts, keeping their pieces hidden. Not having the balls to show off theirs yet. They knew if they made a move, they were getting one between the eyes. They weren't built like León. He didn't care if he lived or died.

"Did you just threaten an officer of the law?" I asked.

León mockingly wiggled his fingers. "No threat, officer. Just reminding you who you are and where you come from."

I was outnumbered eight to one. That was a battle I was not gonna win. Neither was Rambo.

He fucking beat me at my own game, and that pissed me off. I walked back to my car, trying to maintain what semblance of alpha posture I could. That's what they taught us in the academy.

But theory and wisdom are two completely different things. Always try to maintain control of a situation, even when you have none. Deadly force was the last resort.

The Continuum of Force. I wouldn't have minded skipping a step or two. I got back in my car.

"Where are you going, Lopez? Hang out—have a beer with us. We were just about to have some fun."

"Go home, León. Leave these poor people alone. And for God's sake, put on a belt. You look like a moron."

***

The funeral for Don Watts, the scumbag who had been killed in the fields, was held at the Chosen Ones of Christ Church up in Davidson, a converted, defunct Mervyns.

It was a simple place, but you always heard what was going on in there. I shit you not, they turned clothing racks into crosses they venerated, and they used two-for-one clearance banners as altar placemats. It was essentially four white walls, a projector, and enough folding chairs to hold its fifty or so hate-mongering congregants.

I guess the Bill of Rights allows for places like this to exist. We gotta follow it. I might disagree that something like this can take place, but I must protect the spirit of the law. That's what we're called to do.

In this place, they spoke of God's love, not for the whole of humanity, but for the white man. The pastor leading this flock of sheep was Reverend Job Wilson. He stood no more than five foot seven. He wore cheap pastel suits that always ran a little too long down his leg. His hair was overly gelled. A wolf in sheep's clothing. This was a man who wanted to build his church, not for the sanctity of God, but for his own vanity.

I'll hand it to the guy. He was charismatic as hell. Always hollering, jumping up and down, and pointing to the camera as he spoke. He knew what he was doing and wasn't ashamed to build his audience via YouTube, Facebook, or whatever was popular that day.

In the past investigations on him, he was always toeing the line of what was inciting violence and what was just free speech, saying things like, "God honors boldness." And, "Don't let the spirit of offense keep you from saying what you need to say."

Over time, when his message of hate wasn't being received or he felt his audience wasn't growing quickly enough, he got bolder. "Send a message to all the tyrants, globalists, and communists. We will not give America to them. The United States needs to be reborn. In Christ's Holy Name, we pray." All his prancing grew the fire inside of him to deliver to an increasingly more indoctrinated audience.

He gave a voice to their discontent.

We needed to keep a close eye on him, and we did, watching his videos almost every Sunday.

As is the case with most bad people in this world, Wilson and the church justified their misgivings and outright hatred as a way of steering humanity toward salvation. It was them, and only them, who could reclaim the land lost to them, so that Heaven could flourish on Earth when Judgment Day arrived.

You gotta love how these preachers preach "humility," yet record and post on YouTube, Facebook, proclaiming everything that they're saying, with the same conviction, as if it were the Almighty Himself speaking.

Well, luckily for the investigators, this "Man of God" asswipe recorded the whole thing.

And it was broadcast live on social media for their dozens of hardcore followers. His aspirations of bringing the next mega church to San Eugenio would be his undoing.

About fifty to sixty people were there to bid a white power farewell to Mr. Watts.

There were babies born into the hatred and kids of all ages, dressed in their Sunday best, being shaped by it. Too innocent to know what was being done to them.

Then there were the teenagers. They were the ones I feared for the most. The next generation of hate-mongers in waiting. The fury in their eyes, the passion of their worship, and the energy to do something with it all. They had a choice before them, yet in watching tapes like this, their choice had already been made.

These people were scum. And of course, after further investigation, as if a piece of divine intervention, this Jesus preacher would eventually be charged for possession of child pornography, following the investigation of the night that laid ahead of me. He'd find salvation at the hands of inmates in federal prison. Don't know if he came out a changed man. I like to think he faced a hell far scarier than anything the Bible preached for those eight years and beyond.

"We lift Brother Don up to the hands of the Lord, where he will be seated at the right hand of the father." He paused a beat, channeling the best inner pseudo-Hitler that he could. *I bet you he wished he could've fucked Hitler*, I thought. *Would've been a whole lot of Aryan pride.*

"He believed in all this country stood for. He believed in standing for this sacred ground and keeping it pure, the way that our forefathers intended, who too were chosen by God. In a time when our lands and our hearts continue to be infested by the brown curse that feeds our children drugs and disturbs the purity of God's land, we must find a way to come together to honor Brother Don's memory. While these rats take your baby formula at the borders, your white children are left to go hungry and die. We cannot stand by. We must find a way to continue living out the Word of God."

As Reverend Job, that's how his people refer to him, grew sweatier and more indignant, his voice grew louder and more definitive. He was "channeling God," looking up to some false perception of Heaven and asking for violence to come into his heart.

He was looking up when he should have been looking down.

"It is time to put on our Armor of God. As God's soldiers, we must defend our land. Let justice be done." He grabbed a Bible from his fake-wood pseudo-pulpit in front of him, raised it to the sky, and put his arms out like Christ on the cross, shouting, "Let death take my enemies by surprise. Let them go down alive to the realm of the dead, for evil finds lodging among them."

He regained himself. Wiped his brow. Took a deep breath. He looked back out at the people in the crowd, and said as he exhaled, "Psalm fifty-five, verse fifteen. This is the Word of God."

A man who was known among the White Patriots as "Freedom Frank," rose from his seat at the front of the church. He was a large hulking man, dressed in a cheap gray suit that might very well have been purchased in the very same Mervyns department store they "worshiped" in. His suit was a bit too small for him, overly and incorrectly tailored so that it showed off his hulking chest. It was customized for intimidation, to show the work that went into his armor. He wore a dark-blue shirt and a black tie. All of it finely crafted, so that people respected him through fear, upon first sight.

Frank was the opposite of León. He had muscles bulging through his jacket, a long unkempt beard, and a bald head that made him look ten years older than he actually was. He was the personification of intimidation. He walked over to Don's wife and hugged her. They shared a few tears. Frank whispered into her ear and hugged her again. He then shook the hands of Don's ten- and eight-year-old boys, as if they were grown men in their fifties, with a seriousness and sternness not meant for kids that age. Frank turned back to the front, ready to pontificate to the congregation that was soon to belong to him. "Give justice to the weak and the fatherless. Maintain the rights of the afflicted and the destitute."

"Psalm eighty-two, verse three," the pastor responded. A nod of approval from "God." It seemed that Frank could do what he felt necessary to right the wrong.

"The Lord wills that justice be done for Don," Freedom Frank continued. "Not just for Don, but for all who have had their jobs, their livelihoods, their land, and their decency taken away by this brown scum. And what does our government do? They stand by and let it happen. They give them driver's licenses. They give them food and shelter. They educate them. I can't stand by and let tyranny win. That's not what Don stood for."

Voices from the crowd shouted, "speak the truth, Freedom Frank!"

"We have to protect our children!"

"We can't let this last any longer!"

The pastor blessed Frank once more. "God will bring into judgment both the righteous and the wicked."

That was one more means of justification for this self-righteous crusade motivated by fear and hate. Impassioned and capable militiamen, who regularly posted their training on their message boards, ready to carry out *God's Will* now had justifiable cause and the blessing of their demented shepherd.

As Freedom Frank left the "pulpit," a group of about ten men stood and exited with him, all exuding a false sense of power. They met fear with hubris.

"We are the righteous."

It was the shot heard round the world that those guys had been preparing for their entire lives—to die for some fantasy of God and country. This was their 1776, and the revolution had just begun.

***

I saw it in front of the station—his black Prius. He was an environmentalist too. A "social justice warrior." It said so on a bumper sticker positioned under his right taillight.

It had been five years since I last saw that car, and I wished it would have been another five. But I had to face him. We have to face all the things that scare us in life.

Why should I be scared of a whiny, scheming defense attorney? I'd dealt with them a thousand times before. As long as I went in with the same approach as the hundreds upon thousands of low-life defense attorneys before him, then the outcome would be the same. I stood on the grounds of moral superiority, while they had to defend men who they knew were guilty.

Why should an interaction with my son cause me any sort of anxiety? He was soft. He was overly emotional. A snowflake. He hadn't seen enough of life, like I had. When you look at things from a pure facts standpoint, the truth of what you're supposed to do becomes glaringly evident. It's what gave me objectivity in my job and what was about to give me objectivity now. That would make it easier.

I parked my Tahoe in my reserved space. As I pulled up, I saw that his back right tire, below the social justice warrior sticker, was on top of the white parking line. For all my son's self-righteousness, he couldn't park like a responsible human being. I put the Tahoe in park, took a deep breath, and put him in the defense attorney category. A bad-parking defense attorney. I could ticket him now if I wanted to.

He was making this easy for me.

Inside the station, I saw him talking to Jimmy at the front desk, laughing and sharing memories of their past. Uncle Jimmy had kept in touch with him throughout the years. Eric's faux-Italian navy-blue suit, his thirty-five-dollar brown winged-tip shoes, and too much gel in his hair made his SuperShears haircut look like a hundred twenty-dollar salon haircut. But that's what made him so good at his job. He spun the truth in a way that people would believe. He knew it wasn't true, but he presented it as if it were the Bible. His billboards and bus ads with his stupid face on them, God I hated them.

"1-555-No-Deport, *Hablamos Español.*" Yup, that's what the ambulance chaser had on his billboards. One entering town and one leaving. The only way in and out. He didn't even live here anymore. He had a hot shot office in San Jose ninety miles away. He knew what he was doing when he put those billboards there. Lopez and Associates. Immigration attorney. He learned Spanish in college for crying out loud, and now he was presenting it like he'd spoken it his whole life. We didn't speak a lick of Spanish in the house.

How could this be who my son became?

As I passed through the hip-level swinging door at the front desk, Theresa had a hard time containing her excitement. "Sarge, you have a visitor."

"You're enjoying this too much."

"Chisme in person. My favorite," she said with a smirk.

Eric turned around and looked my way. He extended his hand, stone-faced as can be. I was the bad guy. *Can you believe that? Five years of not seeing your own father, and that's how you act?* I didn't care.

"Mr. Lopez," I said.

"Sergeant Lopez," he responded with an all-business monotone.

"Sergeant Lopez?" I shook my head. I was his father, and that's the welcome I got after five years? The vacations. The college education. Still ungrateful. I extended my hand to him and shook his. His hand was a little rougher than I remembered.

He was actually working. That's one thing I could be proud of him for. I know it's how I raised him.

"As Mr. Hinojosa's attorney, I need to speak with him immediately."

"There are no cameras around here. You sure it will mean anything? Should I call a press conference to give it some significance?"

"There's no need for this, Sergeant Lopez. Please, let me go back to his cell."

"I can't let you back there without the arrest record and a statement of retention."

"Under the sixth amendment, Mr. Hinojosa—"

"Oh God, you're gonna start with this crap already?"

"Why can't you be a professional?!"

"A professional! Why can't you just—"

Jimmy jumped in. "You know what, guys? The transport bus hasn't even arrived yet, so why don't we all just simmer down and take a second to breathe?"

I didn't break my stare from Eric. I couldn't. That had got me the win every time before, and it was going to get me the upper hand here. I wasn't the bad guy. He was the one defending a suspected murderer.

"Jimmy," I said, "get Mr. Lopez, Esquire, Attorney at Law, a room to talk to Mr. Hinojosa when he arrives."

"You got it, Sarge. Yo, Theresa, get Mr. Lopez a space where he can set up a desk!"

"Yell at me again and see what happens," she said with her finger pointed at Jimmy. Her presence was always powerful enough to put Jimmy back in his place. "Right this way, mijo," she said to Eric.

Eric walked with Theresa into the booking room.

"So do you miss your dad?" she asked.

"Theresa!" I snapped at her.

"What? Just trying to make conversation!"

This night was fucked. I wanted nothing more than to get it over with. The past was the past, and we had to move on. Lingering on it was not going to do anything. I didn't want to see Eric, and he didn't want to see me.

"Anything good out there, Sarge?"

"Same old, Jimmy."

I rubbed my face from the overwhelming exhaustion, boredom, and frustration. "We gotta get out of here. We gotta do something to make ourselves relevant again. I can't waste away here anymore."

"Jesus, what happened to you out there that got you so philosophical?"

Jimmy looked over at Eric, as Eric looked back at me one more time. He walked into the room with Theresa. "Cheer up, Sarge. Look, we get through the family reunion and everything will be grand. We can get back to living out our last few years as cops, and then you and me, we start a ranch out here or something."

"A ranch? Jimmy, you've never even seen a horse."

"Those are the ones with the long necks, right?"

We laughed. That's what partners do. He always knew the right thing to say to bring me back to reality.

The doors to the station creaked open meekly. We both figured it was another one of the moms from the town telling us that her teenage son had found some fireworks. That we should talk to him. Keep him out of trouble.

"Can someone please help me?" the woman asked.

Jimmy and I turned to the whisper of the voice. The woman's face was beaten to a pulp. Her left eye was nearly swollen shut, blood streaming down from atop her left eyebrow. Any beauty she had left in her had been taken from her, just as her soul had been.

"Jesus Christ. Theresa, get over here!"

Jimmy ran out from behind the desk and over to the woman. She had given her last bit of energy with her plea for help. Jimmy caught her in his arms just before she hit the ground.

CHAPTER FIVE

Sandra

They say time heals all wounds.

How can time heal when it doesn't know heartbreak? When it doesn't know loss?

When I was in the ER at the start of my career, I saw some horrific injuries. Bullet wounds to the stomach, a person who was shot screaming for me to save his life, open leg wounds where you couldn't tell where the skin ended and the bone started.

Ladder falls. Skateboarding injuries. Car accidents. Drunk drivers. Domestic violence.

Time didn't heal those wounds.

I did. My team did.

And sometimes, the scars never fully heal. You just learn to live with them.

It had been five years since I had seen Carlos.

This thirteen-minute drive feels like an eternity. The last time I remember seeing him, he was a shell of his former self.

When I picked up the phone and heard his grumbling voice on the other side, my heart started to race. Every insecurity, every thought that I wasn't enough came rushing back to the forefront of my brain. I had all but forgotten the feeling.

I was still so angry at him. I still couldn't forgive him. I didn't want to. Why should I?

His low timbre was still so soothing. His voice, his presence was all consuming. When he would speak, I would forget all the barriers I had put up, all the work I had done to move past the hurt, and I would be sucked back in. Answering his every request. Wanting so bad to be there for him. Hoping that maybe I could help him find his way back to being Carlos.

When he asked me to come down to the station, yes, I was obligated by HIPPA to help the woman he spoke of. Victims of domestic abuse always meant the most to me.

They were women who lost their power. I wanted them to feel heard. I wanted them to know life didn't need to be this way.

Of the three doctors in San Eugenio, I was the only woman. And to be frank, I was the only one worth their salt in medical knowledge.

He could have called any of them. Yet he called me. Selfish prick. He knew I couldn't say no. And he knew I wouldn't complain.

Of course, I wanted to help the woman out, but at what cost to me? God, I sound so arrogant, but it took so much for me to forget the twenty-six years, seven months, and eighty-five days Carlos and I were together. I didn't want to go back to it. I felt so powerful without him. I had my life back.

Why did time feel the need to force us back together?

I had contemplated this day for so long, wondering if Carlos and I would ever see each other again. We knew we would have to eventually finalize our divorce. Neither one of us had made a move in three and a half years to push it through.

My parents, especially my mom, wanted me to be independent. Seeing the way she served my dad's every whim and need— cooking, cleaning, and taking his condescending tone... it was hard.

I know they loved each other, but somewhere along the lines, Mom gave up. She always encouraged me to make a life for myself. To pursue my passions and my dreams. To make sure I knew what I wanted. She didn't want me to give away my power like she had.

Giving away my power became my biggest fear.

Carlos rocked my world. The moment he handed me cash for the beer, our hands lingered a little too long. Our stares locked. From the moment I saw Carlos, I knew he was the man I was supposed to be with.

Whether I wanted to believe it or not was a whole different story.

He was handsome. He was different from his boisterous friends. He annoyed me, but I somehow loved the fact he did. The sincerity and kindness in his eyes hit me so deeply.

It wasn't love at first sight. No, I wanted him to earn my love. To prove he could be there for me.

Saying it now sounds so juvenile and sad.

Something shifted in my heart. As hard as I wanted to fight it, I knew my life would never be the same. All I wanted to do was give myself over to it and to him.

It went against everything I knew. I didn't think I was ready for love.

Time knew I was ready. It brought him to me. And me to him.

Our relationship was so damn exciting. It was all so new. He took me out of every comfort zone I had.

He was so decisive. So confident. So self-assured.

Because I was still in medical school, I was't sure if this was the path for me.

Carlos was so confident becoming a police officer was what was destined for him. It scared me how he attacked life. He wanted to graduate at the top of his class at the academy, and he did.

He always got everything he wanted. Including me.

The way he approached the start of our relationship scared me. The flowers, the notes, his willingness to drive an hour just to spend five minutes with me during a lunch break. I didn't understand it. Was this guy crazy or was he trying to control me? I really didn't know.

I got lost in him, in the overwhelming power of who he was. I was a strong, powerful woman, yet around him I became a doe-eyed girl. It was unsettling. I had promised myself for so long I would live the way my mom told me to.

It was terrifying.

Next thing I knew, we were married. It was a small ceremony, around twenty-five guests in my parents' backyard. All the decorations were Pick N' Save Specials—honeycomb white paper wedding bells were the go-to. Atop the cake stood a white bride-and-groom cake topper.

Jimmy drank so much tequila he actually stepped into my parents' pool and talked on his broken cell phone. The next morning we convinced him he peed himself. And bless his heart, he wore it as a badge of honor.

It was ugly, and it was perfect. We didn't have much, and we didn't care. We just wanted each other.

Four years later, just as I was getting ready to start my residency, Eric came along.

He was perfect.

I wish I could tell you he was named after some great leader or hero of literature. Or better yet, that Eric was a family name.

Nope. We named him after Carlos's favorite baseball player, nineties Dodger first baseman Eric Karros. I can't believe I let him talk me into that.

Now, I can't imagine Eric any other way. I take solace in the fact Karros is the all-time leader for home runs in Los Angeles Dodger history. The man also had an incredible head of hair. Ditto for my Eric.

We were a happy family. Life went underway.

We took vacations to Orlando to go to Universal Studios and Disney World. There were baseball practices, travel teams, and hot summer days by the river with friends we kind-of-sort-of liked. In between Carlos working graveyards and my eight-hour shifts at the hospital, somehow we always figured it out.

To this day, I don't know how we did it. Whether it was calling for a ride from Uncle Jimmy or Grandma and Grandpa, we always figured it out. And we never missed a game or parent-teacher conference.

Our relationship had balance. We had each other's backs. Life was turning out far different than I had ever expected, and I was loving it.

It was a perfect life, with everything we could have wanted. I wish it would have been enough.

A fire inside of Carlos burned so brightly, pushing him unlike anything I've ever seen. He was always the hardest worker in the room. Thirty-six-hour shifts. Long nights. He did it all.

None of it was ever enough for Carlos, though. He couldn't be content. He needed more.

He always needed more.

If we would've ended up in a cardboard box, I would've been fine because we had each other. I wish he'd felt the same.

Growing up, Carlos never had much. To fill the gap, he just wanted more, and he needed everyone to know things were different now.

A new car every five years. Always wanting to remodel and fix something in the house. Always a presentation to friends of all the things that weren't done yet and how there was going to be "more." Everything—the fireplace, the kitchen counters, the couches—would be "nicer."

Orlando became Turks and Caicos. Motels became five-star hotels. When I wanted to pack sandwiches for a road trip, Carlos insisted we stop for meals everywhere.

I treasured those little moments in picnic areas on the side of the road where we could be a family without the distractions of the outside world. Those sandwiches were soon replaced by generic chain restaurants and Firehouse Onion Wings, or whatever weird menu item was on special.

The insecurity of Carlos's past never left him.

How did we pay for all that?

Carlos took on more OT. He insisted I take on less because he had to "provide for the family." Not willing to admit or take notice that his wife was a, you know, doctor. Making a doctor's salary. He wanted me to work less and take the "burden off" me.

For some reason, I agreed.

I loved what I did. I loved serving my community and working with patients. The "burden" was actually a place of fulfillment for me. His need to embrace his dated form of masculinity put a heavy weight on my soul.

I started to resent him for it.

I look back now with anger for not drawing a line. For not stepping up. And most of all, for not speaking up.

The most powerful thing we have in this world is our voice.

This woman I was on the way to see? Maybe she would find hers again. And maybe I would be able to exorcise the demon that still weighed heavy on my heart.

She needed help.

As I slowly gave up my voice, each night I waited by the phone. Unable to sleep, waiting for the call. I knew what he was up against in East LA every night.

I was there, left by myself, waiting to know if I was going to wake up a widow.

There were too many close calls. When he would call at one in the morning, my heart would sink. I almost always expected it to be Jimmy telling me this was it. But it was always Carlos.

Every time he was shot at. Every time there was a close call, I was always the first call. Honestly, sometimes, I wish I didn't know. The pillows might've been a little dryer.

Each morning when I woke up and the sunlight trickled in through the window, I thanked God I still had a husband. Once I made the bed, it was time to cover the windows again with the heaviest blankets we had. A blue-and-black one with a bison on it blacked out the sunlight the best.

We went on this way for years. Not saying anything. My resentment grew.

Then came the night with the AK. That was my breaking point. I was at my parents' house when I got the call. He always called a little into his shift, right before Eric went to bed, to say goodnight.

An AK-47, as the forensic scientist at the trial would tell us, shot six hundred rounds per minute.

Six hundred rounds.

The standoff was nine minutes. The *what ifs* still haunt me.

Throughout the trial and after, the only one who stood by his side was Jimmy. His *brothers* turned on him and defended Ian. They wanted to stand up for the badge.

Brothers in blue, bullshit.

I didn't see one of his fucking *brothers* stand up for him.

Carlos was determined to give the department a means to escape. Carlos was the one who was ethical and moral. The system failed him.

The brotherhood was more important than his humanity. The worst part of this case was how much Carlos blamed himself for doing the right thing. He refused to be a victim. He was determined to punish himself.

As he punished himself, he punished our family.

Carlos went internal. He pushed me and Eric away. He stopped taking care of himself. He started to stress eat. Tacos and burgers every chance he could. His hair grayed. He would sleep in longer each day. He tried to laugh it off. Like my dad did to my mom, he started to criticize what I wore, what I cooked, and the decisions we were making with Eric. Passive aggression at every point. Anything to distract himself.

Everything that made my husband great was fading away.

Any disagreement we had with him about the case, the harder he pushed back. There was nothing for me to do. There was nothing either of us could do.

He spoke up. He said his peace. And he begged anyone he could to give him a second chance at sticking around. Why he would want to stick around a one-sided relationship made no sense.

I hope that when I see this woman, it will make sense again.

I stayed silent. He needed to come to realize it on his own. That's how I believe growth happens: when people realize it for themselves. Sometimes, it's best not to say anything. Everyone knows what's best for them.

Who am I to judge? Who am I to criticize?

Plus, if I did say something, maybe I was going to push him away. I wouldn't be responsible for our family breaking apart. All I could do was love him the best I could.

I was still so mad at him. But really, I was mad at myself.

When he was told he was being transferred to San Eugenio, I didn't fight him. Everything inside of me knew it was a big mistake, but I didn't say anything. I couldn't. He was my husband, and I wanted to stand by his side, but it doomed us both.

I started to drown with him. I gave up the beautiful life we had before the trial so I could keep our family together.

This wasn't the place for us, and we both knew it. I had gone from a hospital and people I loved to a place where I knew no one and nothing. In San Eugenio, we couldn't even get our hands on a reasonable amount of antibiotics to treat the cuts, gashes, and infections people would get from working the fields. The county, or the state for that matter, didn't deem us worthy enough to spend the money.

I sat and waited. We grew more into roommates than husband and wife. Going through the motions of existence rather than living.

I could see Carlos didn't want to live anymore, and instead of killing himself, he become a prisoner of his own mind. That was more comfortable than actual change.

Comfort is where Carlos lived.

I waited for one of two triggers to click: the one from his Baretta or one from a lawyer in a manilla envelope. I was not going to be held responsible for the dissolution of our family. I was there for Carlos, but if he wanted to, then he could break up the perfection of it all.

Perfection. It's something I've come to realize I couldn't live my life without. There's comfort in perfection because nothing ever changes and nothing needs to change. It gives me everything I expect. It's controllable.

I knew that if I said something, it would change. I couldn't see myself taking such a big leap. Carlos would have to do it if it was something he really wanted.

When he said he wanted to separate, I filed the divorce papers. We have a legal separation. We haven't finalized the divorce.

I don't know why.

When I saw the lights inside the police station, my heart started to race again. What was I going to do? What was I supposed to say? Who was I supposed to be?

Time isn't compassionate. It's not even empathetic.

This woman needed my help. Where time can't be compassionate, I could be.

I had a job to do, and I was gonna make it through because the bullet wounds, car accidents, and drunk drivers taught me how.

Time will continue to tick. Second by second. Hour by hour. Separating me from the past, without actually doing any healing.

I put my car into park.

No operating room in the world could fix the wounds of the past.

I loved Carlos, but I was so angry at him for how he made me feel.

I couldn't give in, and I wouldn't. I've done too much work to let myself go there again.

I didn't want to be a weak woman. I wanted to remember my power.

As I turned the handle of the door, I could hear the gravel in his low voice. It brought me equal parts tranquility and anger. I didn't know what to make of it.

I took a deep breath. My heart pounded.

What will I tell him? Should I tell him how much he hurt me?

The wounds were too deep and the past too thick to think anything but what our present has become. I loved this man. There was no future because the wounds will never fully heal.

I didn't want to open them back up either. Too much time had passed, and I wouldn't let it dictate my healing. This world was on my terms and on my time, right now.

I exhaled and pulled the door open.

I caught a glimpse of him and my heart fluttered. Unacceptable.

Each step I took into the precinct felt like a step into the past. I must move forward.

Take care of your job. Take care of this woman.

Be a strong woman. His life isn't yours anymore. It can't ever be again.

Don't tell me time heals all wounds.

CHAPTER SIX

Lupe

Be the good wife.

Guadalupe Flora Magdalena Sanchez. Originally, Osuna. That changed when I married a Sanchez, and our families became one.

This wasn't the first time, but it was the worst. Before, it wasn't as bad. It was a shove here and a shove there.

Sometimes I deserved it. I was out of line. I talked back, and a good wife doesn't talk back to her husband.

'Til death do us part, and everything in between.

He called me stupid. He called me ugly. I knew I wasn't, but after what he had been through, I wanted him to get it off his chest—all the hate he had for himself. It's what a good wife does. I thought maybe it would make it better.

But, after a while, I started to think, maybe he is right. Maybe I am ugly. Maybe I am stupid. I mean, if I went out on my own and tried to get a job, who would hire me? I was made to be a housewife. It's how I was raised. It's all I've known. Yes, I went to high school, but I barely passed. I was so pretty back then. I felt like I had purpose. And he … he had eyes for me. The football player for the cheerleader. It was a fairytale. One I didn't want to end.

It was so wonderful when we first started dating our senior year. He treated me *como una princesa* as my papi used to say. There were flowers and poems just for me. He held doors open everywhere we went. He made me feel like I was the only person who mattered. And back then, I was.

"It's you and me against the world," he would say. And I felt it so deeply.

When I gave myself to him on prom night of our senior year, I did it because I knew it was forever. Until our wedding night—four years later—we lived in sin, and somehow when our angelita

40

came into the world, it felt like she had saved us from dancing with the devil.

We named her Brava, "Brave" in English. Bravery is what we saw in her the moment she entered the world. *You and me against the world* became *us.*

Us against the world.

I loved him so much, and he loved us. I knew the day would come when we would find everything he had promised. I just had to be patient.

San Eugenio offered us nothing but poverty and an endless cycle of what had come before us. We needed to carve a path for ourselves—one out of here.

"One day, you and me, Bebita, we're going to go somewhere. We're going to leave this place behind. We're going to make something of ourselves. You're going to have everything you ever wanted. Everything you ever deserved. You are *mi princessa.*"

I was. He wouldn't say this every day. Mostly on the days after he had a little bloodied lip, or was out of breath, after he came from seeing his dad. Or sometimes when he was drunk after a day in the fields and needed a little extra care. He hated the fields. But he always promised once he saved enough money, we would go start the fairytale.

He gave me a kiss every morning before he left to go pick. Those four a.m. kisses, as the darkness of the night started to fade, were my favorite. They made me feel so loved, like the morning was made just for me. The kisses when he got home after sunset, mmm, those were special. I could feel the weathered dirt on his hands as he held me in his arms while I finished cooking dinner. The kisses were scented by the sweat from the central California sun he worked under all day for less than minimum wage, his body odor blended with the subtle scents of strawberries and dirt. No thousand-dollar perfume could replace that smell. He worked so hard for us, and I loved him for it. I felt so safe, so secure.

He was right. Me and him against the world.

Then diapers started piling up, and so did the overdue bills. We came close to losing our house many times. He worked more and more, trying to provide.

"This is our home, my family's home, and no one is going to take it from us. No lousy, no-good banker. Not the owners of the farm. No one. I am a man, and a man doesn't let his family suffer. A man fights for what he believes in. A man has strength. A man provides," he would say each time a past-due bill came in.

The kisses started to come only in the evening, several hours after I had already eaten and Brava was fast asleep. The lingering smell of beer replaced the scent of strawberries and dirt. The kisses didn't feel the same anymore. My four a.m. kisses became shakes of the shoulder. Signals for us to make love. At first it was exciting. I was what a good wife should be, a caretaker of her family, her home, her husband, and all his needs.

But just as the kisses had become different, so did the love. So many times, I would lie there, and he would kiss my neck and fuck me, like he was trying to exorcise a demon weighing heavy on his heart.

Then, he would just shake me so he could put it in my mouth. I am a good wife. He was under a lot of stress, and it was what he needed. Anything to make him happy again. Anything to get us back to where we were—what I knew we could always be. The promise of what could be was the greatest gift I could aspire to.

Then the kisses turned into yelling as soon as he walked through the door.

"Why didn't you wait for me to eat, you selfish bitch?"

Or, "Can't you make anything other than the same old shit, or are you too stupid?"

Brava would cry loudest when the plates smashed against the wall. I would hold her and try to settle her.

"What do you want from me, huh?"

"Haven't I given you everything? Haven't I given all of myself?"

"Do something!"

When he had me pinned against the wall, shouting in my face as I held Brava, that was the scariest. Sometimes I wished he would just hit me and get it over with. The thought of what he could do was scariest. Tears ran down my face.

"Are you a fucking baby? Get out of my fucking face," he would say before shoving my face out of the way and punching the wall.

"Knock the crying off, or I'll give you something to cry about!" he would say before he left again.

And he did.

I am a good wife.

The tears made me forget.

The small shoves got bigger. Mostly, while Brava was in her crib. The small shoves across the kitchen turned into big pushes over the couch, leaving bruises all over my arms and legs when I would hit the coffee table or the arm of the couch my parents had given us when we got married. I started to lose my hair, both from the stress and from when he would drag me across the floor. His thick strong fingers always had strands of my hair in them, whether it was in pain or pleasure. I screamed and cried, "I'm sorry!"

I apologized for I don't know what, but it was my fault. I did whatever I could to make him stop hurting. And for him to stop hurting me. The bruises from the couch and the coffee table were replaced by bruises from his back hand. They were always on my body, never on my face. He knew better. I knew better. If it was on my face, our family would be ripped apart. I wasn't going to let that happen.

He'd wake up and apologize. "I'm so sorry about last night, *mi princessa*. You know I don't mean it."

He would start kissing me again, like he did before. He would kiss my neck and enter me again and again. Empty love. As best as I could, I tried to turn off my mind in those moments. Waiting for that last pump, that last exhale, the warm ooze inside of me—a mixture of white and red. He'd roll over to his side of the bed and put his jeans on. After he walked out the door, I could come back to my body.

He was a great father to Brava. On Sundays, we felt like a family. After mass, he would spend the afternoon replastering the holes he made in the walls. We'd go for walks in the park and enjoy time with our neighbors at barbecues and meals at their homes.

He was so joyous on Sundays. He would hold my hand for all the world to see, and I felt his love. I wanted it to last forever with my hand in his, and my head resting on his shoulder.

Brava would giggle when he tickled her. He would hold her in one arm and me in the other and say, "I swear to you both I'm going to be better. I'm going to be the man I know I can be. It's us against the world, *mis princessas*."

And every time, I believed him. How was I not supposed to? He provided for me. We had a good life. He worked hard to give Brava and me everything we needed. I could be better to him. We could always have life this way. I just needed to fix this. And someday, we could go find what was promised for us and be happy again.

On most Monday nights, when I heard his truck pull up at nine p.m. or later—the light from his headlights peeking through the closed blinds, sending the silhouette of a prison onto the living room wall—my heart raced.

I would cover the blinds with curtains so no one could see in. Next, I would close Brava's door gently, so as not to wake her. I would always be ready with my makeup on, a shirt showing my cleavage he loved to grab, and his dinner on the table, just how he liked me and our home. Anything to not set him off. Anything to make sure the neighbors didn't get curious. Anything to show our home was not broken.

I wanted them to believe in the Sunday promise as much as I did.

But nothing worked. He got angrier. The beatings got worse. I learned how to go somewhere else in my mind when it happened. My nonreaction brought his fists down with more fury, but I knew better than to fight back. Fighting back would mean our family was broken.

A broken family could not be real.

One day, I worked up the courage to tell him I was going to leave him if he didn't stop.

"Go ahead. Who is going to want a fat, stupid, used good like you? Tell me. What are you going to do? Get a job? Take Brava. Go ahead. Make a life for yourself. See how well you survive. You're nothing without me."

He was right. Every last bit of it. I didn't know what it was like to work outside of the house. What man would want a divorced woman from a failed marriage. A used good. I didn't look like I did when I was the cheerleader and he was the football player. What would make me valuable now?

I couldn't go to Papi. He died a few weeks after Brava was born. Cancer. If I went to Mami for advice, she would say to me, "*Mija,* you need to hold it together for the sake of Brava. She can't grow up in a home of divorce. How would God look at her? How would God look at you? Sometimes, when you're married you need to go through rough patches like this. At least you have your husband. I don't. You should be grateful."

I heard every word she said, and she was right. I needed to be a good wife. What would I look like to everyone if I failed? Men beating women has been around forever. Why was I special? Why did I deserve anything different? I was a mother. I was a wife. I was great at being both, and I should stick through this. Mami was right. Every relationship had rough patches, and I wasn't going to be responsible for breaking up my family. Being the only divorced woman in San Eugenio? No, *gracias.*

Shake, fuck, push, hit. Shake, suck, drag, hit. Routine. Every day—except Sundays. His day to rest.

He loved me, and I loved him. Life could change. I needed to stick it out.

One night, he hit me so hard in the stomach I threw up all over the kitchen floor.

He pulled me by my hair and told me to mop it up. "Pick that shit up. The least you can do is keep this kitchen clean!"

So I did ... with my hair. Just as he asked. Just so he would stop. As I did, he passed out on the couch.

This wasn't right, and something needed to change. I ran over to the phone and called the cops. Just to scare him.

Sergeant Carlos Lopez arrived. We stood outside of our home. The neighbors watched as the red, white, and blue lights from his SUV lit up the street. I was so ashamed it had come to this. I gave my statement, and he gave his. People were watching. My worst fears had come true. I was a failure.

"Mrs. Sanchez, charges aren't automatic. Would you like to press charges?"

I looked around at my neighbors. I saw the disapproval in their eyes. I couldn't take their judgment. Their happy families. The disturbance I caused. I upset my family, my community, and I couldn't live with that stain. People would talk. People would know I was a failed wife. People would know he wasn't as great as they thought he was. I needed to protect him. I needed to protect Brava. I needed to protect us.

I needed to keep the dream alive.

"No, I'm fine. Really. It was just a misunderstanding. I just got scared. I'm so sorry. Every marriage has rough patches, right?" I said to Sergeant Lopez, holding Brava in my arms. He spotted a bruise on my arm and looked at my wet hair. I smiled at him.

"Mrs. Sanchez, this doesn't need to continue. I can help you. I just need you to press charges."

"She's teething, and it can get really tough. I think she's about ready to chew through some ice." I laughed.

Sergeant Lopez didn't find it funny.

"If there's anything you need, please don't ever be afraid to stop by the station," he said. He stared into my husband's eyes with a look that could kill.

As Sergeant Lopez walked away and got back into his car, I tried to shout everything—all the pain, the hurt—but nothing came out. My voice stopped. It was like I could no longer speak. My husband took Brava from my arms gently and held her in one arm and me in another. He waved to Sergeant Lopez with a smile. He looked over to our whispering neighbors, and in Spanish said, "Sorry, everybody. Food got a little too hot, and I yelled. You know how it is. See you tomorrow at work."

As he turned us around and we walked back into the house, my heart sank. I knew what waited for me when I got back inside. And the next day, and the next day. I needed to get to Sunday.

I started getting text messages throughout the day. All day.

What do you mean you're at the store? Tell me, who you are fucking?

No. You don't miss my calls. You pick up when I call. I don't care where you are. Is that understood?

How's my day? Like every other day. It's hard, stupid. You're gonna get fucked good tonight.

How am I supposed to TRUST YOU? TELL ME!!!!

When he got tired of texting, it was phone calls. I always felt like I was on eggshells. Anything I said might set him off. I had to be good, and I didn't want to set him off, or worse, let the anger boil inside of him for when he got home after the bar. It's not a life I wanted. I wanted to live mine … with him. But I wanted to feel like myself again. I didn't know who I was anymore, and I hated it.

So, what had brought me to the San Eugenio Police Station?

I got courage.

And so did he.

I saw his headlights pass through the blinds. I was cooking him spaghetti. The water boiled atop the stove. I decided not to put on makeup and wore a shirt that hung from my shoulders down. Nothing hugging my curves and nothing to make me desirable. Maybe this would work. He could still have his dinner ready for him, and I didn't have to be perfect anymore. I could be me. My heart raced as I waited and hoped.

The door opened. He was a little drunker than normal. He never stumbled. This night, he did. "*Hola, mi amor.* Your dinner is almost ready," I said as I stirred the noodles.

He didn't answer. He went to the couch and took off his work boots.

My back turned to him. I stirred the noodles. I took a deep breath. "Your dinner is almost ready."

I heard his boot fall. The hair on the back of my neck stood up. His footsteps changed from muted silence to heavy steps as they went from carpet to the vinyl of the kitchen floor. My heart beat faster and faster. My breathing shallowed. He held my hips. The side of his face right beside mine, just like he used to when he would kiss me when he got home. The smell of strawberries and weathered dirt completely gone. Now, the sweet scent of fear.

"What the fuck did you say to me?" he whispered in my ear, as he put his hands on my shoulders and rubbed them softly.

"Dinner is almost ready." A tear ran down my cheek as I closed my eyes. I continued to stir.

His hands slipped up my shoulders to my neck, squeezing as tightly as he could. "That's what I thought you said."

I hit his hands, as I gasped for air. I grabbed at anything I could as I struggled to breathe.

"You think I'm stupid, huh?"

I grabbed the boiling water and tilted it onto his foot, burning his and mine.

"You stupid bitch!" he shouted as he grabbed his foot, and I gasped for air.

"I'm so sorry. You were hurting me. Let me get something for your foot."

He looked at me. He wound up and slapped me across the face so hard I fell to the floor. I saw nothing but white before I felt the vinyl of the kitchen floor. When the white went away, all I saw was him huffing and puffing, and his fist up in the air, ready to land right on my face.

And it did.

Hit after hit, repeatedly to the right side of my face. He held my hair, each time he was ready to hit me again.

"Why do you make me do this?! Why?" he shouted as he took deep breaths between each wind up. "Stop making me do this. Stop it!"

He cried, tears running down his face.

I gasped for air. I could taste the blood from my lip as I tried to breathe. "I'm sorry."

"I don't want to do this anymore!" he shouted as he reared back.

The first thing I saw when I woke up a few hours later was blood from my face making the water from the pot on the floor take on a reddish hue. I thought of Moses and the signs of God's wrath on Egypt. I spit out whatever was in my mouth. I got up quietly and saw he was asleep on the floor with a few cans of beer next to him. I walked over to check on Brava, who was fast asleep. I was so desperate for something to change that I left her there.

I'm trying to remind myself, for all that he did to me, he was at least a good dad to her.

I walked out to his truck as best as I could and faded in and out as I drove. Next thing I knew, I was waking up in a police station, sitting at Sergeant Lopez's desks, speaking to him, and waiting for Dr. Lopez to arrive so I could go home.

Things felt different the moment I got to the police station. Reality hit. I didn't want to press charges against my husband, but I asked if maybe someone could talk to him so this would stop. Maybe someone could see the truth of what was going on. I mean, how often do we avoid facing the truth? How often are we willing to look away from a broken home? I at least was willing to take responsibility and take the power back by coming here. I hoped maybe they would be able to talk sense into him.

I would never leave him. I couldn't be the one who broke our family apart. I couldn't keep blaming him for what was wrong with our home. Everyone wants to blame everyone except themselves. I wanted to be different. I wasn't willing to lie to myself anymore. I wasn't going to be stupid anymore. I could save our Sunday dream, the future life we once had, and be the good wife I was always meant to be.

I want to share this poem I wrote.

The Beauty and the Beast.
Tale as old as time.
We applaud one another for this great experiment we created together.
Living in harmony. It's beautiful. Everything we ever dreamed of.
Nothing could ever say it was broken inside.
Inside, it was hell.
The foundation you thought was there, destroyed by anger.
The fury no one talked about, slowly crept up to the surface.
No matter how the beauty cried out to be heard, to be listened to, to be remembered,
The hate, the anger, and the injustice were never dealt with.
So she suffered in silence as the days carried on,
And as the house seemed to be the shining example of all that was possible in this life.

But the beauty could not be stopped. She had to rise up. She had to be known.

It could only be dealt with if she turned into it and showed the ugly side.

She had to look herself in the face and see everything she didn't want to see.

The bruised and the battered. Everything that didn't work.

Until one day, she asked herself, will the Beauty become the Beast?

—Guadalupe Flora Magdalena Sanchez

CHAPTER SEVEN

Carlos

When I met Lupe Sanchez, I found out how deep self-justification could run, so much so she was able to take beating after beating and still stick around. How someone could stay for all of it and call it "love," I'd never understand. People need to see the reality of a situation. Stop running from their problems and face them head-on. It's the only way to live.

I think if Lupe would have owned up to it all, she wouldn't have faced the hurt she did. But then again, people gotta do what they gotta do to keep themselves sane enough to live. In my opinion, it's no way to live. Truth can set people free—if they choose to acknowledge it.

I've never been one to hide the truth. I think we can lie to ourselves all we want to, to try to find some sort of truth that makes sense for us. Eventually, the capital T "Truth" always finds its way out. Maybe it's not lying to ourselves. Maybe it's a type of justification for our past. It's part of the reason why I ended up here.

It's what Eric and Sandy could never understand about me. It's why I was so honest with them all the time. I wouldn't be serving them if I wasn't.

"Mrs. Sanchez, we can't help you if you don't tell us anything."

"I know he loves me."

"Can you tell me what happened to your eye?"

Lupe sat in the light-brown, faux leather chair that had a tear in the back, exposing yellowish foam. She couldn't look up at us, her eyes fixated on the ground, searching aimlessly for some sort of reason as to why this continued to happen, maybe even looking for a way out. I remember back in East LA seeing so many of these women. Bruised and battered. Over and over. Crying. We'd do everything we could to convince them to leave,

51

or at the bare minimum, suggest they should leave. But they never did. They lived in the comfort of the abuse. Speaking up would mean stirring the pot. And that was a greater offense than seeing the light for themselves. Sounds odd, doesn't it? You can't force them. No matter how badly you want them to change. It was nonsensical to me that people would rather live in shit than try to go where the grass was greener.

"I know he loves me," she repeated.

"He's got a funny fucking way of showing it," said Theresa, unable to look our way.

"That's enough, Theresa," I said in the most calming tone I could muster. "You can press charges. All you have to do is tell us exactly who did this to you, and we can get you out of this. Please, Mrs. Sanchez. This will continue to happen over and over again. We can make this stop. We just need to know what happened. How it happened. When it happened."

"She doesn't need your high and mighty ideals, Sergeant Lopez," Eric said. "She needs to talk when she's ready. She doesn't have to say anything to you."

Eric never could mind his own damn business.

"I was wondering when Oprah was going to chime in," I said.

"Are you seriously this stupid? You think you're helping her by berating her?"

"How am I berating her? I'm just doing my job. You're not her attorney, so maybe you should just shut up and go back to your little office."

"Fellas! Is this really the time?" Jimmy said, trying to bring us back to reality.

It was easy to lose myself when Eric was around. "I'm sorry, Mrs. Sanchez," I said quietly.

"Is it okay if we call you by your first name, Mrs. Sanchez?"

I didn't know why Theresa asked that, but it felt right. It wasn't much, but something changed in Lupe for a second. It was the first time she looked up from the floor. Her shoulders perked back. I was used to observing people when they were lying to me—the way their body would change when they weren't being honest. The ways they would look away and squirm in their seats.

Their stories would flip-flop. But this was different. This was a type of body language I wasn't used to.

"Yes, I would."

"Lupe, why don't I make up a room for you here, and you can stay with us for the evening. Let things get figured out a bit. Would that be okay with you?"

"Yes, please."

I don't think there was much else Lupe could say. She seemed removed from herself and reverted into a type of default autopilot mode. I read once it was a "trauma response." Repeating the comfort of pain. Unable to say anything else other than what we need to be true. Who knows? Shrinks are quacks anyway.

"I don't think that's the best idea," I said.

"Where else is she supposed to go? You want to send her back home? So this can happen again?" Theresa shot back.

"We don't know that to be true. She hasn't told us who it was."

"Bull fucking shit! We know it was her scumbag husband!" Theresa looked over at Lupe and caught herself mid-explosion. Lupe began to crumble again, her shoulders rolling forward, gravity pulling her head down. Almost as if she believed Theresa would hit her. "I'm sorry, Sarge. I was out of line. Please do as you see fit," Theresa said quietly.

"A woman needs help, and you want to turn her away?" Eric broke the tension with his petty chime.

"This isn't the place for her to stay tonight. Your murderer is coming in. We're going to have our hands full."

"Sarge, I'm going to have to side with the Billboard here. I think it's the right thing to do."

I wanted to help Lupe. I really did. I just had to stay focused on the well-being of the people I commanded. It wasn't going to be a peaceful night with Hinojosa here. These things always have a way of becoming bigger than they are ever meant to. But there was something about this woman I couldn't say no to. I don't know if it was the fact I hadn't seen denial to this level, or if it was just the compassionate side of me—one required of all the best police officers.

"You're right. I'm sorry, Lupe. I just want to make sure everyone is okay, including you. With what we have going on tonight, I just—I just want you to be okay."

She nodded. "Thank you."

"We'll finish your report tomorrow."

She shook her head no.

"Don't let him scare you like this. We need you to speak up. We can protect you."

A tear rolled from her eye. She wiped it away. Theresa walked up to her and placed an arm around her.

I threw my pen and slammed my hand down on my desk. Lupe nearly jumped out of her skin. I shouldn't have done that.

"Nice one, Sarge," Theresa said as she shook her head.

As hard as I tried to hide my emotions, I was never very good at it. I couldn't write the report anymore. I couldn't listen to any more of the fabricated story of it being a fall she took down the front two steps of her porch. Or the fact that she said it was concrete. Didn't know concrete had such precise aim or could put that much fear into someone.

I couldn't figure out how to help her. It made me furious. It's what I was meant to do—help people. I always knew how to fix these situations. This one I couldn't get through to. It became easy to spot, having seen so many of these over the years. Lupe's story was similar to so many women who reported it to me and in some baffling turn of events wouldn't admit it was their boyfriend or husband. Let us do our job. Husband goes to jail for a few months, maybe a few years. Send the woman to a shelter for a few weeks and some therapy, and she'd be good as new—ready to find a life for herself.

Then there was the other option. I saw too many of those. We were too late for some. Those memories I can't get out of my head. I didn't want the same outcome for Lupe. I don't think she did either. She wouldn't have shown up to the station if she did. When people want help, when they want something to be different, they show up. No matter how much they say the opposite.

As Theresa comforted Lupe, Jimmy leaned over to me. "What are we going to do, Sarge? We can't just let this go. We know what happens next if she says nothing. At the very least, we gotta get her looked at."

I knew what the answer was. My heart started racing. My chest tightened.

"I know. I needed to make a call."

Except I hadn't made the call right away.

One moment, I would just stare at the phone. The next I typed up reports of what I had seen earlier in the day. Looked at the phone. Sorted office supplies. The highlighters and pens at different desks had suddenly been disorganized, and I needed to organize them. Looked at the phone. Had the numbers shrunk? Checked our ammo. It was low. It always was.

I had looked back at the phone. I always answered the call. She would too. That's what scared me the most. Sandy and I both lived our lives in service of others. No matter how much she hated me, she wouldn't say no to someone in need. She was the only female doctor around for miles, and frankly, the only good one. The only person I could have called.

But it was bad enough the boy was here. I didn't want another person who abandoned me to find themselves here and needing to "fix" me again. I didn't need fixing. I wasn't the one who left. Hinojosa was enough for the night. Add one ungrateful kid and wife—uh, ex-wife—to the mix, and it was enough to make me want to retire immediately. I didn't want to do this anymore. But I had to put my ego aside and get this woman the help that she needed. It was what I was called to do.

You can't linger on the past.

I had picked up the phone. As I bent down to push each number, my hand had shaken a bit. It was weird. I had been in a number of gun fights. Made calls to parents to tell them their kids were in the hospital after a drunk-driving accident. This had felt harder than the rest of those things. But I'm never one to back down, and I sure as hell wasn't going to back down from Sandy. I had punched in all the numbers, and the phone had rang three times until the receiver on the other end picked up.

"Hello."

Sandy's tender voice on the other side of the phone had sounded a bit lighter than the last time I heard it five years ago, proof her life was better without me in it. Hell, mine was too. We didn't need each other then, and we sure as hell didn't need each other now.

We had a job to do and a citizen to take care of. I'd say if there was one thing connecting me and Sandy, we were always there to serve our community. She couldn't understand. She chose to abandon me after the trial. She didn't care when I needed her. She just walked out. But I don't give a fuck anymore. It's in the past.

Honestly, I can't remember much else past me dialing the phone. I trust I did my job, told her the details of what happened. I know I was professional. Kept my cool. I was a cop. It's what I was supposed to do. Keep the situation calm. I wasn't going to hide from it.

The details aren't important. The important thing is I did my job. Not like she would care. I needed to get it done with and get her to the station to help out Lupe. Brief, cordial exchange, and we can move on with our lives. This chapter could re-close, and I'd be done with it forever. One night, and Sandy, Eric, and I could all go back to our lives. Better off without each other, than with each other. All I really wanted was peace.

It was 7:36 a.m. when I landed in Kuwait; 6:03 a.m. when I saw the second plane hit the tower on 9/11; 12:01 a.m. when the first bullet went past my head the night in the alley.

Those are times you remember change your life. I'm sure if I tried hard enough, I could probably remember what time Sandy and I got married or the time Eric was born, but those memories are too far gone for me to try to dig for. I doubt they cared about them either.

It was 11:14 p.m. when the bus arrived. The Davidson County Sheriff's Department logo ran across the side above silver exterior. You could make out horizontal bars through the tint of windows. Why they didn't put a high-profile prisoner in an unmarked car, in a multicar convoy, or SUV, I don't know. Maybe they were trying to hide him in plain sight. He was the only passenger on this bus.

Jimmy and I stood out back. Jimmy propped the back door of the station open with a small gray trash can. It didn't have a liner in it. Might have been a puke bucket for the remains of a

San Eugenio cocktail. This place didn't have door stoppers for Christ's sake. Didn't matter one way or the other if the door was open. The Titanic was pulling into port.

The bus let out a hiss as it came to a stop.

"Here we go, Sarge."

Those guys on the bus were always ornery. We used to call them "Triple A with Guns," a bunch of low-ranking cops who barely squeaked by the academy and now had a tried-and-true little-man complex. Every time a prisoner came off one of those buses, you could tell how these guys had to make their presence known in some way. They were pushy. Condescending. Obnoxious. They let the prisoners know this was the new reality they were walking into—decisions were going to be made for them from here on out. It would make their lives better.

Officer Carpenter was one of the best at assuming all those traits and so much more. Everyone knew his ex-wife had an affair with his captain. She was just as miserable and somehow even more annoying than him with her cackle of a laugh.

I shudder to think of her orgasm.

Carpenter was a borderline alcoholic, an overweight slob, who barely could fit his shirt into his waistline. You could always expect a small sliver of the shirt to be outside of his belt. He had a crewcut he spiked like an idiot that would make an eighties movie bully jealous. He was constantly broke from his days at the dog track. He held his shotgun like it was his child. His kids had left him too. I couldn't blame them. Smart kids. He didn't care what you looked like or where you came from, he was an asshole to everyone—the right guy for the job.

It was dreary on those buses. Cold and callous. The seats were hard and an uninspired plastic blue. The locked gate between the prisoners and bus driver made the whole thing claustrophobic. Talk about losing hope quickly.

The bus driver unlocked the locks from Hinojosa's ankles. Then he moved up to his wrists and uncuffed those. Carpenter's shotgun never wavered from the side of Hinojosa's temple.

"Make one wrong move, and I'll blow your head to Kingdom Come. You understand me, you illegal fuck?"

Hinojosa nodded.

"On my command, you'll stand up and walk over to the door. Three, Dos, Uno. Up."

Hinojosa got up and shuffled his way to the front. His pace was slow. Diligent. Calculated. Almost as if nothing in this world has ever bothered him. Carpenter got off the bus first, his shotgun pointed at the door.

"Nice to see you again, Carpenter."

"Fuck off, Lopez." Carpenter's gaze never broke from down the barrel. One sudden move, and I do believe Hinojosa would have found the insides of his head sprayed all over the gravel.

"Good to see you, too."

"Hey, Hoagie Hero," Jimmy greeted. "We're going to be stuck with him for the night. Not you. So make this transition bearable or go find another cop to bang your wife."

I could never say that stuff as a sergeant. But Jimmy could, and he knew it.

God, it felt good.

A bead of sweat fell down Carpenter's chubby brow. The man was always tense, ready to fight or have a heart attack. You never could tell. I think he knew the gravity of the situation far better than anyone. The department saw he was really good at this, despite all his flaws, and kept him in this box. I think the misery of the cage never left Carpenter.

Hinojosa stepped down the three steps of the bus and touched down into San Eugenio. His eyes never broke from the ground. He was maybe five foot six. Not an ounce over one fifty soaking wet. This is what we were supposed to be afraid of? This is what was causing the divide in the country? This immigrant? This brown skinned, meek, cold-blooded killer? Another Latino giving someone like me a bad name. The good ones. Didn't matter what size or shape they came in. What was in their heart is what scared me most.

"Transferring custody of Prisoner 9161821 to San Eugenio. This piece of shit is yours now," Carpenter said.

"Book him, Jimmy."

Jimmy grabbed Hinojosa by his arm and led him to the back door.

"I really do think you'll love your stay here. We just replaced the carpeting and painted the walls to really bring out the mahogany furniture. We have a full margarita bar. It's a really wonderful place. You have many choices, and we appreciate you choosing us at the Grand San Eugenio."

Carpenter begrudgingly lowered his gun. "Transport will arrive at zero four hundred. Patrol units enroute. If you need anything, well, suck a dick."

"Good to see you've changed, Carpenter."

"Following orders, Lopez. Just glad we get to keep all the pieces of shit I know locked up together for one night."

"Get back on the bus, Carpenter, or you'll be late for school."

Carpenter laughed. He turned his husky butt around and huffed and puffed his way up the stairs. Walking up the three steps of the bus doorway made him exhausted. A nice consolation prize for us.

"Move out!" Carpenter shouted to the bus driver.

The doors closed behind him. An asshole like him practiced that move a thousand times. Honestly, it looked pretty cool.

Cops are cops. We know what this badge has cost us. Carpenter was no different. He was just an enormous prick. As the bus drove off in the night, the taillights were lost to the dark and foggy mist.

I turned and made my way back into the station, securing the door behind me. I walked back toward my desk, wondering what the hell I just signed up for.

"It's nice to see you, Carlos."

My heart stopped. I hadn't seen Sandy in five years, and she was as beautiful as the day she left. I didn't care. There was nothing more to do between us. Any hope for our future died the day she left me to find a better life for herself. Her hair had a few streaks of gray in it, but she looked refreshed as she tended to Lupe's wounds. She blamed me for everything that went wrong in her life. Now, since I wasn't a part of it, she got everything she ever wanted.

"Thanks for coming down," I said to her, not knowing what else to say.

"I'm a doctor. It's what I do."

"You can't be behind the front desk. You're a civilian. Please go wait in the lobby," I responded confidently.

"Are you serious? You called me. I'm treating her. You asked me to be here. I am not going to leave the side of my patient."

"I don't care. It's procedure. Until you're authorized by me or one of the other officers, you can't be back here."

I don't know why I said what I said.

"You gotta be kidding me," Eric said, butting in with boundless disgust. "It's Mom. Grow up."

"We're separated. Don't you know the legal difference between the two, Mr. Lawyer, or is there not enough money in breaking families apart? Get back to the office."

"No, I'm meeting with my client, and I don't have to do anything that you tell me without due process of law."

"I let her back here, Sarge," Theresa offered. "Didn't know it was going to turn into World War III. Y'all need some therapy."

"There's no point to it, Theresa. It's not something any of us want. There's no future for us. Carlos didn't want it when we were together, and I don't want it now. I've moved on with my life."

"Excellent. Something we can agree on."

Sandy walked over behind the front desk. She kicked open the little swinging door by her hips and stood behind the counter, tapping her fingers.

"Feel like a big man?" Eric asked.

"Stay out of this, Mr. Lopez. Go back with your client and do your due process bullshit."

"I'll talk to you in a bit, Mom."

"Sounds good, honey. If you need me, I'll be in the grand foyer."

"Theresa, can you check her in, please?"

"Uh, I already did, Sarge," said Jimmy.

"Then why didn't you say anything?"

"Seemed like you needed to get something out."

I walked over to the swinging door and held it open for her. I'll always be a gentleman and serve, even when I'm at my most angry. She didn't even acknowledge me. She walked over to Lupe and asked about her wounds.

"I'm sorry you had to see that, Mrs. Sanchez. It wasn't very professional," I said.

"It's okay, Sergeant," Lupe responded meekly.

"I'm sorry, Sandy. It's just ... today ..."

"I don't want to hear it, Carlos. Just please let me care for Mrs. Sanchez in peace. I'll take her home, and we'll be out of your hair," Sandy said defensively.

"You can call me Lupe."

"Lupe." Sandy smiled gently. "You're safe now."

Sandy always knew what to say.

Lupe wiped a tear from her eye. "Thank you."

There was nothing else for me to say. The only thing I could do was make sure the doctor and Lupe had everything they needed. There would be no saying sorry. No making up for past mistakes. No repairing of broken relationships.

Just people ready to move on with their lives.

CHAPTER EIGHT

Ian

Hate and fear make the world go 'round. They're what I took solace in during my ten years in prison. No commuted sentence for a brother in blue. Ten years with the low-life thugs and degenerates I swore to protect the community against—many of who—I helped put here. Somehow, I, Ian McGinnis—sheepdog of the herd for seventeen years—was considered the same as the wolves.

How's that for justice?

No one listened to me when I tried to explain why I shot the spic—I mean, gangbanger—in the head. He deserved it. I was protecting and serving.

Tell me why I'm wrong. I want to know. The piece of shit had a rap sheet longer than a CVS receipt. Assault, battery, domestic abuse, child endangerment, possession of illegal weapons, drug trafficking ... should I continue? And that was all before he was twenty-three.

But I was supposed to let him back on the streets so he could find his way to another AK-47? Another way to beat his kid who he never showed up for? Or better yet, get money by having people shoot shit into their arms? I'm supposed to stand by and let it happen? No chance.

Enough is enough. I thought of all people Lopez would get it. After all, we were more than brothers in blue. We came up in the academy together. Spent so much time with each other's families. Hell, I remember even taking over the PlayStation controller from Eric. I loved playing video games with him. Especially NFL Blitz. That was a fun one. It let the anger out.

And Sandy. Sandy was amazing. I heard Carlos let her go.

Moron. I wouldn't let that perfect ass out of my sight. But what else should I expect from someone who sat on the stand and said what he did about me. He knew we couldn't let scum back on the streets. He knew the cycle. These guys don't give a fuck about prison. It's a mark of pride.

But he looked me right in the face and signed my death warrant. No one—and I mean no one—sees me as a cop anymore. I'm bundled with the rest of the low-life scum. He was the rat, and I was the one who was punished. Brotherhood my ass.

Ten long years of wondering why my life was taken from me. Why my kids no longer talk to me. Why my wife divorced me via mail in jail … cunt.

I loved being a cop more than anything in this world. The judge didn't understand that when she handed down my sentence, when my family left me, and when the department took away my badge. The camaraderie, the purpose, the thrill, the power—all of it.

Carlos took it away from me.

But now, I was ready to speak the truth. And Carlos needed to know; everyone did.

One way or another, I was going to be heard.

I was going to take my life back.

It wasn't a decision anymore, it was fate. I was going to be the cultivator of justice I was always meant to be. I was going to be judge, jury, and executioner. Truth was my power. When the truth is behind you, how can you fail? What is more powerful than truth?

Fear.

Fear is what kept us alive all those years at Fort Comanche. It kept us from losing the ones we love. Fear of death is what gave us all the procedures we had. It's why we were so well trained. To prevent death of one another and ourselves.

But no matter how much we try to prevent it, we're destined to meet it. We can't stop fate.

It's what keeps us in relationships and what takes us out of them—the fear we will die alone or we'll never get what we deserve. You know what we do deserve? Truth. Once we uncover the fear, we get to the truth. I wasn't scared anymore. Everyone would know my truth. *The* truth.

The fear of being lost to the annals of time is perhaps the greatest possible motivator we can have. It trumps all else. And the fear of being forgotten is what I used, and what I knew would be most effective when I met the white trash piece of shit, Freedom Frank, and the head of the beaners, El León.

I planned a trip up to visit my friend Carlos in San Eugenio. I wasn't sure what I was going to do when I saw him, but it was meeting these two gentlemen that made the vision become much clearer. I went into the dark, just as I had back in East LA. What did I have to lose?

These men and their band of criminals met at an abandoned tractor-storage facility about twenty-five miles outside of San Eugenio. I never forgot how to infiltrate. I had the added bonus of friends on the inside telling me what was going down. I had to think like a criminal to get what was mine.

"The only thing we owe them dirty-skinned spics is a fuckin' bullet to the head and a ride back to Mexico," Freedom Frank said with a smooth confidence as he held on tight to the AR-15 nestled against his black bulletproof jacket-covered torso.

"This is our home! You terrorize us, all while we do the work none of you lazy gringo putas want to do!" El León shouted.

"Your home? Your home? This is a white Anglo man's country. Founded by white Anglo men. Thomas Jefferson. James Madison. George Washington. Did you learn about some fucking Pancho Rodriguez or Pedro Garcia anywhere growing up? Oh shit, I forgot. You can't read. This ain't your home, boy, and you're sure as shit not going to replace us!" Freedom Frank said this with all the definitiveness he could muster. It was what he believed. Hell, even I believed him.

"Let's fuck these bitches up. This is our home!" El León shouted as he pulled back the chamber of his AK and pointed it at Freedom Frank's face.

Freedom Frank never stirred, even as El León had the barrel of his AK inches from his nose. Part of me thought his calmness was what irritated El León the most. What's scarier than a man who doesn't fear death, but instead, almost welcomes the opportunity of it? It is the trait I valued in both men the most and why they were both what I needed to get this job done. I needed the stoicism and leadership of a calm, collected white man. And I needed someone who would keep the attack moving forward with the fiery, unyielding passion of a relentless spic.

"Easy, Lion. There is a proposition for all of us to get what we want," I said as I pushed up the barrel of El León's AK slightly to break the tension. Both the White Patriots and El León's gang, Muerte, stood at the ready, waiting for the other one to make a wrong move. And there I was, in control of the situation. It was all so beautiful. I don't know why they listened. But my guess is they were willing to listen to anyone, so long as they could get the control back in their lives.

I was the opportunity.

"Maybe I should just waste your pasty ass so you shut the fuck up."

"Typical spic. Unable to keep his cool. You take out another white man and you're dead where you stand. You understand me?" Freedom Frank said as he racked a bullet into the chamber.

El León set off a flurry of .39mm rounds. A strobe of flashes and bringing everyone's barrels up to one another. A final stand off before we were all dead.

The members of Muerte stood there with their .357s, Taurus .38s, .9mm Glocks (same ones we used at Fort Comanche), and other illegally purchased firearms. It was the perfect representation of who these men were—messy, disorganized, violent, and illegal.

Freedom Frank and the White Patriots held their AR-15s, M&P Shields, Springfield XDS, and M&P 15s right back at El León and Muerte. All their men were trained. Their weapons were legal, and waiting for their opportunity.

"Look, gentlemen, if we kill each other now, you become a headline for the eleven o'clock news for one, maybe two days max, and then you're forgotten about. You leave your wives and kids with nothing but a bad memory of you and how you went out. Nothing lasting," I said.

El León and Freedom Frank lowered their guns. They signaled to their people to do the same. We were getting somewhere.

"Make it quick, gringo." El León's curiosity got the best of him. In that moment, I had won, and this was all going to end in my favor. The way I deserved to have it.

"You owe each other vengeance, yes. But most of all, you owe each other a chance to be remembered."

"You better start making sense real quick," Freedom Frank said as his finger neared the trigger and resisted pointing the gun at my face.

"San Eugenio Police Station." They all looked at each other, inquisitively, waiting to hear more. "Lion, there is an opportunity to get rid of the man who has made your life a living hell, when all you want to do is live. Am I wrong?"

"Lopez goes against his own blood. He deserves to die." El León was falling further and further in-line with what I knew, from the moment I saw him. His heart was full of hatred.

"Frank, is it wrong of me to say you're owed something for the death of your brother, Don Watts?"

"Blood for blood will make things right," Frank said as he looked at El León. He started to see an opportunity.

"I share that belief. You have to make a stand and show these transgressions against your people will not be tolerated. You'll take the power back in your hands. The government can't fail you again and won't have the chance to in the future." I struck a chord with Freedom Frank. "You want what I want, a chance to be remembered. If you do this, you and your White Patriots will be known as the ones who stood for something."

"So we give one of ours to help a white who hates us?" El Léon jumped in.

"I think it's only fair, León. One of yours killed one of his. I don't think any of us wants a war. Why would you want to risk losing more of the ones you love and swear to protect?"

Freedom Frank and El León looked at each other with a sense of agreement.

"Well, here, gentlemen, I'm proposing something that gives us all everything we want."

"And what exactly is that?" Freedom Frank sneered.

"We attack the San Eugenio Police Station and kill everyone inside—Lopez and the immigrant, included. No witnesses. All our story—how we want it to be told."

El León and Freedom Frank laughed hysterically. I didn't understand what was so funny. I had never been more serious about anything in my life. Not the academy. Not my marriage. Not my kids. This was what I wanted.

"Shoot this piece of shit, homes." El León signaled to one of his cholo homeboys.

"You laugh because you're scared of the truth—life might be different if this actually works. A part of you knows this is exactly what you need."

El León's shit-eating grin left him. It always happened when what I said landed with a low-life gangbanger like him or my bitch wife. The energy of someone shifts when you speak to a deeper truth or something someone doesn't want to acknowledge. It showed on both El León and Freedom Frank's faces. I was in the right. My destiny was on a path to fulfillment.

Maybe those ten years behind bars were exactly what I needed to lead me to my true purpose—to help others be heard once and for all. To be a leader.

"What's in it for you?" Freedom Frank asked matter-of-factly.

"I want to be remembered as the good person I know I was. Because Lopez took everything away from me. Because I believe in the justice I deserve, you deserve, and Muerte deserves. And mostly, because like you both, I don't want to be forgotten. This is the only path left for us to define our destiny."

El León looked at Freedom Frank with a subtle sense of agreement and attrition. "How do we do it?" El León asked.

"I used to be a cop. I know when and where Lopez and Hinojosa will be and what they will have available to them. I know what tactics they'll use and how they'll go about protecting themselves. We have numbers and guns on them. All they have is location. It will be annihilation with minimal risk to any of us."

"What about backup?" Freedom Frank asked.

"Let me worry about that."

El León stuck out his hand toward Freedom Frank's. "One night, together. We do this, and our beef is squashed. Deal?"

Freedom Frank and El León shook hands.

Fear proved to be the most powerful unifier of all. And I was in control.

The three squad cars HQ had sent formed the perimeter. Two cops to a car. It's so sad how little the tactics change over time.

Police training evolves at a glacial pace. It all played into our favor and made it easier for us to take what was ours. I watched as pairs of Muerte and White Patriots quietly approached the sides of the cars—cooperation among those who deserved their chance.

They were efficient. It was amazing how quickly these guys started working together.

"Eagle One in position. *Estamos aqui.* We're here … on your mark," calls whispered among the radios.

I took one last look at my brothers in blue. It was my last chance at redemption as I knew it, to turn back to a comfort that had always been there for me. But they had turned their back on me. I didn't care if I knew them or not, when one turned, they all turned, and I was a pariah. They lost their sense of justice, and they all deserved to die for it.

"Execute," I called through the walkie.

Low-tone gasps. Some stirring. The frantic kicking of a dashboard. Muted gurgles.

Gone was the blue line. I crossed it. I was on the right side of history.

"Clear. Clear. Clear," came over the walkies in rapid succession.

The night was ready to begin.

Seeing as the whole town essentially ran off one grid, killing the power to that building was easy. I watched as two Muerte scaled up the light tower like fuckin' brown lizards and knocked out the main transformer running power into the building.

The station went dark. A dim light flickered on, but their backup generators wouldn't last them long. Silhouettes of people in the station scrambled as we looked on, waiting for our moment. I could hear Lopez's muffled speaking. Even in old age, the low timbre in his voice carried as it always had. His voice commanded respect as it had back in the East LA days, even if its muffled sound had a sense of defeat to it now.

"Forty-two King. Come in, Forty-two King," came over the radio. "I repeat. Forty-two King, come in."

I looked down and pressed the button to the cell phone jammer I had purchased from an old friend who had set up shop as an arms dealer. Like me and Lopez, he was a Devil Dog too.

All cell phones went dead. All their communication went through us now. And the best part? They didn't know it.

"Forty-two King. This is the precinct you are quote, *protecting*. You either get your act together, or I will personally turn your wife into a lesbian. You got me?" a female voice said over the walkie.

"This is Forty-two King."

We had disguised a White Patriot and a Muerte each as San Eugenio Police Officers. They got a script and everything to fit the part, all to give any wanderers, onlookers, or exceptionally brave—or stupid—citizens someone to refer to and keep our cover.

"Forty-two King, how's everything looking out there?"

"All good out here, San Eugenio. See your lights are out."

"Good spot, genius. You guys getting cell service out there?"

"Ten-four. We already called the power outage into HQ and the city. They'll have someone out here in two to three hours."

"You told them we're a police station, right?"

"Ten-four. Not the only ones with power outage. We'll keep you updated on the status as soon as we hear more."

"You just learn ten-four? Stop saying it so much. You sound like a douchebag."

"Forty-two King over and out."

The White Patriot smiled at me in his new dress blues. It was all going so smoothly. He and his Muerte partner saddled up for the evening outside of the road leading into the station, ready for anyone who might try to mess up our fun and interrupt our chance at making history.

Muerte and the White Patriots started to take their positions all around the building. Slowly, they descended on the police station, emerging from the surrounding emptiness, almost as if they had been planted and sewn there for this point in time. The White Patriots wore military garb from surplus stores, wanting to play soldier for a day. Muerte sported their plaid shirts, wife beaters, and oversized jerseys.

Either way you looked at these guys, they all had an image to put on, an image that projected strength and cool—at least in their eyes. It was their time to test their unearned ego.

There's a difference between shooting bottles in the backwoods and holding a gun in your belt in actual battle. We'd see who the real tough guys were and who earned the chance to be here.

I hopped in the back of Freedom Frank's truck, Muerte and White Patriots surrounding me, peacefully coexisting. Guns at the ready. Chomping at the bit. Ready to begin the siege.

Freedom Frank powered on the LEDs at the top of his truck. The spotlight outshined the moon. I took the microphone of the bullhorn. I looked up at the American flag that Freedom Frank had on the back of his lifted truck. I watched as Old Glory majestically flapped in the wind.

This is what America had come to. Righteous vigilantes and vaqueros, like me, Freedom Frank, and El León, all taking power back in our own hands. The system would work for us again. And if it didn't, we were going to make the system and those who hurt us pay. We weren't going to be silent anymore. We weren't going to take it lying down.

This was our country and our time to stand.

The whistle of the bullhorn let out. I put the microphone up to my mouth and smiled from ear to ear. "Fort Comanche. Brothers in blue. Calling Lopez."

Not a sound. I could feel the fear from inside the station as the silence became deafening.

"Fort Comanche calling Lopez. Brothers in blue. Fort Comanche calling Lopez."

I felt the anger. The hatred.

"Ian!" the booming voice rang out. "Ian, I have my family in here."

Freedom Frank and El León smiled, sharing the sense of knowing the destiny we all believed so strongly in was about to be fulfilled.

"I know, partner. We're here for all of you. They deserve to know the truth, and they're all going to die when they know it."

Hate and fear had brought us together before. And I was proud to know it would bring us together again.

CHAPTER NINE

Carlos

"Get away from the windows!" I shouted as I pressed my body against the wall and tried to keep the exploding shards of glass from getting in my eyes. Beretta in my hand, ready to fire back, shots went off all around me.

Desert Storm wasn't as bad as this onslaught. I don't even know if Saddam had this much ammunition. Bullets of all shapes and sizes whipped through the precinct—bursting through light fixtures, tearing up walls, and leaving us all wondering what the hell was happening.

Honestly, all this carnage kind of made this godforsaken place look better. If anything, it needed to be torn down, and these assholes were taking care of it for us.

"What's the plan here, Sarge?" Jimmy called out in a weirdly calm tone. I guess it made sense. We had been through this before against the AK.

"They're going to have to reload in a second here. And when they do, we're going to unload everything we got on 'em."

"Doesn't sound like a plan, but you got it, Sarge!" Jimmy smiled as he waited in the corner.

"Carlos, what do we do?" Sandra asked, huddled under a desk with Eric.

"Try not to get shot. Mrs. Sanchez are you okay?"

Lupe nodded her head in assurance as she covered her ears.

"Anyone of these m-fers comes through the back, they'll get an additional asshole." Theresa shouted with a 12-gauge pointed at the door.

I heard footsteps as I peered out the window. "Flank 'em, flank 'em," and "*A la derecha.*" Voices boomed throughout the night in between the bursts of fire. This was a full-blown assault. Calculated. Specific.

As I watched these guys point and shoot toward us, they had an aura of invincibility. They had numbers on us, and if they had known how little ammo we had and how scarcely unified we were, they would have taken the station in about ten minutes. Ian was too smart. He knew better. He wanted this to hurt.

There was a brief pause in the fire. Silence.

"Sarge, I don't like the sound of silence," Jimmy said as he held his gun out from the corner of the window.

"I got five on this side in firing positions. I'm making out a couple of pistols and one or two rifles."

"Same here, Sarge. This ain't the last of them."

"No shit, Sherlock from Seoul," shouted Theresa.

"You just gonna stand there pointing at nothing, or you going to come help out?"

"Someone's gotta watch this door, or you'll become Korean barbecue," Theresa snapped back.

I looked over at Eric, curled up in a ball with his mommy's arm around him. Unable to move. Unable to fight. Unwilling to fight.

It was time for him to step up. "Eric, I need you to grab one of the desks with Theresa and barricade that door while we're waiting for them to move."

Eric looked up in distress, his hair still finely quaffed and quivering slightly.

"Now's not the time to pussy foot. Do you want to live? Yes? Then, get your ass up and go help her."

Why did I have to repeat myself for someone to want to live? Eric looked over at Sandra. She whispered something to him I couldn't hear, and he crawled out from under the desk like the scared kid he was.

Pathetic.

"Wait for my command. Try to keep your head below the windows. Jimmy, covering fire, in three … two … one … Go!"

Jimmy and I unleashed everything we had in our mags. Each bullet met with what felt like a hundred more in return. Eric did as he was told. When he was close enough, he dove to where Theresa was standing. He crawled over to her side, and she got him behind the wall.

"Got your boy, Sarge," Theresa said.

We ducked back behind the wall. Bullets continued to send holes through the walls, bust up chairs, and demolish the piece of shit computers we had on our desks. Maybe the county would spring for some snappy ass Apple desktops—wishful thinking.

"It looks like they're retreating. Sarge, they're running back. We did something right."

"Nah, Jimmy, you know better than I do they were just sizing us up. Everyone okay?!"

"Good! I'm okay. *Esta bien*," everyone responded, except Eric.

Theresa and Eric slid a desk from the bullpen over to the back door. You could hear every inch of the move against the shitty broken tiles.

"Put a little muscle into it, kid. Lifting up an entire race has to count for something," I joked. Eric just stared as he got the desk into final position with Theresa. "Come on, it's been five years. Take a joke."

"Oh Sarge, noooo. Read the bullet-riddled room," Theresa shot back.

"Are you insane? Do you understand human emotion whatsoever, you absolute ape of a human being?" Sandra asked as she got out from under the desk.

"Calm down. We need to break the tension. Trust me, I know how to survive. I'm going to get us out of this. We need to stay relaxed."

"That's your problem, Carlos. It's always been your problem. Everything is a joke to you. You never want to address the reality of a situation."

"Now's not a time for therapy, okay? There's a bunch of homicidal maniacs out there who want us dead. Not to mention, all of these little minions are being controlled by my ex-partner. This isn't my first time in a shootout. You just want to be right all the time. Well guess what? This is my area of expertise. I've been here before. So we do as I say. Do you hear me, Doctor Lopez?"

"Don't speak to my mom like that, you condescending prick!" Eric charged toward me with his chest puffed out like a high schooler who was about to get into his first fight.

"There he is. Now we're getting someone who wants to fight. Where have you been?" I asked mockingly yet with a sense of pride.

Eric and I stood face to face. I felt the anger in his eyes down to my bones. I didn't know why. He was the one who started it. I was just trying to keep us alive and tease him a little. After all, I hadn't seen my son in five years. If he couldn't take commands and a little teasing, how were we ever supposed to make it out of here?

"I'm not scared of you anymore, you fat old has-been," Eric said near the brink of tears.

Jimmy stepped in between us. "We already have enough people trying to kill us out there. They don't need our help."

"He's right, Sarge. And you don't pay me enough to be a family counselor. I got enough shit of my own." That broke the tension a bit and got a chuckle out of everyone. This was Theresa's gift.

"Alright, how many guns we got? How much ammo?"

"Let's just say the Alamo had better chances," Jimmy responded.

"Shit. Alright, Theresa, I need you and Eric to go to the ammo room. Get everything that we have—rifles, flashbangs, handguns, bullets … lots of bullets—and whatever else you can. Everyone except Hinojosa gets a weapon."

"Copy that, Sarge."

"That's your idea? To give a lawyer, a doctor, and a housewife guns? And we're all just supposed to be Navy SEALs and shoot our way out of here? This isn't a fucking movie, Stallone. This is real life," Eric said.

"What's your plan, genius? Hug our way out? Tell everyone how wonderful they are and hold hands singing *Kumbaya*? In this world, you need to fight. You need to stand for what's right. There's black, and there's white. There's no need to make it complicated," I said, still holding back everything I really felt. I couldn't annihilate the boy. I needed to talk some sense into his snowflake mind.

Time heals all wounds, right? Bullshit.

Sandra walked up to me. "Carlos, there must be something else we can try. Please. We don't need to do this."

I looked into her eyes ... so much sincerity. I had forgotten what it felt like to have her look at me that way. If there was someone who could level an army with a look and extract the truth, it was Sandy.

"Sandy, I need you to trust me, please. I know I can get us out of this."

Sandra backed away and never broke her gaze from me. She quickly grabbed my hand and squeezed it. I didn't know what she meant by it, but a sense of peace came over me.

CHAPTER TEN

Eric

"We need to fight. Everyone grab a gun!" Carlos shouted as he roamed the station back and forth, trying to keep things under control.

"Fight?! Are you a fucking psycho? Who or what are we supposed to fight?! There are three people in here with firearm training and four civilians," I said back to him. "Don't make us suffer for your mistakes."

"Did you not hear they want us all dead? All of us. *All* includes you, college boy."

"You paid for my college, you fucking idiot. We need to get out of here." I scrambled, not knowing what to do or say, flustered beyond my comprehension to think or do much more.

I made a mad dash for the door, hoping someone would listen to reason and logic. There was no reason for this to happen. If it continued, we'd all end up dead, and our attackers would end up in jail for a long time. Surely, they had to understand. I looked at the open door.

My way to freedom.

As I neared the entrance, a floodlight shone through. In a silhouette, I saw something raise up. I stopped in my tracks. This was the end of the road for me.

As I saw a flash, I hit the ground hard.

If Carlos had ever wanted to be a linebacker in the NFL, he missed his calling. The full force of Carlos's body falling on top of me sent me into next week and, to some extent, knocked some sense into me. As I hit the ground, bullets flew right over top us. Everyone took cover behind whatever semi-meaningless cover they could find—plastered walls, desks from the seventies, decrepit windowsills—nothing could provide sufficient protection from the seemingly never-ending onslaught.

As the shooting went off around me, I covered my ears and closed my eyes. Maybe if I didn't see or hear anything, this would all somehow disappear.

When the shooting stopped and I opened my eyes and uncovered my ears, I felt a heaviness on my chest. Carlos was on top of me, trying in vain to shield me as best he could. For a moment, I remembered what it was like to have a father.

"Are you okay? Did you get hit anywhere?" Carlos asked me as he pulled himself up.

"Yeah I'm fine. Get off of me, please," I responded as I felt my body cautiously, searching for any new, unwelcomed holes. Carlos's fat, dirty, cut-up thumbs wrapped the inside of my white Armani shirt. He shook me as ferociously as he could to jolt me back to reality.

"What do you think you're doing? Why won't you listen to me? You're going to get yourself and everyone in here killed," he said with a mixture of anger and worry in his eyes.

I remembered the same look back when I had broken a neighbor's window with a baseball. I had tried to put my hand through the opening in the broken glass to grab it. Fortunately, he stopped me.

"Get off me!" I yelled as I pushed him off. "I can make a deal with them. This is what I do. Why can't you just trust me?"

"What part of 'we're all going to die' did you not understand?" Carlos asked.

"They have to listen to reason and logic. If they keep this up, they're all going to go to prison for life or worse. They can't be that stupid."

"The only one being stupid here is you, putting everyone's lives at risk. These men want you, me, your mom, the criminal, Jimmy, Mrs. Sanchez, everyone dead. Period. End of story. There's no reasoning."

"This isn't some sort of Western, Carlos. You don't get to go down in a blaze of glory. You've had your opportunity before. I'm not going to be a part of it," I said with everything I had in me, hoping to whatever God was out there this would sit with him.

How could he be so blind? How could he not see all he was trying to do was to serve his own personal glory? He wanted to live out some fantasy he had seen in some movie to make up for how shitty his life ended up. We were all pawns in this.

"Eric, listen to your father," my mom said in her tone that could silence Dodger Stadium during a World Series game. There was a way my mom spoke when she meant business. It could stop the world in its tracks. It came from a place of deep truth, no matter how much I wanted to ignore it.

She watched on as I got off the floor, trying to pull myself back up and regain whatever dignity I lost.

"The floor is yours, Sarge. Lead the way." I refused to let him win, his reward for raising a kid to be as tenacious and determined as he wanted me to be.

Carlos took center stage. He wanted this moment. He needed this moment.

"We need to buckle in for the night. Jimmy, we need to secure a perimeter. Barricade every door."

"Copy that, Sarge."

"Theresa, get everyone in here a gun."

"Copy, Sarge. We don't have much."

"What do we have?"

"We have two shotguns, one case of shells, about two hundred 9mm rounds, one door breach, and two ARs."

"That's it?"

"Honestly, Sarge. We ain't got shit," Theresa stated matter-of-factly.

"Well, we have the defensive position. This is our home, so we have tactical advantage over them. We just need to hold on until zero four hundred, and reinforcements will arrive. We can do this," Carlos reassured everyone. "Jimmy and Mrs. Sanchez, I want you to cover the back door. Theresa, you'll be with me, roaming the front doors and the windows. Sandy, Eric, I want you to cover one side window each."

Everyone started moving to their assigned positions. Jimmy went around, checking every door to ensure he hadn't done something stupid like leave one unlocked. Lupe and Mom started barricading the doors, while Theresa assembled and handed out the guns. Even Roberto—with his hands cuffed—moved chairs and desks best he could.

Yet there I stood not moving, thinking I was the only one who might have an ounce of sanity left.

"Have you all gone fucking crazy?! We can't beat these guys."

Everyone stopped the preparations for a moment.

"Are you really thinking we can fight these people? We have two old fat cops, a woman who just went through a horrifically traumatic experience, and an undocumented worker who is the most wanted man outside of these walls. What do we think we're all going to accomplish?" All my words seemed to fall on deaf ears.

"Jimmy, shotgun," Carlos said.

"Incoming," Jimmy said as he tossed Carlos the shotgun. Carlos caught it and racked it. I pushed it away.

"What am I supposed to do with this?"

He shoved it into my chest.

"Point the barrel at anyone trying to kill you. Pull the trigger. Eight shots. Just like when you were a kid. Be smart," Carlos said sternly.

"No, I'm not doing it. I'm an adult now. You can't force me to work with this shit like you did back then."

"Eric, please just listen to your father!" Mom screamed out. "Please, just for tonight, let your father help you."

Mom walked close to me. The look in her eyes told me everything. Now was not the time for bullshit. There was one way out of this. This wasn't something I wanted and wasn't something I was ready for. But, as I've learned in this life, these are the times when the true measure of my being and soul are determined, whether I'm ready for it or not. It's the type of trust I had to put into the powers in this universe.

I was searching for whatever *that* power *was* now.

"Mom, I don't want to do this. I can't do this. I can't take a life. Neither can you," I said as I allowed the shotgun to find comfort in my hands.

"It's not a choice, Eric. You owe it to everyone in this building and to yourself to fight."

Looking at Carlos, I responded to her, "Everything's a choice, Mom."

Something struck a chord with Mom. When I said this, she looked over at Carlos, who didn't take notice. As he lifted his head, Mom quickly looked away.

Carlos exhaled. "Then, choose how you see fit. Watch us die or watch us try to live."

Carlos looked deflated, just as I intended him to be. All the anger and resentment boiled over. I wanted nothing more than to hurt him. And hurt him I did. But something inside of me was unsatisfied. I got what I wanted, yet I stood there with a gun in my hands, and my father walking away as though the fifty plus men with guns outside were the least of his worries.

"No worries, kid. I'll show you how to reload. Ole Jimmy's got you." Jimmy comforted me as he walked me over to my position near the window of Carlos's office. A glass pane was the only thing between me, murder, and the Almighty.

I looked back at Carlos as he walked away to his position, ready to defend a dilapidated Alamo not deserving of defense, had it not been for the people inside.

Carlos knew this place was bound to fall apart any moment, bullets or no bullets. He wasn't dumb. He was too afraid to let it go. This place felt like his last beacon of hope. His last opportunity to run away from everything torturing his soul.

"We don't have much ammo. Try to shoot at only what you can hit. Jimmy, Theresa, and I will give you all a crash course on your weapon. For now, just keep the barrel pointed out and shoot at whatever moves."

I saw Mom walk up to Carlos. "You know, he's just angry. This is scary for him. For all of us. And let's be honest, this is just about the stupidest idea there is." Mom laughed.

So did Carlos. It was their first brief moment of connection in at least seven years.

"He's the only one who's complaining and fighting me."

"Did you want your son to be a principled man? Yes or no?" Mom asked Carlos.

"I just want him to be able to protect himself."

"He can, Carlos. He always has been able to. You have to trust him now," Mom said as she rubbed his back. She caught herself midway through the backrub and pulled her hand back. Carlos looked up and smiled slightly.

Carlos looked over at the AR-15 Mom held in her hand. "You still remember how to use that thing like I showed you?"

"I remembered how to deal with you after all those years. I'm sure I can remember how to use this other stupid thing too," Mom said with a smirk.

"Be careful, Sandy," Carlos said as Mom walked off.

"Always."

As we settled into our positions, I looked out from behind the windowsill. I could see Muerte and the White Patriots conversing among themselves. As I looked at them, I wondered if their sole intent was to kill me and me only. I knew how ridiculous it sounded given everyone in here was a high-value target. The fear was going to prevent me from doing what I needed to do, whether it was against my moral code or not. But maybe, it was this moral code stopping me.

There was no time to think. With each passing second, each moment, each shuffle among the bushes, death was a step closer to me. If this was going to be my last hurrah, I didn't want it this way. Something inside of me would be unresolved, and the worst part was, I couldn't figure out what that was.

The footsteps of White Patriots and Muerte came closer to my window. My heart began to race. The beat of my heart almost kept lockstep with their boots hitting the asphalt, faster and faster.

I gripped the shotgun tighter and tighter, hoping maybe, just maybe, they would rethink their whole blood pact and give us a way out. My vision blurred. My breathing grew shallower. Everything suddenly felt tight.

Pop, after whizz, after pop went off. Pieces of plaster fell everywhere around me. Glass shattered. The ferocity of the noise was equal only to the constant flashes outside.

"Hold your positions," Carlos said just above a whisper.

It was no match for what came back at us.

It wasn't fair. Round after round in rapid succession.

I pointed the shotgun out the window. Members of Muerte converged on the front where Carlos and Theresa did the brunt of the fighting. Jimmy fired shots out the front door as he kept his eye on the back with Lupe. Lupe's eyes locked on the door for any movement, almost like she was waiting to see if her abuser—whether she would admit it was her husband or not—was going to walk through the door.

I think part of her wanted it to be him.

As they moved toward the front. I saw them start to point at the window I was at. It was another way in for them they hadn't seen yet. I peeked out, far enough to catch a glance of them. As if he sensed someone watching him, a stalky, strong Muerte turned. He carried a pistol of some sort alongside his gray Dickies shorts. His wide face and buzz cut sat above a slither of tattoos. He looked like he could kill me with one punch. He smiled. He signaled over to a few more Muerte and yelled something in Spanish over the thunder of gunshots.

I translated in my head. They knew I was soft. They knew I was their way in. It was an easy victory for them. I started to crumble to the ground, hoping against hope they'd make a mistake, or that if they saw me, they might show mercy to me. I don't know if it was cowardice or bravery or both, but I couldn't shoot the gun.

I took a few deep breaths, clenched the shotgun. I looked around at everyone else fighting. They had taken this duty seriously, yet here I was folding before them. I couldn't stand down and let these people die mercilessly.

Maybe there is compassion in killing. You, me, or anyone doesn't know what we're capable of. We don't know how we will convince ourselves what we're doing is right, until we're in it.

Wisdom is in action.

When I looked at Roberto—the one person Carlos had not given a gun—my mind started to shift. I saw him, sitting across the station from me, no gun in his hand. Handcuffs on his wrist. Waiting for his chance to prove himself to the world around him. The calmness in his demeanor brought me a sense of duty I always wanted to pursue. It renewed my sense of purpose, regardless of how much taking the life of another human would haunt me the rest of my days.

I owed it to Roberto. I owed it to everyone in this building.

I got up, racked the shotgun, and moved toward the window sill. As I pointed my gun out, the burly Muerte man peeked up from below. I caught a glimpse of tattoo on the right side of his neck. In cursive, it read *Rosa*.

"Hola, amigo," he said as he pulled himself up.

Next thing I knew, he was on the ground with a hole in his stomach and blood flowing from his mouth. The barrel of my 12-gauge had smoke coming out of it, but I had not a single recollection of how my finger got to the trigger or how he now had a hole in his stomach. All I knew was he was breathing his last breaths.

Other members of Muerte gathered around him. Just like me, they were in disbelief I had shot him. They rushed to his side to help him. Arbitrary attempts at CPR looked more like they were just hitting him. All in futility. There was a hole in his stomach. The show was as much for them as it was for him.

He shot us one more menacing smile, like he knew something we didn't.

Then he was dead.

There's something no one ever tells you about killing someone. I'm not talking about physically killing someone; I'm talking about death of a spiritual nature. With one pull of a trigger, I took away everything from him, everything he ever loved. Every regret he had. Every chance he could have had to turn his life around. Everything he could have done.

I thought about the pain I brought on his family. I thought of the people who loved him.

I thought of the name *Rosa*. It could have been his wife, his mother, or his daughter. Someone meant something enough for him to mark it permanently on his body. And I took this man away from one of them. All of them.

Our choices brought us here.

His friends, or maybe they were just loose acquaintances of a forced fraternal nature, dragged his dead body away. He knew when I pulled the trigger, I would never escape this.

What I had done to him would live with me forever. No matter how much longer I lived.

The shooting stopped. I threw down the gun.

I cried.

Carlos heard me, and his head snapped in my direction. "Jimmy, cover the front!"

"Ten-four, Sarge!"

I don't know how many more Muerte and White Patriots started to climb through the window. I just felt a rapid fire of bullets and the air leaving men's mouths. I felt the shotgun abruptly pulled out of my hands in one move. I heard the shell go into the chamber, followed by a pump and a boom. Pump and boom. Until there was the eerie silence.

"Clear!" Theresa shouted.

"Sarge, they're retreating!" Jimmy yelled back.

"Everyone good? They're not done. Hold your positions." I felt a tug on my arm and heard a soft but stern voice. "Get up, Eric."

As I uncovered my eyes, I saw Carlos standing over me, supreme disappointment in his face. "Get up, Son," he repeated as he held out his hand.

I hit it away and cried harder.

"Jesus Christ, get up, Son. Not going to be the last one you kill tonight. We need you."

His lack of understanding pissed me off. I quickly wiped away the tears, regained my composure, and tapped back into my anger.

"Is this what you want? You want to go out in a blaze of glory? Prove to yourself somehow you're worthy of some fuckin' 'Cop of the Millennium' trophy. You're just as much of a killer as they are. And now, because of you, so am I." The anger emerged in every possible way I could take him down. I wasn't even trying. It flowed out of me at this point. I didn't have to think. Anger, hurt, and resentment had become second nature when I was around him.

I couldn't control it.

"No, I want you to be a man. I want you to protect the ones you love," Carlos responded.

"Am I a man now because I killed someone? Does shooting a gun make me worthy of manhood? Does it tell everyone how much I'm protecting them?"

"When will you understand I am trying to save your life? And if not save it, then at least give you a chance to live. What else can a father do?"

I stood there stone-faced, not an ounce of energy left in me. I stared into his eyes with a form of exhaustion so pure, he read everything I felt. "Do you really want me to answer the question?"

"I'm okay. I'm okay. I swear." Theresa's words started to fade with each false statement she made.

Jimmy had her in his arms and started to lie her on the ground. "Sarge! We need you here now. Theresa's been hit!"

Carlos snapped his head around. His shoulders slumped as soon as he caught a glimpse.

He hobbled over to Theresa as fast as he could. I followed suit, shotgun still in hand.

"Jimmy, keep your eyes out front. Eric, watch the door with Jimmy."

Carlos swapped with Jimmy as he watched over Theresa.

"Sandy. We need you!" Calls of desperation from Carlos's voice I'd never heard before.

Mom hurried to Carlos's side. She checked Theresa's back. As soon as she felt the exit wound, the look in her eyes said it all.

There was nothing she could do. The bullet had clipped Theresa's heart.

Every second became precious.

"There has to be something," Carlos said, looking at Mom. She didn't seem to know how to respond to him. Although they had been separated for over five years, Mom knew how much Carlos loved his deputies.

Theresa saw it in everyone's eyes. "Well, I think I got a couple of them, right?"

Carlos, hard as he fought it, couldn't keep the emotion off his face. Theresa was like a sister to him, someone who told him like it was. Both the good and bad angel for him, she helped him to better understand the choices he made. Her wisdom just happened to be wrapped in lewd obscenities and harsh reality.

The harshest of realities set in now.

For all the bad in Carlos, I knew his greatest fears were losing someone he loved dearly and knowing there was nothing he could do to fix it.

"Hell, yes! I saw a few of those motherfuckers hit the ground hard," Carlos told Theresa.

It was the truth. She had. She protected and served.

"Sarge, just make sure Bella knows her mommy loved her," Theresa said, clinging onto her final moments.

"She'll be taken care of, Theresa."

"I know she will. Hey, Jimmy?"

Jimmy turned his head as he leaned against the wall facing the exterior. He wiped away a tear. "Sup, Theresa?"

Theresa raised her middle finger and flipped him off. Jimmy laughed, and so did Carlos.

"I love you too, Theresa," Jimmy said with every ounce of a final goodbye he could muster.

"Sarge, thank you … for everything," Theresa whispered with her last few breaths.

Her eyes closed.

She was gone.

Her hand went limp where Carlos held it. He kissed it. Then he put it down.

Carlos covered her face with his jacket—one last goodbye to his friend. He held back a tear, took a deep breath, and commanded, "Everyone get back to your positions. They're going to come back for us."

I knew that Carlos didn't want to take responsibility for Theresa's death. For now, he needed to remove himself from any emotion he felt.

It's what he was best at.

CHAPTER ELEVEN

Eric

Carlos always said he lived his life with no regrets. I find it hard to believe anyone in their lifetime can live a life with no regrets. But I took him at his word. And taking him at his word that he *lived with no regrets* was the most painful thing I could have imagined him saying to me.

What about how he left me and Mom behind? Not a single part of him would do it differently? To make a different choice for a different life? One to keep us together? A decision not leaving him isolated at this station? A decision not leading to us now fighting for our lives together?

I watched Carlos as he looked out the window and tried ardently to push away the fact he had just lost his friend. His observance of the threat outside was a distraction from the exploration needing to happen within.

"*Agua, por favor,*" Roberto stated at a volume just above a whisper.

"Jimmy, get Capitán Killer some water please," Carlos blurted out with disdain and duty, both of which he lived with as a cop who believed in the strength of the thin blue line.

Immobile and inflexible.

Jimmy, taken aback by Carlos's crude brashness that was even too much for him, responded, "Sarge, it's okay for us to grieve Theresa."

"Grieve what? She's dead. She died protecting the station. What else is there to say about it? We have a job to do. And the job right now is staying alive," Carlos said without missing a single beat, almost as if he had it preplanned.

"Looks like you're doing a pretty fucking good job at it so far," I said.

"Eric, enough!" Mom said.

"You're going to defend him?! One of his best friends just died, and now his response is to insult a man who we don't know with any certainty is guilty," I snapped back.

"It's okay, Sandy. Let him mouth off. It's what he's best at. If it weren't for all his bullshit self-promotion, we wouldn't be here," Carlos said, stone-faced, his gaze not breaking from the assailants, waiting for any attack unfolding from outside. And from within. Both were inevitable, and both ones he had to resist or give in to. Giving in was neither in his nature nor mine.

Jimmy handed Roberto a cup of water. Roberto struggled to grab it with both hands as they remained cuffed. Carlos didn't even have the decency to uncuff him while the attacks were unfolding.

"I can't believe you. A man who was so adamant about teaching me the meaning of justice, about right and wrong, can't give this man the courtesy of what is a fundamental constitutional right."

"He's not a citizen. He's an illegal criminal. The only reason I haven't fed him to the wolves out there is because I swore an oath to uphold the Constitution. And he, unfortunate as it is, is granted those basic rights and protections. I intend to see it through or die if I need to," Carlos said, impassioned. His body was now almost completely facing me—just not enough to take his watch off the front.

"You don't get it. The less you see him as a person, the more you're one of them out there. You're just putting a different lens on it, making it seem like it's not you doing this," I said, standing my ground.

"I'm the problem? Who was the one out there like Al Sharpton, screaming out front of the steps of the police station, riling up everyone with the *Latinos are victims* rah-rah bullshit you were spewing. It's you who divides us. It's people like you who get people like them angry. And it's people like you who force people like me into a position where I have to stand in between it all. You have a problem with it, then fight your way out like a fuckin' man, instead of crying like a pussy and having me come save your ass."

"Enough!" Mom yelled. "Both of you. I don't care who did what. We're in here together. The more we fight, the better chance we give them, and the sooner we die."

The room fell silent. Mom didn't use her voice often. But when she spoke, people listened. And when she got angry, there was a different gravitas. Mom had a love for all humankind in her heart that people couldn't help but listen to.

"Lupe, this better or worse than a telenovela?" Jimmy quipped loudly.

After a brief second of the elongated tension, Roberto laughed so hard he spit out his water. The whole room busted up with laughter.

It was a nice reprieve, a moment to feel like people again.

"At least in telenovelas, people have sex. No one is getting any in this room. And it shows," Lupe quipped back.

We all laughed harder.

We all admired Lupe Sanchez. Amid the horrible shit she had gone through, she still exemplified the strength of the human spirit. No matter how broken we might feel nor how unjust the world might be, moments of laughter and the human connection it offered could never be dismissed, no matter how hard anyone tried.

Carlos and I both relented. We returned to our positions. Jimmy hesitantly took Theresa's spot at the front with Carlos. "It feels weird being here. I hope I can do the job she did."

"Let's hope," Carlos said as he turned away, his attention back to the front.

Jimmy looked over to his friend of twenty plus years and said, "Sarge, she died fighting for what was right."

"I know, Jimmy." Carlos's attention unbroken, he took a deep breath.

"Here for you, Sarge. Just, 'ole Jimmy with a pair of ears and an open heart, ready to listen to his friend."

Carlos smirked. He couldn't let the facade break. "We got a job to do, Jimmy."

"It's no easy see someone die," Roberto said in his broken English.

Everyone's attention turned to Roberto, whose only words of the night prior had been his request for water.

He was meek. Broken. Voiceless. In this position, none of us knew whether he was actually innocent or not. Someone had to stand up for him, and I was willing to do it.

The status of his innocence did not matter. His presence here was bigger than all of us.

"Sergeant Lopez, I have a daughter. I'd do anything to make sure she safe," Roberto said.

"Including kill a man?" Carlos responded, intrigued enough to listen, though not without his filters.

"You mean like you?" Roberto asked, his confidence wavering.

"Oh snap!" Jimmy yelled.

Carlos relented a moment as he gathered his thoughts. "How old is she?"

"*Tres años*," Roberto answered, staring at Carlos's profile, as if he was challenging Carlos to look another human in the eye to see him for all he was. In matters of the family, or anything really, I came to understand Roberto as a man of extreme diligence and unwavering integrity.

"It's a fun age. They're just starting to see the world for real, and they don't shut up."

Roberto laughed in knowing agreement.

Toddlers really are the worst. But then again, going through new phases of life is fraught with awkwardness. Kind of felt like this whole night was our toddler years, full of relentless interactions and untimed, unmitigated rage. However, I felt we were all trying to see life for what it was for the first time. And the confusion of seeing the world anew made us all stumble through.

Carlos looked Roberto square in the eyes for the first time. "It's amazing how far we go for our children. I feel like people are capable of anything when pushed."

Roberto nodded. "It's not easy see someone die."

Roberto then told us what had happened the day in the field. How he killed that man, and why he killed him, never straying from the fact he was the one who killed him. He readily admitted it.

He was working the strawberry fields. As was always the case, the sun was beating down on him. It was a little stronger than it normally had been, or at least, it had felt that way to him. The sweat came out of his hair from underneath his beat-up trucker cap a little faster than usual.

He had been feeling the pressures of wanting to provide more for his family. It had been three years since he and his pregnant wife crossed from Mexico into the Arizona desert.

His daughter was born a few short months later. She was a naturalized United States citizen. That's what made the numerous attempts at the brutal week-long desert crossing worth it.

An ambitious man, he was growing impatient with what he believed was the slow pace of his development in America. With what he believed was going to be his key to success and happiness—money, a new car, and a house. I'm not so sure he understood the trappings of the American dream. It might have been better to stay in Mexico. Still, regardless of if he wanted to be or not, he was a beacon of hope for many.

But for swarms of other people across the country, who admitted it or not, a dead illegal was better than a living one.

He pushed and pushed and pushed, picking day after day in the fields. Trying to save enough so he could provide a better life for his wife and daughter. And if he was really being starry-eyed, he wanted to take on the daunting task of becoming a US citizen. If nothing else, he wanted to ensure his daughter would have the chance to be the American he never was.

That's why he worked so hard. Why the blisters on the inside of his thumbs hurt a little more each week. Every passing moment was one moment further away from the dreams he had for his family.

He could deal with the racism, the below-minimum-wage pay, and the unfair treatment by the exploitative foremen of the fields, so long as it got him closer to his dream. I can't say whether it was healthy or not. Whether the pursuit of something so undefined and so elusive was worth fighting for, I can't say. It was something he needed. And it was why I was willing to fight for him, whether with words in a courtroom or side by side with a gun in a Podunk police station.

Here I am getting caught up playing hero ball, just like Carlos. Then again, I was the one who stood up for him. I was the one willing to take his case.

If you want to be the change you see in the world, then be it, right?

I digress. This is about Roberto, not me.

As I mentioned, the sun shone brightly that summer day. Roberto was hunched over, as he was every day for twelve to fourteen hours a day, picking. He held a pair of shears in his hand because the strawberry plants needed to have their old foliage trimmed. He and his friend laughed about how hot it was. "When it's that hot, *we all start to get a little loopy,*" he said.

Suddenly, the sun went dark. His plant sat in a shadow, and so did the one or two rows next to him. When the shadow came, he knew it could be one of two things—the foreman telling him to stay longer for the day or members of the White Patriots coming to harass them. The foreman played nice with them, not because he empathized with their cause, but because he didn't want any trouble.

In the background, a raised Ford F-350 rumbled, and Roberto knew his weekly harassment had arrived. And he was tired of it. These shakedowns. For what? Just to be obnoxious. To try to reestablish some sense of flailing power. This wasn't the "great America." This was a nostalgic sense of segregation and outright racism in which the white man had all the power. This was an evolving America where people like these guys and their families were becoming rarer by the day. However, they wanted to do everything they could to hang onto the past and be as loud as they could for their last stand.

Roberto had only been here a few short years, but he was already tired of it.

"Look at what we got here. Another spic on American soil, taking American jobs," the shadow said with intimidating arrogance.

When Roberto looked up, he saw a hulking man in silhouette. He looked down to gather strength, then up over at the raised F-350. An American flag situated on a PVC pipe faux flag stand waved in the slight breeze.

Roberto stood, three to four inches shorter than Donald "Don" Watts, who used his height to his advantage. Roberto saw a Nosler M21 rifle slung over Don's shoulder, one Don used to hunt for elk and wild pigs. Next to him was his younger brother William "Billy" Watts. They were different men with the same goal—keep America safe from "intruders" and maintain the power structures of Anglo America. They were there to intimidate and restore order.

"Billy, ain't it funny? Here we are trying to put food on the table with a hunt. And these fuckin' spics are out here just enjoying the sun," Don said with a sinister laugh.

"Please leave us alone. *Quiero trabajar*," Roberto said as he tried to walk away.

"We can't hear you with all that mush mash *Ay papi* Spanish you're speaking. Don't no one understand you. Not in America," Don said as he caught up to him.

"I want to work."

"See that's what I'm talking about. Spic comes over here illegally, and he wants to take a potential job of a white man, in a white man's country. Can you believe this shit? This is what America has come to," Billy said as he stopped Roberto.

"Leave me alone, *por favor*," Roberto said, trying to avoid eye contact and escape the situation any way he could.

The more Roberto didn't engage, the angrier Don and Billy got.

"Didn't you hear what I said the first time? You speak English and only English in this country. Do I make myself clear?"

Roberto, proud as he was, had enough. He was done with these weekly harassments. He was done sitting idly by. He was done feeling less than.

Roberto stopped and stared Don right in the eye. "*Es un pais libre*. It's a free country."

Don smiled, took a deep breath, and took the rifle off his shoulder. He racked the bolt, slipping a 7.62mm round into the chamber.

Don had been waiting for this moment. It was made clear in all the online propaganda—a moment like this would be the time for the White Patriots to shine. The time to declare he was powerful again. To prove all the hate he had in his heart was righteous and just. To prove his superiority to the brown man. It was the power he needed after having felt powerless his entire life, whether at the hands of his alcoholic father, the bosses who laid him off time after time in factories as more automation took over, or the politicians who promised him the world but left him with a road of empty promises and more hate in his heart.

Don raised the barrel of his M21 to Roberto's face.

The foreman turned his attention away, needing to go fix something that didn't need fixing. It was the worst kept secret in San Eugenio that the White Patriots had somewhat of an affinity for the foreman. They were angry he had hired so many Latinos and Latinas to do work they didn't want to do. So much so, he gave them free range to harass these guys, not a single word to be said to the police for fear of retribution. In a way, he gave them protection.

"What are you doing, brother? I thought we were just using the gun to scare," Billy said nervously.

With equal parts fear and anger in his eyes, Don looked down the barrel of his gun at Roberto. "I'm taking a stand because no one else will. I won't be replaced. I have my place here. In America. My home."

Roberto didn't falter. He stood there daring Don. If this is what life in America was going to be, he was going to face it head-on. He didn't want to be scared. He didn't want his daughter growing up being scared either. He wanted a place where she could not just survive, but live. And if that meant standing up here and now, even if it meant giving up his life, so be it.

"I want you to leave, and get your ass outta here. I don't want to see you here again. Do you hear me?"

Roberto didn't respond.

"Come on, brother. Put the gun down," Billy pleaded.

Don shoved the barrel into Roberto's cheek. Roberto squeezed the shears. All the laborers in the field stared, none wanting to help, most assuredly, for fear of deportation.

Stay silent, stay in America.

Don swung the butt of the rifle at Roberto's left cheek, sending Roberto to the ground, hoping against hope everyone in the field would take notice, and he could be in control again. "This is the last time I'm going to ask nicely. Leave."

The gun trained right on Roberto.

Billy tried desperately to pull Don back.

Roberto grabbed his face. He felt blood rush to his forehead. He grabbed the shears tighter than he ever had. Anger pulsating through every inch of his veins.

He was done.

Roberto knocked the barrel away with the back of his hand, causing Don to shoot an errant round into the ground, the shot ringing throughout the entire central farming valley of California.

It was a signal that life was never going to be the same for Roberto or his family.

As Roberto held down the barrel of the gun, he screamed, a scream equal parts anger and need as he shoved the gardening shears through Don's chest as hard as he could.

Don Watts died immediately.

Roberto looked at Don's body face-down in the dirt, the crimson of his blood mixing with the light brown of the soil. Roberto still held the shears in his right hand, blood running from the point of the shears down the wooden handles and into his palm, wondering what he had done.

He had taken a stand. And a man's life.

He sacrificed everything, everything he worked so hard for. His chance at a life in America. His chance at a normal reality. Gone in the blink of an eye. Yet, he had stood for what he believed in. A flood of emotions rushed to the front of his mind. Unable to act the way he would expect himself to, he yelled at Billy, "Leave! *Ahora!*"

Billy looked at his dead brother's body. He hopped in the truck and drove off. Roberto watched as the truck faded into the heat waves emanating off the road.

The laborers all took off. Roberto understood they couldn't be associated with this. They couldn't risk it.

They left Roberto and Don alone in the strawberry field, each getting exactly what they wanted. Now left with nothing but heat and time.

Roberto sat, wondering if he had chosen differently, would any of this have been better. A quick death or a slow burning one? Either way, his choice impacted the lives of so many others.

He didn't want to be noticed. He just wanted to be seen as a person.

Carlos walked over to Roberto, pulled out his keys, and gestured to Roberto to hold out his hands. "*Dame sus manos.*"

Roberto offered his hands, and Carlos unlocked the cuffs, putting them away in his utility belt.

"Jimmy, give Mr. Hinojosa an AR."

"Copy that, Sarge," Jimmy said with a giddy smile on his face.

"You're still going to stand trial. You're still going to face the full extent of the law. And if you so much as try to run off or do anything stupid, I'm going to shoot you. Do you understand me?"

"Yes, Sergeant Lopez." The first look of hope appeared in Roberto's eyes.

"You deserve to stand trial. You deserve a chance. And if you want to start to make amends, you can begin by helping us survive the night," Carlos said, not wanting Roberto to see in his face any of the flexibility his actions were offering.

Jimmy handed Roberto an AR-15.

"Keep watch out the window," Carlos stated as he walked back to his post at the door.

"Yes."

Carlos resumed his watch. I sat there wondering if this decision was one he would regret, maybe not at that specific moment, but sometime down the road.

Regardless, it was a decision he couldn't make now. The only thing he could do was try to live. Maybe continuing to live would be something he would regret. There was a lot of pain to sort through, not just in him, but in all of us.

Maybe regret is the answer. It just needs a different perspective.

CHAPTER TWELVE

Alejandro and Delfina
"Ganarselo"

It's the motto we've lived our life by. Earn it.

That's what we Latinos have been asked to do. It's who we are. We earn every day God gifts us on this Earth.

Del and I, we earned the life that we created for ourselves.

Kids these days don't seem to want to *ganarselo*. This whole world doesn't seem like they want to earn it. Every damn person wants to be right. Nobody wants to do the work of going to find the answer. Every damn person wants every damn thing right damn now without the work.

My hands, Delfina's hands, they built this life that we enjoy today. Our hands tell our story of our success in America. Our hearts are what guided us.

Somewhere along the way, this town, this country lost its way.

People are always telling me and Del to slow down. "You move well for your age. You two do so much for your age," they say. What? Do they think just because we're old we're supposed to quit? *Mierda*.

Alejandro and I have seven grandchildren, ages three months to twenty-nine, four of whom have graduated from college. Our children and grandchildren are the greatest gifts God has given us. They are who we've built this life for.

As a matter of fact, we're just on our way home from Fresno right now from seeing a few of them. Alejandra's quince is coming up in three weeks, and we want to make sure she has a nice time. I don't like driving home this late because he gets tired and …

I do not. Aye, *amor*. Just let me, please.

Go ahead, Mr. "I know everything."

If God gives you success in life, you owe it to the world to pass those blessings on. Del and I have built properties not just in San Eugenio but across the Central Valley. We have modest homes and a few apartments. They've afforded us a good life. Many of them are homes to people working the fields, people who were just like me.

I remember in my teenage years, my dad always wanted me to have a job. So I did really the only job that was allowed for the Mexicans in those days—I picked. My favorite was working the tomato fields. I liked them too much. It's why I got fired all the time. I didn't know you weren't supposed to eat them.

Once is an accident; four times *es un pendejo.*

Aye, honey, *por favor.*

Well go on then, Mr. Know It All.

Even if some people didn't have their papers in order, we wanted everyone to have a nice place to live. As long as they treated the homes and us *con respeto*, we did our best to give them a chance at establishing themselves in the US. We wanted everyone to feel like they were home.

That's what San Eugenio was to us. Home is something you build and something worth fighting for.

It started with our first liquor store on Olive Street. Del let me convince her to buy it in 1982 with what little money we had.

I worked the register while Alex made the deliveries. It was a piece of the town. Just as my dad's grocery store was to Santa Barbara in the thirties. We loved it. It was us. Most of all, Alejandro and I loved to share stories and help some of the lost kids of the town.

Our store was where field workers bought their beer after a long day, where the tequila was purchased for the aunts and uncles attending their nieces' quinces, and where so many kids bought their after-school snacks, Snickers, or premade tuna sandwiches. Those snacks might have been the only meals those kids would eat all day.

Honey, you did more than that. She's being modest. She would throw in a piece of fruit, a drink, or both to make sure they had enough to eat. She always remembered what it was like when we had fifty dollars to our name, and we couldn't hold down jobs.

Our family was growing, and we couldn't get our footing. But, when you're a parent, you figure it out.

This liquor store, those families, and those kids—they were the heartbeat of this town.

We loved when one of the kids who would regularly come into the store graduated from high school. It was like seeing one of our own children graduate. It felt like one day, they were barely able to see over the counter, but the next they were walking across the stage at graduation.

We never missed a San Eugenio High School graduation or football game. We loved being there to see these kids grow up. Only about 70 percent of the kids in San Eugenio graduated high school. It was a damn shame, but that what was normal in the Central Valley for Latino kids at that time.

Often I would come back from a delivery, and I'd see Del helping some kid out with homework. We'd check in on their grades, make sure they were going to practice for whatever activity they were involved in, but most of all, check that they did what they needed to do for their families, keeping the kids honest when it came to their dedication to school, sports, and their family life. If we wanted to see the story around Latinos in America change, we had to do our part.

Something happened to San Eugenio. Picking wasn't an opportunity anymore. I don't know if it was the corporations and the big machines they brought into the fields or what, but the town became poorer.

Over the past few years, the kids who stopped by the liquor store weren't there for snacks or advice anymore. The parking lot became the place where the kids would hang out, smoke a little marijuana, and drink a few beers they would steal when the Tuesday morning shipments came in.

No matter how many times Alejandro tried to reason with them, teach them, or guide them, his words didn't seem to land anymore. The kids had become less respectful and more defiant. His stories weren't heard anymore, and his advice on things like the importance of wearing a belt seemed to fall on deaf ears, as the sagging pants were living proof.

If I see another teenager's chonies above his belt ...

Most saddening to us was the kids seemed to lose respect for themselves. Alejandro's tolerance and temper became shorter. This wasn't the town we remembered. After all, we had accomplished everything we ever wanted. Because of what we built, we didn't have to worry about money on a daily basis. We had a great family. We sent all four of our children to college and supported our community.

Del was concerned these kids weren't just drinking but getting into something bigger. Each week the kids looked a little different; their faces had aged in different ways. They looked less and less respectable. And they couldn't seem to keep their pants above their *nalgas*.

We started from nothing. We worked hard for what we had. Del graduated high school; I barely made it out of six grade. Our parents each pushed hard for us to have a chance here. Yes, Del drives me crazy, but she is the greatest love of my life.

We wanted to help break the rhythm of the past for Latinos. We wanted the younger generations to do the same, have what we made. If they felt like it was something they wanted, to push it forward. We Mexicans worked hard, and we earned our right to be heard.

That's why Alejandro had kept on top of Carlos for so long to fix the problem. If they were no longer going to listen to love, maybe they would listen to force. What those kids outside of our liquor store represented wasn't just mischief. It was a step backward. Somehow everything we worked for was being stripped by the kids. We didn't want that to happen. We didn't want these kids following the same story expected of Latinos.

It feels like these kids were no longer just bored, but they had something to prove. They were abused at home by fathers who tried to escape their poverty and brutal working conditions at the bottom of a bottle. Their mothers' stern obedience to traditions and ways of living left them behind in a world moving forward faster than they could keep up with. Work was becoming harder for their parents to come by as the farms became more automated. Plus, their immigration status limited their options. These kids were the products of an educational system that didn't care about them. It was becoming harder for the state to make sense of why they were granting funding to the area.

Not being white kids, they were fighting a losing battle. They were being left further behind with each passing day.

They were losing hope.

Their choices became simple: Join their parents in the fields, move out of town and try their luck elsewhere, or join one of the small-time gangs popping up. Nothing more. Nothing less.

Jose Chiquito, or at least that's what his abuela called him, fed off kids like this. They were just like him.

Jose goes by El León or something goofy like that.

He sat in the parking lot of our liquor store many times, often in silence, trying not to be noticed. He was one of those kids who Del always tried to drop an extra treat in with his snack. But he never looked up. He always had holes in his shoes or in his shirt. He would buy whatever snack he could with what little money he had and walk out the door. Never looking up. I can't imagine the shame that he must have felt.

He was one that, as he got older, we saw less and less of. Even when he was little, and even though he didn't say much, most of the kids pretty much stayed away from him, almost like they were scared of what was inside him.

Poverty and hardship, from sunrise to sunset, was all these kids had known in San Eugenio. It's why they started these *cliquas*. A *community of power* seemed way more inviting than sweating and breaking your back for twelve to fourteen hours a day in the fields.

The few who made it out of San Eugenio pretended like it never existed. They used their upbringing as the basis for college essays, that would then provide them full scholarships to some of the top academic institutions in the world. We were proud of them, but once they saw the world promised so much more than San Eugenio had to offer, they never looked back. And frankly, why would they when there was no hope here?

We would check in from time to time with some of the kids, but most of them sort of forgot about us. We never expected a thank you. We just always hoped that they might bring back some of their successes to their community. But can you really be upset for someone wanting to forget the past?

Those humble origin stories played well during publicity interviews, in their respective Ivy League newsletter as an example of their "emerging diversity," or as the *Face of Progress for Latinx People in Business*. They were the rags-to-riches stories.

We wanted to help break the cycle and give credit to those kids who *ganarselo*.

Alejandro was always so persistent with Sergeant Lopez.

You need to be, honey. That is how we were successful.

Aye, callate. My turn.

Alex would call Sergeant Lopez because he had enough of these kids. He was tired of them stealing. Tired of them taking, drinking, and causing problems. We have no issues with kids who want to be around to do good, but those days are gone. With the texting and the *cliquas*, it's not what it used to be at our store. We might even close soon and leave San Eugenio. But a part of us still believes in this place.

This is our home.

"Send them somewhere else and make sure they don't come back," Alex would always say.

As I told him all the time, you can't fight fire with fire. But he only listens when he wants to, what he wants to listen to.

Como?

Aye, nada. Keep your eyes on the road.

He was so stuck in his ways. The harder he pushed these kids to leave, the more they wanted to stay and bother him.

It's his job, honey.

Enough!

Do you see what I have to put up with?

As much as Alejandro can be a pain in the butt, he and Carlos have a deep respect for each other. They share a lot of the same values around working hard and serving the community.

Well, Carlos hasn't been returning my phone calls, so we're going to pay him a visit on the way home. He's not going to ignore me.

At midnight? *Esta loco*.

Carlos needs to return my phone calls. A man doesn't dodge hard things. I want something done, *now*! If we let these kids keep going, we'll keep losing what we built. I want things back the way they were. The only way we can achieve that is if we work together.

This is what I'm talking about. *Mira*, he gets on his high horse, and now, we're on our way to the police station at midnight. Why mess up a great day by getting your blood pressure up? There's nothing he can do right now.

It's just going to take a second, *amor*. Why are there so many cars out here? I didn't even know this police station had this many cars. Carlos hasn't mentioned anything about this. This is why he needs to return my calls, so I know what's going on.

Aye, honey, pull up to that car and ask those young men what's going on.

Who is the new guy and *quien es el gringo*? When did they get the Crown Vics? Those will never make it through these roads. Those smiles remind me of *El Cucuy*.

"Good evening, folks. How may I help you this late in the evening?" a brown officer said with his hands behind his back.

"I came here to talk to Sergeant Lopez. He said he was going to get rid of the kids hanging out in front of my store," I said back.

"That's unfortunate, sir. I'm sure those kids are just looking for somewhere to belong," the brown cop replied.

"Well, they can belong somewhere else. I run a good business, and I don't want some cholo slacker hanging out in front of the store, smoking dope and drinking shitty beer."

"*Ya, no mas*! Speak to Carlos another day. Nothing good will come out of this tonight," Del said.

"*Hola Señora*," the cop said with a smile. "You know, your wife is right. At this hour, I know Sergeant Lopez is tired and just under siege at this moment."

I looked out at the station, seeing all the cars and SUVs with their high beams on, all directly pointed at the station. "Who are you? Where's Jimmy? I know every cop in this town, and I've never seen you."

"I'm not from here, sir. We're all here just for the evening. Training exercises."

"At this hour?" Del chimed in.

"Yes, the department requires us to get in a certain amount of evening training hours. The San Eugenio precinct just happens to be the most appropriate place to do that, seeing as it is isolated enough to ensure we don't disturb fine folks like you."

"Hmm. Never heard of anything like that before," I said. There was something strange about this kid. I took off my seatbelt and reached for the door handle. "You know, I'll be one really quick second. I just need Sergeant Lopez to hear me out."

"Aye, what are you doing, honey? *Vamos a casa, ahora!*" Del shouted.

"Let me do what I need to do, honey!"

The officer put his hand on the door and held it shut. "Please listen to your wife, sir."

As he held the door shut, I got a glimpse of why he had his hands behind his back. The Desert Eagle slightly jostled out of his hand, and I saw the barrel. Those weren't department issued.

"You know, I'll try Carlos another night." I moved my hand toward the gear shift.

"*Gracias a dios,*" Del exhaled. I didn't know what to say to her.

Delfina, you are the greatest thing that ever happened to me. *Te quiero mucho.*

Stop being weird, honey. Please, let's just go home.

"Help! Help us!" I heard the muffled shouting in the background.

"What was that?" Del asked, looking over at the police station.

I threw the gear into reverse.

POP.

Del's head went slowly onto my shoulder, the gringo's gun smoking.

My love.

"*Ganarselo,*" the cop said.

POP.

My head landed atop Del's. Our car slowly rolled forward and off the road into the ditch.

Together, we had built our life. A life we were proud of. And together, we were meant to leave.

Ganarselo. Earn it.

CHAPTER THIRTEEN

Freedom Frank

This is a white man's country.

It's a country founded by white men, for white men. And these globalist commies want to do nothing but make sure we're divided. Their goal is to destroy America. It's why I protect my race and our chance to be heard. It's why I earned the name Freedom Frank. I believe in the freedom of the white man. I'm not going to watch our culture be eradicated any longer.

What happened to the America I used to know? I know we can make America the great place it used to be again. We can regain the strength of this country, not the neoliberal commie-pussy haven the left wants us to be. That's not what America is, nor the values she stands for.

We are being replaced. Plain and simple.

It's happening every day faster and faster, and I'm supposed to roll over and take it? No. It didn't happen in 1776, and I sure as hell ain't letting it happen now. We're supposed to fight tyranny and oppression, stand for liberty and the flag. Yet, the liberals, the government, they want us to let everyone in. Brown scum. We're supposed to leave our borders open and be a beacon of freedom for everybody else? No, I don't think so.

I mean, look at tonight. We're here because an illegal killed one of my best friends. Don was a good man. A God-fearing man. He had a family, just like me. I think about Becky living the rest of her life without her provider and Donny Jr. and Clayton growing up without a father. Because of that fuckin' spic, those kids are going to grow up without a father just like the fat-lipped niggers.

Not on my watch. We are the protectors of the herd. We're going to keep our community together, and we're going to stand up for one another. We're not going to murder each other like the niggers do. We're not going to rape women like the Mexicans.

And we sure as hell are not going to let these boys grow up soft like the faggot queers the liberals all want us to be. Don's family is going to have a chance at life, liberty, and the pursuit of happiness. It's in the Declaration of Independence these liberal commies are trying to take a shit on.

America will be strong.

"As a father has compassion on his children, so the Lord has compassion on those who fear him." Psalm 103:13 was my dad's favorite verse; one he used to recite often. It's what he used to say when he took his belt buckle to my back every time I acted up.

He'd say it every time he committed adultery on my beautiful mother. It was his way of keeping us in control. I mean, he was being a man. He took what he wanted and took control of his life.

He was right; it was the Word of the Lord. We cannot contest that. If we weren't supposed to be strong, then God wouldn't want us to fear Him. I know my father loved me. I know he did his best.

He said the Word of God, but I don't know if I ever believed him or if he even really believed it. Something was incongruous. Every time the silver belt buckle hit my back and the prong dug little holes into my skin, I thought about what those words meant to me. There's strength in pain. And my father was the best at delivering both strength and pain.

He left us.

He left us when I was twelve. Twelve was also the first time I fought back. I was bent over his sawhorse in the garage. I can still feel the splinters in my arms as he reared and yelled, "So the Lord has compassion for those who fear him."

Over the previous six years, I had gotten really good at timing the hits and preparing for the pain. Momma was out working late one night. He stumbled into the house, laughing, with a waitress from the Waffle House down the street under his arm. I stared him down. I had enough of his two-timing. This was the one thing God didn't want from him. But he betrayed God's trust in him.

When he and the floozy saw me staring at them, they quieted down. He walked over to me.

"Francis, Carol here is a, uh, friend," he said holding back laughter. Carol thought it was hilarious.

I continued to stare at him.

"You got something to say to me, boy?" Do you?" He grabbed me by the arm and took me to the garage. He threw me against the sawhorse. "You know what to do."

I slowly gathered myself and bent over, waiting for that buckle.

He always took two deep breaths before he'd do it. "Discipline your child, and he will give you delight to your heart."

"Proverbs 13:24," I said.

I heard the slight clank of the belt buckle. He was winding back, and he began. "So the Lord has compassion …"

I knew I had one deep breath before the belt buckle hit my back. Before it landed, I turned and caught the belt. My father tried to take it out of my hands, but there was no way I was letting go. I'll never forget the look in his eyes. Nothing was funny anymore. When I saw the fear in his eyes, I felt the power inside of me for the first time.

I took the belt out of his hand, and I pushed him down to the ground into some empty paint cans. I stood over him, and I finished the verse for him. "On those who fear him."

And I fucking hit him once.

And again.

And again.

The belt buckle struck his face, the prong digging little holes into his cheeks, leaving his face as bloodied and cut up as he used to leave my back.

Like father, like son.

"I'm doing this because I love you. You will fear me, just like we fear you. And how I fear the Lord. This is compassion, Daddy. This is compassion," I said, trying to catch my breath.

He laid there, whimpering and rolling around. He got up and walked out the garage door. He took the whore with him. We never saw him again.

He stopped loving me and my mom. He lost his power over us. I, on the other hand, felt what it was like to have power. To know what it was like to be feared. After that, I always wanted to have that in my life. I liked it. I got the high. I wanted people to fear me.

Because fear, as the Bible said, would lead me to be a more compassionate man. If I could instill fear into the niggers, spics, Chinks, and Jews, I'd be emblematic of God's love.

They could exist elsewhere. Just not in America.

I met Don at the first football practice of the season a few days after my daddy walked out the door in Charlottesville. He left me, my momma, and my baby sister, to fend for ourselves.

I felt lost, and Don felt like family to me. We were linemen. The way he hit me, and I hit him during Oklahomas, there was meaning behind those hits. Coach said he hadn't ever seen kids our age hit the way we did.

After a couple of practices, Don's momma invited me to his house for dinner. I didn't know if she did it because she felt sorry for me or what. Word had gotten around about what my daddy had done. I started to feel like a charity case. But Don and his family were different.

They had a wonderful home. Two American flags on opposing posts heralded the way into their front door. When I got inside, their table was covered from end to end with plates of food. A portrait of their family dressed in all white hung above their fireplace. They smiled together. Their home was far different from the chaos I grew up in. It was so clean and pristine.

Their couches had no holes in them. They had pillows with sayings like *The Lord your God will be with you everywhere you go* and *God Bless this home*. If I remember correctly, I think Don's momma made those.

This is what life could be. At dinner, no one yelled at each other. They ate in peace. Don's parents loved each other and seemed to care for one another. It was different.

I wanted a home.

After dinner, Don's momma thought it would be a good idea if we went to meet one of their rich lawyer friends at his house. When we entered his house, he shook Don's and my hands and looked us right in the eyes. He made us feel like we were adults. I felt like I belonged.

When we walked into his study, I saw it was lined with beautiful mahogany bookshelves. Among the shelves of books was a pile of *The Turner Diaries*. He said he handed those out as gifts to visitors and friends and would give me a copy if I wanted one. He thought it was good for boys like me to know what being a good American meant.

Through the dense cigar smoke, I could see a red flag. On it was a black symbol I hadn't really seen before.

I walked up to Don's dad and I asked him, "Mr. Watts, sir, what's that black symbol?"

He said to me, "Well, Frank, I'm here to raise the identity consciousness among white people. That's the symbol of power. It's a reminder of what we're here to defend and the livelihood we're meant to strive for—keeping the pure race, the white race, in power. It's a representation of the anti-communist liberal ideals America should strive for. The ones the niggers, spics, Jews, chinks, and faggots all want to dismantle. We have to protect our values. It's called the swastika. You want to protect our values, don't you, Frank?"

"Yes, sir," I responded.

Mr. Watts went back to his conversation with his lawyer friend. I saw them laughing and smiling, smoking their cigars, among their group of prestigious friends, pillars of their community in Charlottesville.

For the first time, I felt like I knew where I was. I now understood how fear drove compassion. I had a greater purpose than I could have envisioned. It was God's love at work. I knew I belonged. The life I wanted was right in front of me. A sense of security and belonging was mine. I didn't need to fear anyone alone anymore. We could be feared together. We could be compassionate men together. Together, we could protect our families, our heritage, against the people who wanted to destroy it.

I was going to become a symbol of God's fear—and a symbol of God's love. It's why I became a lawyer. It's why I spent all those countless hours in the gym. It's why I train for self-defense with my AR-15. I am a protector of liberty and the promise of tomorrow.

Charlottesville brought me here. Donny brought me here. My daddy brought me here.

I'm willing to not see color tonight, so long as we get the job done. Once the spic and the cop are dead, we'll get back to ensuring the rest of these bastards that try to cross these borders, don't take any more from us.

This is our home and we're not going to let it be taken over, and we sure as hell aren't going to be replaced. We stand on the right side of history, and when Judgment Day comes, the Lord will look at us with favor and grace. We're called to defend this land. "Blessed be the Lord, my rock, who trains my hands for war, and my fingers for battle." Psalm 144:1.

I am a soldier of Christ. I am ready to defend myself from the tyrants inside or outside. There is no man whose word is more powerful than God's, no matter how these liberals and *demoncrats* want you to believe. My "tolerance" and my "love" are expressed through the defense of God's will. And God has called me to defend His Name. His Word. His Land. His People.

I am the righteous. I will show my righteousness. Those who infringe upon the righteous will feel the wrath of God. Righteousness knows no color. Only right from wrong. Those are the rules of a white man's country. God has blessed us. Tonight, El León and his brown buddies are the righteous. We are united in one common cause. Against one common enemy.

To be feared is to be loved.

To make them fear us is to love.

I am a symbol of God's love.

CHAPTER FOURTEEN

El León

Mira, there's nothing you can say to me to change my mind about how I feel about nobody. Why should I? This mindset, this way of thinking is what got me to where I am today. I run these streets. I run Muerte.

I'm taking the power back—not just for me, but for my people. El León is *el rey* of this jungle. You understand me?

My people have taken generations of abuse and slaughter. Slaughter of our bodies and of our spirits. I'm not going to allow us to take it anymore. That's why I started Muerte in the first place. We will break the cycle of poverty. We will elevate us to the next level and leave the past behind us. We have the power.

"*¡Viva la Raza!*" All that shit, it's just words. I'm putting power behind my words, and I always will.

Fuck this fuckin' place.

San Eugenio exploits our people for the betterment of the white man and the fuckin' millionaire and billionaire pieces of shit running this country. They can't have me, and they ain't gonna have me. They won't have us.

It ends with me.

It ends with us.

Fuck my moms and my pops. Moms bailed right after I was born. Said she couldn't handle it. Pops drank himself stupid.

The fields take your soul, leaving you nothing.

I guess I get why they both did it: Moms because who the fuck would want to stay here? And Pops, because what the fuck else are you supposed to do when people keep taking advantage of you? All these fucking farm corporations did.

We picked. They profited.

"Have something to say? Go ahead, I'm sure ICE would love to hear."

"Want more pay? Find another job."

"You're working too many hours? Sun too hot? I got a new swarm of you crossing every day."

It was easy for them to exploit us.

And me? I was supposed to be some sort of dreamer? For every immigrant kid that graduated from Harvard and thanked their mom and dad for the sacrifices they made, there were a hundred of us living the reality we did—going nowhere.

Driving their fucking Teslas, competing for who the best Latino would be. Always talking the talk, but none of those motherfuckers ever came back. They never gave back to the places they came from. There were a few pictures at charity events. Pictures they got to post to their Instagram, in-between vacations to Aspen or wherever the fuck their wannabe-white asses would go.

Fuck them. They became part of the system exploiting us. They traded their virtues for six- and seven-figure salaries. Who could blame them? I can. They forgot who they were and where they came from. Just like Lopez.

"But, what about Cesar Chavez and labor rights?" You can believe the fairytale, but when someone wants to cut costs, they'll find a way. When someone wants to cut corners, they will. The small farms were too small to regulate, and the big corporations had enough money to pay off government officials to turn the other way and keep cutting costs. It was all bullshit, but it was the price of doing business here. And people say I exploit?

Fuck 'em. I give people a shot.

When my moms left and my pops died, I was left all alone. I was seven. Sent to live with my *abuela*. She lived down the street from the house my pops rented from Ramon Salazar, the owner of Salazar Farms.

My *abuela* and *abuelito* came here first, and Moms and Pops crossed a little after they had set themselves up. They promised them a future. They were better set staying in Mexico. At least people spoke the language there. Maybe Pops wouldn't have drank, and maybe moms wouldn't have left. But what the fuck do I care? It's in the past, and it's up to me to change the future. I'm going to show we matter.

Abuelito built the home *abuela* lived in. He died when I was five—pancreatic cancer—so it was just her when I moved in.

Abuela loved me. I was her *Jose Chiquito*, Little Jose. She did the best she could, but we had fucking nothing. She always tried to keep me fed, but I don't remember a day growing up where I wasn't hungry going to bed. Even with the one-week past expiration groceries *Abuela* used to buy, we never had enough.

Holes in my thrift-store shirts. No money to go to the movies or play sports. Nothing. Any money went to any of *Abuela's* drugs she needed for whatever she was sick with at the time. And whatever was left over went to whatever food I could pick up.

I spent a lot of time at friends' houses for dinner, whenever they could spare it. My friends' parents gave me clothes because "respectable men don't wear clothes with holes in them."

It was embarrassing, man. Being the charity. The poorest kid among the poor kids.

Can you believe that shit? I didn't have no fuckin' home. My home was wherever I could eat and sleep. I did the best I could, and for a kid that was orphaned at seven, I did good. I made a vow to myself I was never going to beg for nothing again. I ain't mad at *Abuela*. The fucking government, these *pendejo* drug and insurance companies felt no pity for people trying to make a life for themselves in America. Isn't this the land of opportunity? If you believe bullshit like that, you're a bigger *pendejo* than those fools.

The streets are where everything made sense. They made everyone the same if you're tough enough to survive. I did what I needed to do to survive. Stealing food from the liquor store. Selling shitty ass grass to the guys as they headed home. Giving *Abuela* what she needed however I could.

I remember one time when I was like fourteen, we was at the doctor for a cough she had, and I was filling out the forms for her, 'cause she don't speak no English. The nurse, or whatever the goody-two-shoes white bitch's name who worked the front desk, called her out. "Señora Ramirez, can I please see you at the front desk?"

I told *Abuela* in Spanish as she started to fall asleep, "I need to talk to the lady. I'll be right back."

She nodded. I wasn't sure if she was still going to be alive by the time I made it back. I went up to the nurse's desk and said, "My *abuela* is Señora Ramirez. I'm her grandson."

"Well, it looks like Señora Ramirez's insurance is no longer valid. Usually this happens when you're behind on your payments. We won't be able to see her today unless you can meet the one hundred and fifty dollars cash-visit price."

"There has to be something you can do. Dr. Ochoa has been seeing my *abuela* for thirty years, please. She's very sick. Just look at her." Gringa bitch never once looked up at my *abuela*. Even when she coughed. She couldn't be bothered.

"I'm so sorry, sir. You're going to need to take it up with your insurance company."

"Don't you guys have some oath or something?"

The nurse looked over at my *abuela*. "Does she have urgent medical needs?"

"I don't know. I just brought her for her appointment."

I looked at the pen that sat on the counter, the black ink on its sharp point.

I could shove this through her neck and make the ink red, was the first thought in my head.

"Please, can I talk to Dr. Ochoa? He'll understand," I said as I walked to the door. She got up from her chair.

"I'm sorry, sir. I can't help you. Do not go through that door!" she yelled, moving in front of me. "When will you freakin' people understand this isn't how things work in this country?"

Can you believe that fuckin' bitch? I couldn't. I looked her in the eyes. A rage took over me. I pulled that pasty white bitch's fucking hair down to the ground so hard her stupid ass scrunchie came out.

"Please stop! Don't hurt me!" she cried as I stood over her. I wanted to take the scrunchie and strangle her with it. I wanted to shove that pen through her fucking throat. I bet she'd let *Abuela* see a doctor then.

"Please. There's nothing I can do. Please stop, or I'll have to call the cops. Please just leave," she begged. I liked that she begged. She finally knew what it felt like to have to beg for your life. That's what I did every day.

As I pushed *Abuela's* wheelchair out of the office down the sidewalk toward the house, she didn't make a sound. For once, it wasn't hot as shit. I talked to her about whatever came to mind. *Abuelo*, the liquor store I used to visit, or *Wheel of Fortune*. That was her favorite.

When we got in front of her house, she grunted. Like she wanted me to stop, so I did. "*Abuela*, are you okay?"

She nodded gently and smiled. She coughed softly once or twice. Then she took one last big gasp and called out, "Ponchito."

And she was gone.

No one helped her. No one helped me. No one helped us. I was without any family, and now I had to find my own.

At fourteen, I was *un huérfano* again. But this time, I was going to build my own family. I was going to choose them. And we were going to be strong.

Since no one helped us, no one was going to push us around no more.

I needed to be *un león*, a lion, for my community. And there wasn't going to be no one in my way. I was going to do everything to make sure we were always protected. Always in control. Cause no one—and I mean, fucking no one—would be ready to stand up for us. We had to be strong. This was the death of pity. It was the death of us being a victim. "Chiquito Jose" was dead.

Muerte.

People used to laugh at me because I was so skinny. They don't laugh now when I stick a piece to their forehead to get them to pay me my fucking money. Nah, they don't fuck with El León now. They know what's inside, and I'm still as hungry as I was growing up, ready to eat whatever's in my fuckin' way.

You can believe that, bro.

El León was born.

Muerte and El León were everything I wasn't, but everything I will be, and what my people will be—heard, rich, and powerful. I planned to put the power back in the hands of the powerless. Ain't no one gonna stand in our way of what we're gonna get, and we're gonna get it anyway we need to—drugs, women, guns. All of it was for the people. So those workers could live a life out of the fuckin' fields.

The stronger Muerte was, the stronger we were as Latinos and our influence could spread. It's just our neighborhood now, but we're gonna get money, and we're gonna get the fuck outta here. We're gonna leave the people here in power.

And that night, that night was *the* night. *Coño de puta madre,* Lopez would be gone. He was the last obstacle. One of our fucking own holding us back? That motherfucker needed to die, and if we had to give up one of our own to get it, so be it. We had to fight with these *coño gringos*, we will. We all had to make sacrifices. *Mis hermanos, y hermanas*, are ready to do what's necessary. Muerte will be remembered. Live or die, the people will know what we stood for. *Nuestras voces sean escuchadas.* Our voices will be heard.

This is a brown man's country.

Ain't no gringo going to keep it from being what it 'posed to be. *Esta es mi casa, mi familia, y mi vida.* This is my home, my family, and my life.

El miedo es amor.

Fear is love.

CHAPTER FIFTEEN

Eric

As the deafening silence took over the evening, we all held the positions Carlos had assigned to us, the watchful eye, though we might as well have been blind.

Lupe and Jimmy were placed together near the back door to ensure no one burst through the door like some sort of zombie apocalypse.

They were two people who wanted so much more for their lives but never had any idea how to get it for themselves. Rather, they had allowed life to take them away, holding loyalty and allegiances to people and relationships no longer serving them. I don't know, maybe it was wrong of me to have such presumptions and judgments. It's what I saw and how I perceived it.

They sat there through the night. Lupe with her face battered from the beating she had taken and Jimmy in all his Jimmyness looked at each other with a sense of depth and intensity I don't think either one of them had experienced before. For the first time, they were being seen for who they were. Maybe it was the nature of the situation we were in. With death bearing down on us, I do believe some sort of clarity came before us. I know those with near death experiences talk about the clarity they found in the moments leading up to their encounter with death. However, right now, there was only an understanding that there was no real exit from this situation. When we're faced with extraordinary circumstances, we're met with an incredible opportunity to confront the life we lived and wanted to live. It was a life that would no longer exist in the coming moments.

They sat across from each other on the cold, dirty tile floors. Their weapons laid in their laps, pointed at the door. Even during rest, their guns were at the ready.

"Was this the first time?" Jimmy knew the answer. He wanted to see if she'd say it herself.

"No."

"It's a hard position you're in. I can't imagine how difficult it must be."

Lupe nodded, barely able to look Jimmy in the eyes.

"If you can, Mrs. Sanchez, I'd ask you please keep your eyes on me."

"I know the truth," Lupe said.

The truth was Lupe had always known what she needed to do. But for her, and for all of us, a different type of courage is required in the most difficult of situations, especially when it involves matters of the heart. Lupe was entirely capable of making the decisions. I'm not sure she ever challenged herself in that way.

Tonight was different.

"How many men do you think you clipped today?" Jimmy said sheepishly.

Lupe tried to hide the grin on her face. It felt wrong to have one in this context.

"Probably like four or five."

"Be honest, it felt kind of good to get revenge. It's okay. You can be a bad bitch in here, and we'll be cool."

Lupe smiled.

"You know with all this fighting and everything taking place tonight, I don't think I've seen someone so unflustered. I mean, I've literally been shot at with an AK-47, and I was nervous as shit."

What Jimmy hadn't understood yet was the skillset Lupe had crafted over her four years of marriage. The will to endure. The need to endure. But most of all, the need to escape in the face of unthinkable pain. She had to keep it together for her daughter. She couldn't let him win. She couldn't let him see the pain he imposed on her. It was the bit of solace she took in her life. No matter what, he would never take her spirit from her. Perhaps, the feeling of the gun in her hand provided some sort of respite. Some sort of release she so desperately needed. It so happened that who she was releasing it on was a group of hyper-aggressive men with no ability to regulate their emotions.

Then again, I don't think Lupe ever wanted this. I don't think she ever needed it. She was a woman of deep internal peace. But the peace had been interrupted by the relationships she chose and the years of being told to be "the good wife."

Little did I know how far off my interpretation of her was.

"How much worse have these been getting?" Jimmy asked hesitantly.

"Usually a pair of sunglasses will cover this up. But tonight, something inside of him snapped. He let it go. It started with the normal shoves. The shoves turned to slaps once he saw the tears started. It was a signal he had gotten through. The torture in his soul of knowing he had won. My pain brought him fulfillment. But to exist in that pain, he needed to let go of his own. I was his outlet. I never cry. My tear set him off. One single tear."

I would have expected Jimmy to be stunned into silence, but there was a deep level of understanding between them.

"As far back as I can remember, I was always under a watchful eye. Told to be and do the things that I should. Grandparents who pushed me so impossibly hard because they wanted more for their kids than they had. That's why they came to this country. Yet here I am. Fat. Waddling when I walk. And in a place that may as well be the pit of America," Jimmy relented.

"How do you get through?" Lupe asked.

"I accept it. I accept that these were all decisions that I made. The truth is, I never wanted to be anything more than Jimmy. I like Jimmy. I like who this guy is. As fat, loud, and obnoxious as he may be. I know the choices I made. And I'm glad that I did. Because to me, being here and helping these people, standing for what's right, I wouldn't change a thing.

"So what should I be doing?" Lupe responded.

"Stop asking me what you should do or who you should be. It's your time to shine, Mrs. Sanchez. I've watched you tonight. You've had the shit kicked out of you by your 'husband.' Beat within an inch of your life, yet here you are, fighting for your life and standing up for others. When others would have said this was too much for them and quit, you didn't. You stood here and you fought because of who you are. You made a decision to leave. Albeit the place you chose to go to couldn't have been worse."

Lupe laughed, a brief breather from the horrors of the day. That was Jimmy's skill. He could find humor anywhere and everywhere when people needed to find it.

"This is your life, Mrs. Sanchez. I don't know if we'll be here much longer or what happens next, but you've taught me what it means to endure, what it means to persevere, and what it means to be strong, simply by being you."

Lupe started to tear up. What Jimmy said was true. It was what she needed to hear. She had believed all those things, and she knew them deep within her, but sometimes, the voice of a stranger helps us see objective reality. That's what Jimmy was for Lupe, an objective voice.

"Mrs. Sanchez …"

"Call me, Lupe," she said and cocked her gun.

"Okay, that was dope."

Lupe and Jimmy laughed.

"Sorry, I had to make it look dramatic. I'm actually very against violence in general."

"Well, it worked." Jimmy looked at her endearingly.

Lupe and Jimmy turned away from each other, pointing their weapons back at the door, propping them up on the broken-down desk that served as the last barrier standing between them and the Almighty.

They shared a gaze that held more than just friendship behind it. A slight smile peeking out each side of their mouths. An acknowledgement of the deep love they found for each other in these fleeting moments. I don't know if you'd call them friends. Or if you'd call them star-crossed lovers. To me, it was an acknowledgement someone on this planet had understood who they were. For all they were.

Lupe looked over to him. "Jimmy, I need a moment. Will you be okay?"

Jimmy nodded. "Of course."

They smiled at each other once again. Lupe stood and handed her gun to Jimmy.

She walked over to the center of the station where she could be seen by everyone. She took a deep breath, mustering what strength she had left to say the things she needed to. The look in her eyes was palpable and leveling all at once.

"Sergeant Lopez, thank you for the safety, care, and protection you offered me this evening."

Everyone laughed at the irony of this statement, including Lupe.

"When I came into the station this evening, I knew I needed help. I couldn't go on living the way I was anymore. This night has been messed up. But in so many ways, it has given me freedom."

Carlos was confused by all this. Hell, even I was. This place felt more like a prison than it ever had before. Even more so, there were goddamn bloodthirsty semi-humans outside who wanted us all dead.

"I understood it was okay to be wrong. I am a victim of abuse. I have the power to change it because I am responsible not for what happened to me, but how I choose to move forward. I lived under a deep fear that if I left my husband or if people found out what he was doing and he was arrested, I would have nothing in my life. I would somehow lose my identity. My family would be gone, and this perfect fairytale life I wanted would somehow be gone."

The eerie silence of the night took on a whole new power. Her words rang throughout the evening, as she touched something deep within our souls, the source where deep definitive human truths lay, at times dormant, only to be awakened from their slumber when we were ready to listen.

And we were all tired of sleeping.

"This is my life. I detest violence, but having a release for all the anger has somehow helped me to see clearly. I don't care about looking stupid anymore."

Lupe took a few steps toward Carlos, who stood near the front door. Ian's floodlights from outside gave her an angelic glow. She walked through the room, almost floating through the air. She stopped right in front of Carlos and looked him square in the eyes.

"My husband did this to me," Lupe said definitively.

"And we will absolutely arrest him as soon as we get out of here. He won't hurt you anymore," Carlos responded as an inner peace triggered Lupe's honesty.

"I'm taking responsibility for my life and for my mistakes, for where I was wrong. That is my power. And I want to use it now."

"Did I do okay, Mrs. Sanchez?" Carlos asked.

"Call her Lupe!" Jimmy yelled from across the room with a smile on his face.

Lupe smiled back at Jimmy.

"Acknowledge the pain inside of you, Carlos. Acknowledge the truth. My husband hit me, and it wasn't the first time. And if I go back, it won't be the last. I haven't wanted to admit it for so long, but I see now, acknowledging the pain is where my freedom is."

Carlos sat with this, the truth emerging, but the memories and the stories of what he had built up to protect himself forced it back down.

"Acknowledge what hurts, and it won't bind you anymore. It's then we can be unified together. It's our only way to survive." And with those words, Lupe walked away, back to her post with Jimmy. She knelt behind the fake wood and aluminum table. Jimmy handed her back her gun.

In an instant, Lupe had become the most destructive force of Carlos's life, one who would tear him down to build him back up stronger and more durable than ever, if that was something he wanted.

When I think back on who is responsible for the hope we found, I think Guadalupe Flora Magdalena Sanchez was the one who gave us hope. Hope that if we stopped looking for one another's flaws, regardless of how this night turned out, somehow life would be okay. Somehow, even if we faced death, we would feel alive in all our humanity.

Lupe helped us to find out what everyone in that police station feared most that evening. It wasn't the guns, the gang members, the AK-47s, or the AR-15s. It wasn't the thought of death. No, those were child's play in comparison to what we were afraid of.

We were afraid of letting go of our perception of the truth, our perceptions of one another. Because if we did, it would affect our ability to live. With nothing but death facing us, I think for the first time in a long time, we were all able to look inside and see that whatever future laid in front of us, we were in control of how we lived our lives.

And for those remaining hours, live, was what we were going to do.

CHAPTER SIXTEEN

Eric

"Carlos! Carlos, my dear partner. Come on out. I have some friends who want to meet you. They want to get to know you a bit more," Ian said through the bullhorn, bellowing through the night sky, among intimidating laughter. Freedom Frank and El León held their guns pointed at the front of the police station, sharing nefarious smiles at Ian's conniving energy.

That energy brought them a sense of unity.

Carlos had been sitting while Ian strategized what to do next, trying to gather himself. His half-sleep, half-alert state was something he was well seasoned in. It was a skill he ardently acquired over his time as a police officer. I can only assume he learned it every moment he was away from us, working those long nights and hours.

He missed so much.

"Sarge, your best friend is out there looking for you," Jimmy said with his gun facing the front, having taken watch for Carlos.

Carlos rubbed his face in exhaustion. His hands were marred in the remnants of gunpowder. His face was covered with a layer of sweaty moisture.

He slowly picked himself up from the floor. With heavy exhales and cracking in his knees, reminding him of all the beatings his body had taken over the years of running through alleyways, hopping fences, and falling to floors. His body was done, and every moment he pushed beyond mandatory human functions was an act of sheer will. His body was rife with so much pent-up emotion, it didn't know where to find an outlet.

"I hear him, Jimmy. Whatya think we got here?" Carlos asked, almost as if it was another casual call the two of them were on.

"Based on the guns they have pointed at us and Ian standing there with a bullhorn laughing like a smug asshole, I'm going to say it looks like he wants to surrender," Jimmy smiled.

"Well, why didn't you say so, Jimmy?" Carlos laughed back with trepidation.

Ian stood with the floodlights and headlights behind his back. "Sergeant Lopez! I have a proposal for you. Why don't you come on out, and I'll tell you all about it." Around him stood a mixture of White Patriots and Muerte. Some were ready to shoot; others had their guns slung across their shoulders or stomachs in postures of bravado.

Carlos looked out. "I can't do that, partner. The moment I step out, you'll kill me!"

"Has our relationship fallen to that point?" Ian responded.

"When you said you were going to kill my family and you started shooting, I'd say I trusted you in a different way."

Ian feigned heartbreak and grabbed his chest. "Oh Carlos. How could you?" The White Patriots and Muerte laughed at his showmanship. Ian regained his sense of reality and stood back up, a condescending smile on his face. "I'll tell you what, we'll put our guns down for a bit, and I'll come to you. You have my word."

"I need something better, brother," Carlos said, holding his gun on Ian.

Ian placed his AK on the ground and put up his hands. He slowly started to walk over to Carlos, hands in the air. He signaled to Freedom Frank and El León to put their weapons down.

"What are you doing, brother?" Freedom Frank asked, looking down his barrel to the front of the station.

"If I get shot, finish them. For now, put down the guns. Trust me," Ian said as he continued toward the station. Freedom Frank and El León followed orders and put their weapons down. They signaled to their brothers-in-arms to do the same. White Patriots and Muerte alike followed suit and put their guns down one after another, finding peace in coexistence if only for a moment in time. No matter how futile and false it was.

"Come on, brother. You owe me one, and you know it. Ten years in a prison cell for doing what was right. Ten years because you turned your back on the badge. This is an olive branch."

Carlos considered this. The AR he had trained on Ian's chest lowered. What he had never considered—restoring some sort of trust with someone he was so certain was the reason his life had fallen apart—was becoming a reality. Perspective changes when facing death, I guess.

"Stop right there, asshole!" Jimmy screamed with his gun still fixed on Ian, causing Freedom Frank and El León to move toward their weapons.

"Still following orders like a good boy, huh, Jimmy?" Ian shot back with an aura of peace in his voice, knowing Jimmy wouldn't kill an unarmed man like this.

Jimmy looked over at Carlos, who had all but put his weapon at his waist. "You're not seriously considering this, are you, Sarge?"

"Jimmy, put the gun down," Carlos said as he put his AR on the floor in front of the door for everyone to see.

"Do whatever the hell you want, but I ain't putting mine down. This motherfucker is here to kill us. I don't care what he says. Nothing good can come from this." Jimmy trained his gun on Ian.

"Come on, Jimmy. Just like old times." Ian approached the front steps. He stopped for a minute, not as certain Jimmy wouldn't drop him. He wanted permission from Carlos to enter, as he had been taught in negotiation situations.

"Jimmy is going to keep his gun pointed on you. Any funny shit, and Jimmy puts one in your head. Is that clear?"

"Crystal. This is a peace offering, so I don't see why there would be any need for it. But do as you must. I am the good guy here."

Jimmy laughed. "How the hell can you call yourself the good guy?"

I walked up to Carlos, my shotgun under my shoulder. "You can't do this. This is insane."

"First you're 'Mr. Let's Negotiate,' and now you have a shotgun under your shoulder like you're some sort of soldier," Carlos said.

I thought for a second and considered what I had become. "I've seen what people are capable of."

Without missing a beat, Carlos responded, "You're just scratching the surface, Son. You have no idea what people are capable of."

Mom came running up to Carlos, gun under her arm as well.

Carlos looked at us, then around the police station at Theresa's dead body, the shattered glass, the broken furniture, the holes in the plaster, everyone in here, armed.

Everyone.

All in the name of "protection."

"What have I done?" Carlos whispered.

Had he stood for what was right, or had he willed people so hard to be just like him?

"Carlos, I know you feel responsible for what happened to Ian. But you did what was right. His chance at redemption faded away the moment he let the first bullet fly," Mom said with pointed, definitive direction, pleading with him to maybe, for once in God knows how many years, listen to her.

Carlos looked at her holding a gun. He looked at Lupe. And at Roberto. All these people had so many hopes and dreams. His family stood in front of him, ready to fight for him.

"I have to do this, Sandy," Carlos said with a sense of resignation to everyone in the station. "If Ian does anything suspicious, you drop him, Jimmy."

"With great fucking pleasure, Sarge." Jimmy said, even more focused on Ian than he had been before.

"Ian, you do any funny business, and you're dead. Do you understand me?" Carlos yelled.

Ian kept his hands up. "Hey, what's fair is fair. Can I come in?"

Carlos opened the door.

Ian walked in.

Jimmy searched him, the barrel of his gun never leaving Ian. "He's clean, Sarge."

Ian looked around. "Yikes, this place is a shithole. I would say our remodeling helped out a bit. This is where you've been for the last ten years, Carlos? And I thought I was in a prison cell." Ian pointed to Carlos, scanning his physique up and down, seeing how broken Carlos had become in the ten years since they had last seen each other. "Now this is making a lot of sense."

"Get to the point or get the hell out, Ian," Carlos said, overtaken by a flood of emotions. This was a man he once loved dearly. They had been through and seen it all. Carlos thought he would never see him again, not after the judge sentenced Ian to ten years in state prison for voluntary manslaughter.

Yet here he was.

Carlos tried not to love him anymore, but he couldn't. There was too much history there Carlos couldn't let go of and hadn't yet dealt with—good and bad.

Ian held out his hands to Sandy to give her a hug. "Sandy, still as beautiful as I remember. My God, time has been good to you."

Mom didn't respond. She only grabbed her gun tighter. She was over this, and Ian saw it in her eyes. "Ooo, still as feisty as I remember."

"Mr. McGinnis, this is your last chance at having any way out of this without spending the rest of your life in prison several times over," I said to Ian.

Ian laughed and clapped his hands. "Oh my, is that little Eric? Should we round up the sticks and get in a game of Madden for old times' sake? Still calling me mister. You raised a good one here, Carlos."

"I'm a lawyer. I'm ensuring you understand the consequences of your actions so you know the choice you're making."

Ian put a hand to his mouth. "Oh Carlos, you must hate that. Your boy becoming an attorney. The apple doesn't fall far from the tree. In your case, I'm guessing the daddy issues here made sure the apple was a football field away from the tree." Ian put his finger on the barrel of my gun. "A twelve gauge. Wow, you got a lot of faith in him."

I didn't know how to take this. Was he being serious? Had Carlos actually trusted me? I didn't know enough about guns. But that answered a question I never thought about asking. "Did

Carlos think higher of me than I thought he did? All this pain I held onto, was I doing it to myself? I had so finely crafted a future without Carlos in my life, yet here I was five years later, still asking the same question I had been all my life.

Jimmy held his gun at Ian's head, his intensity, brewing thicker by the second. "Just say the word, Sarge, and I'll blow his head off, do us all a favor, including him."

"Cut the crap, Ian. There's only so much I can do to hold him back."

"Everyone is so tense. This should be a happy reunion. Come on now, it's a celebration. The truth is coming out! We're all getting what we deserve!" Ian danced mockingly. He stopped as he saw no one else was willing to so much as give him a breath of air. "Okay, since you're all a bunch of tight asses, here is my offer: Carlos, give yourself up. And bring the illegal with you. Let us kill you both, and everyone else gets to live."

Jimmy racked his AR. "I'm fucking doing it, Sarge."

"Kill an unarmed man? A cop, nonetheless? That will go over well, Jimmy."

"You're not a cop anymore. You gave up the privilege when you shot that gangbanger in the head."

"Yet here you are, wanting to do the same thing. Plus, you kill me, and all those people out there, they're not going to hold back. They're going to keep coming until all of you are dead. Blood is what they want. It's the only thing that will satisfy them."

For the first time, Jimmy lowered his gun. Ian was right. They had all the leverage. Somehow, this was some form of mercy. This was something he wasn't ready to decide on yet. It's much easier to decide when to live or die when given the choice.

"Now's your chance to be a hero, Carlos, the way you always wanted to be. Sacrifice yourself and give others life," Ian said with supreme confidence. He knew, above all else, Carlos's capacity to serve others. It's what drove him into this career, and what he had learned about him in all the years working together. Those streets had a way of revealing who you were.

I looked at him as he reflected. "Carlos, you can't seriously be considering this. This is insane. He's going to kill us all as soon as you're dead."

"It's a risk you're going to have to take. Look, with this, we all get what we want. I'm still a cop at heart. I don't want to see any more innocent people die. There's no need for it. I'll be headed to another country as soon as we're done with them, and the others, well the others, know how to fade into the background. It's what they do," Ian responded. "What do you think?"

"They're going to kill us. Our only chance to survive is to fight them," Mom pleaded with Carlos. He was too far gone. He wasn't going to listen to her.

"Seems like you have a lot of family issues you need to sort through. I'll give you ten minutes to solve whatever familial quarrel you've got going on here. If I don't hear from you by then, well, it's farewell for you all." Ian walked toward the doors. He turned back to Carlos. "Partner, I forgive you."

He turned his back and walked out. It was clear, regardless of how right Carlos felt he was in reporting what Ian had done, he still hadn't forgiven himself for exposing another cop. It's not what cops did. They protected each other.

Jimmy pointed his gun at Ian again as he walked away. Outside, Ian put up his hands and celebrated, pumping his fists in the air. El León, Freedom Frank, the White Patriots, and Muerte, all picked their guns back up.

The clock was ticking.

"You're not seriously considering this, are you?" Mom asked. "Carlos, no. You're not doing this."

"What do you care? You and the boy, you left. If it gets you and everyone else out of here, we have to." Carlos held back what was boiling over inside. "I dedicated my life to the greater good, and if you, the boy, Jimmy, and Lupe can get out of here, you can live your lives, and maybe something positive would have come out of this."

"Tell me what good this is going to do," Mom shouted back. "Huh, tell me what?! Don't just stand there. Answer me!"

"Maybe you'll remember why you loved me!" Carlos burst out. One piece of the truth came out, one of many still waiting to be uncovered.

The room fell silent, as everyone in the station considered this.

"Is that what all this is for, Carlos? For me to see why I should love you? I've never stopped loving you. Not for one minute. If you think killing yourself and an innocent man is going to make everything better, you're wrong," Mom said tenderly.

"I have a duty to uphold. That's what you respect … uh, respected about me. I was a man diligent to his word," Carlos said, a look in his eyes asking for forgiveness.

"If you think that was the only reason why I loved you, you really did not know me at all," Mom cried as she walked back to her position. "Do whatever you want. Live. Die. I don't care. I'm still going to fight."

Carlos watched her walk away again. The bolder his actions, the further it seemed he moved from everything he ever wanted. Him being a martyr was never going to solve anything.

"This is stupid, and you know it," I said to Carlos.

"Now you want to be a big man and fight?"

"No. Regardless of all the bullshit between you and Mom, you made a promise to uphold the law. To not give this man a shot at a trial is just wrong." For the first time, I shed some of the anger. What he said to Mom made me realize there was a lot more to this than I thought there was. Maybe all those things I had felt about Carlos were wrong. Maybe not wrong, they were just covered up by endless amounts of baggage ten therapists wouldn't be able to unravel for a few years.

"The billboard is right, Sarge. We gotta fight. Ian's going to kill us all regardless. If we're going to die, at least we gotta do it on our terms."

If there was one thing Ian did during his visit, he further entrenched Jimmy in his beliefs and his will to fight. Frankly, that was a big mistake on Ian's part. It brought back everything Jimmy remembered about Ian. "And honestly, Sarge. Just fuck that guy. He used to beat Eric at Madden when Eric was like five. If that doesn't scream 'piece of shit,' I don't know what will."

Lupe walked up to Carlos. "Sergeant Lopez, if there's one thing I've learned through all of this tonight, our fights, whatever they look like, we can't go at them alone. We need people by our side to help us through it all."

"Mrs. Sanchez, I can't let you do this. To keep fighting."

"My name is Lupe Sanchez. And Carlos," Lupe looked over at Jimmy with pride, then back to Carlos, "I don't need your permission for shit."

"God, that's hot," Jimmy smirked. "We're all behind you one hundred percent, Sarge. This is what is right. And you know it."

Carlos looked over at Roberto. A tear rolled down Roberto's cheek as he kept watch from his corner, never breaking his concentration. Carlos walked over to him. "Roberto, we haven't asked you. You're the other one who this directly involves. I can't make a decision for both of our lives."

"Fight. I no want *mi hija* to be afraid," Roberto paused for a moment to gather himself, "If I die, *quiero que ella sienta que me fui en mis términos. Estoy a tu lado.*"

Carlos didn't know what Roberto said, but he didn't need to. It was in his voice. It was in the way he carried himself. The only acceptable answer was to keep fighting. Let the fates be what they were meant to be.

He wasn't used to not having control, control of his emotions, of his life, but most importantly, of his story, of his side of things. In his mind, there was no other option. If he chose to engage in martyrdom, it would have been an act of cowardice. Not because he would have said no to violence, but because he went against the very things he stood for, what he believed in—justice, in all its forms. Deep in his soul, he was a man who believed in people, and he was a man of boundless hope. Somewhere along the way he lost that, but slowly, he was remembering who he was.

And it wasn't because of some act of bravado. It was because of the people next to him. He was remembering what it meant to be connected to people again, what it felt like to actually be alive. It wasn't some big moment, some action, or facing death that was going to make him feel alive. It was the people beside him and his connection to himself and his past. And being alongside these people was where he would find his well of hope again.

In remembering where life was, Carlos no longer felt the need to commit suicide thinly veiled as martyrdom. He remembered what he was fighting for.

Carlos took a deep breath in and said to everyone in the station, "Okay. We fight together. As one. We're going to fight until the bus arrives. And we're going to get out of here together. And if we don't make it, we know we did everything we could."

For the first time that night, everyone started to believe. Everyone felt, like maybe, holy shit, we might find ourselves out of this situation. And we would be the victors.

"Let's fuck shit …" I tried several times to pump my shotgun to give us a cool movie moment. "Let's fuck shit …" I tried again, arduously, to get the damn thing to pump.

Jimmy stepped in and helped me pump it. "Let's do this together." The gun clicked and loaded.

"Now who's playing hero ball?" Carlos asked me with a smile on his face. It had been five years since I had seen Carlos and seven since the last time he smiled at me. I had forgotten what it felt like. I forgotten what it looked like, the pride in his face, knowing that his son hadn't completely abandoned him in every way.

Carlos walked over to the front door and raised his AR-15 back out toward the front. Jimmy, on the other side of the doorway, pointed his gun at Ian. Carlos looked back at everyone. He nodded. We all gave him a nod in turn.

I couldn't believe it, but we were behind him. All of us. All in.

Carlos turned back to the front, looked down his barrel, and shouted, "Ian, I'm going to have to respectfully decline your offer. Whatever you throw our way, we'll be ready to handle it together."

Ian clapped his hands. Freedom Frank picked up his AR-15. El León picked up his AK-47. Their followers followed suit. The guns all pointed at us again. I had forgotten what it felt like to be staring down death, if even for five minutes.

Ian loaded his Beretta. He slipped in the mag and pulled the slide back. "Partner, I hate to see it end like this, but this was the way it was always destined to be. You, the hero cop."

Carlos's destiny was on the horizon.

And we were by his side.

Within moments, bullets pierced the walls.

CHAPTER SEVENTEEN

Eric

"Everyone good?!" Carlos yelled out.

The fight was short, but it was intense. Even when I felt like I knew what to expect, the only thing I could expect was the unexpected.

They attacked from all angles with different weapons. Their movement patterns were never the same. It was clear that Ian had given them different tactics to use. And the only thing we could trust was Carlos's and Jimmy's ability to spot and yell out the maneuvers.

Cops fighting against cops.

Brothers in blue … bullshit.

And yet, I continued to kill. Kill to survive. Kill to protect.

It was still killing. With each pull of the trigger, I was taking another human's life.

What no one ever tells you about killing is after the first time, you grow numb. I didn't think about it after that. I just killed. I killed, and I killed.

White Patriots and Muerte would approach and …PUMP … BOOM.

PUMP … BOOM.

PUMP … BOOM.

Each time I hit someone, regardless of who they were, I felt less and less. It was no longer intentional. It was all reactionary. A reaction to survive.

Yet there was something so powerful about it. It was like I controlled the universe. I held the lives of men in my hand. I could easily give it and take it away.

That was false bravado, never considering they could just as easily take it from me. I had for so long been against this, but when it happened, it was almost addictive. I was in a position of power. I had to respond to no one. No one I had to agree with and no one I had to answer to. I held all the decisions right in my hand. I controlled my destiny. I controlled my world.

The pump and pull of the trigger were all I needed to choose. And for once, I had the right to choose my life. I no longer had to be privy to someone else's whims, emotions, or thought processes. All this was mine. In those moments, the demons were gone. I was God of my universe.

It felt wrong—going against everything I had so firmly believed in.

I guess I never knew what I was capable of. Against the wall, with no way out, I saw a different side of myself, one I did not believe was true. But fundamentally, it was.

By my account, I killed three. I don't even know who or what they were or even what they looked like. They were just dead. It all happened so fast. They were but a number in a body count. The higher it climbed, the more chance we had of getting out.

To me, that was real power.

When the fighting was over, we were still all together.

Somehow, some way, we all survived. We looked at each other, the shock of what was happening more or less gone, and we celebrated, holding our guns up to one another and giving out low-level congratulations. We didn't want to get too confident, no matter how confident we felt. Now we were a unit, a force to be reckoned with.

It was the power of community.

And it wouldn't be the last we heard from them.

It was Jimmy who helped me to understand this. "They kept coming through the door breaking it down. I would shoot. Lupe would shoot, and it was like nothing would slow them down. They were like goddamn zombies."

Zombies was right. These people had become so full of hatred and anger they were mindless. The only thing they had on their mind was to kill.

"It's their M-O, Jimmy. They're here to kill. And the more we understand that, the better position we'll be in to defend ourselves." Carlos looked around the station, checking to see if there were any glaring holes in the defense. What he originally believed to be the greatest vulnerability, the people in the station, was now its greatest strength. Now it was the structure he was worried about. That building couldn't keep them out much longer.

Walls almost had full-blown holes in them. They were cracking so much they were ready to break. Windows were near nonexistent. And most of the doors were all but off the hinges. It would only be a matter of time before this makeshift fortress would do more harm than good. We needed to find a way out.

"This place can't take much more. We gotta go," Carlos said as he pulled a piece of plaster from the wall—noticing how far gone it was. "This place can't hold us much longer."

Jimmy looked at his watch, "It's one thirty. Bus is arriving in two and a half hours. We can hold on."

"Jimmy, you know as well as I do, they're going to go bigger. They're going to find a way in here," Carlos responded.

"What should we do then?"

Carlos looked out the shattered window toward the ditch, where the shot-up car sat. The ditch it rolled into wasn't so deep as to render the car unusable.

"If I can make it to the car, I can create a diversion long enough so someone else can get in the cruiser and get help. Jimmy, you ready?" Carlos asked confidently.

"Suicide mission to save the world? I'm in," Jimmy responded.

Carlos smiled and gave Jimmy a fist bump.

For some reason, I was hurt. This plan was illogical. Him needing to be a hero went against everything we just talked about. But it bothered me watching Carlos ask Jimmy to go with him.

Hadn't he seen what I had done?

"You two guys are going? Shouldn't Jimmy stay and be the one experienced person here to defend the station? If you both die, we're a bunch of random people with guns," I said to Carlos, trying not to show my hurt.

"Hmm, good point. Hinojosa, why don't you come with me? And we can do this together. And if they kill us, they get what they want, and we both still go out on our terms."

Roberto looked over at me. He could see me seething. I didn't need to say anything.

He looked at Carlos. "No, *puedo*. I stay." And he sat back near his window, rifle in hand, looking out the window, waiting to see what happened.

"You gotta be fucking kidding me!" I shouted.

The whole room stopped and looked over at me. I wasn't expecting that kind of attention. But then again, how could I not? Yelling, "You gotta be fucking kidding me!" is a pretty big showstopper.

"What? What is it? What's your problem?" Carlos asked.

"My problem? My problem?! Do you fucking hear yourself?"

Carlos stood in silence, not registering it. In fact, I couldn't either, I just knew I was mad.

"You and Jimmy? You're both so grossly out of shape and you waddle when you walk. No offense, Jimmy."

"Meh, accurate," Jimmy said.

"And we all just told you not to give yourself up like this, yet you want to run out there and get yourself killed?"

Carlos didn't react, which made me more upset. Why wasn't he listening to me?

"And then ... and then, you want to go with Roberto, who we all said we need to protect. What the hell is the matter with you?"

Carlos stood there. Taking it all in.

Mom walked to be by his side. Even in her most begrudged state, she still stood by Carlos. I was drowning myself, and they had to sit there and watch it all unfold.

"What, are you just going to stand there? Mom, do you hear this? Are you just gonna stand by and not say anything like you did the whole time you two were together?" I didn't understand.

"Do not talk to your mother that way," Carlos sternly shot back. One thing Carlos wouldn't stand for, above all else, was disrespect to Mom.

Hell, normally, it was something I wouldn't stand for either.

"Why do you choose everyone else but me? I've fought hard. I'm in better shape than anyone else here. I can help too. I'm not a fucking child."

Even screaming, yelling, and cussing, I couldn't get my parents to listen to me or understand me. I wanted to go into my room and slam the door shut again. I thought I had outgrown this phase, but it was never really gone. I was twenty-nine going on thirteen because I hadn't faced what I really wanted—to be acknowledged by my father.

"And you're not going to stop this, Mom? What is the matter with you both?"

Carlos and Mom looked at each other. No matter what had come between them as husband and wife, the one thing they wouldn't change was doing everything they could to raise their son right.

"Are you done?" Carlos asked matter-of-factly.

"Yes." I exhaled.

"Eric, I'll never stop being your dad. No matter how much you hate me, no matter how much you think I hate you, I will do everything I can to protect you."

"I'm a grown, man, Carlos. I can take care of myself. I'm supposed to be taking care of you."

"Just like your father, you're not listening," Mom said. I looked around the room to see everyone's eyes bored into my soul with looks of sympathy, which I hated. I didn't want people feeling sorry for me. I wasn't Carlos.

It hit me.

In a night where Carlos had looked like and been the asshole, I most assuredly was starting to look like a maniac. Most of all, when I looked into Mom's eyes, I saw the truth.

Carlos put his hand on my shoulder. "It's okay, Son."

I ripped my shoulder away. I held back tears. And I let him have what was in my soul. "Why were you gone, huh? Why couldn't you have stayed? And now when we need you most, you want to leave again. How is that fucking fair? Huh, tell me?"

The tears slowly emerged.

Carlos gathered himself. Pain was no longer a theory. It was here, and it needed to be addressed now.

In that police station, Carlos had created and lived in a perfect, impenetrable place. The more those walls crumbled, I saw his perception of the past do the same. Try as hard as he could, he couldn't make himself out to be a victim anymore. His son's pain was voiced. And he felt every bit of it, in a way only a father who truly loved his son could.

Carlos faced a choice. He could continue to ignore what he knew to be true and be the victim of his circumstances. Or he could die a victim of the world he constructed. Yes, an external force might kill him, but it would have been he who had done the killing.

Or he could confront reality.

Carlos looked at me, so broken, so vulnerable. "I'm sorry you've had to hold onto all of that for so long, son."

I couldn't look him in the eyes. If I did, I'd start sobbing again. I'd have to look into myself. And for as much as I wanted Carlos to take accountability for what he had done, I wasn't ready to take ownership of my role in this. "Thanks, Carlos."

Carlos then did the stupidest thing he could do. "Eric, do you want to come with me?"

I smiled. My thirteen-year old self felt acknowledged. Carlos was giving me everything I had ever wanted—recognition and respect.

Recognition and respect. It's why I put my face on billboards, bus benches, and TV ads. It's why I felt the need to be the loudest in the room. I wanted to be seen, and I wanted to be heard by one person and one person alone, my father. This need drove me. Whether I was cognizant of it or not, I still don't know. But I lived with the burden and those choices pretty much all my life, and especially the past ten years as Carlos phased himself out.

That's when I realized I was my father's son.

I was my father's son.

For all the pontificating and big actions I had done. For all the criticism, fair or unfair I laid on him, I hadn't yet taken responsibility for my role in Carlos's descent. I had been on the sidelines watching.

And here's the thing, I was going to continue watching, while "participating" because I needed to still feel sorry for myself. I had to continue to tell myself this story so I could function and survive. Choosing differently wouldn't satisfy my ego and match up to what I held onto for years. I wasn't ready to let go until I received some form of retribution for all he had done wrong to me.

I looked up at Carlos. I built up my defenses inside of myself strong enough to put on a tough exterior. "Yes, I'd like to. When do we go?"

I put my shotgun on my shoulder and walked over to him, hubris in each step.

"Now," Carlos said. "The longer we wait, the more time we give them to come in here and overrun this place. Jimmy, Lupe, I need you two to watch our six and provide covering fire out of the back door."

Lupe and Jimmy both nodded. No one wanted to stop us. For as much as everyone thought we needed to handle our shit together, this wasn't the way to do it.

Go to therapy. Go on a fishing trip. Literally, do anything but a suicide mission. We had built a false sense of comfort for each other, and as much as they wanted to step in, they knew, outside of killing us, we were going to do this. There was too much hurt. Too much pain. This feigned peace might give us some closure before we died.

Mom walked over to me. She grabbed me by the shoulders and looked me in the eyes. "Eric, you're too smart for this. Don't do this. If he wants to kill himself, let him. There's nothing you need to prove."

My mom was right, but I wanted to do this—for my ego. I had to save face with everyone in there, but most importantly, with myself. The decision had been made, and that was what was going to make me feel better. "Yes, I do, Mom."

Mom looked at me desperate, trying to break through as she had done so many times before. "Then go. Just know if you die," she took a deep exhale, "you won't be dying in peace."

I stared at her, knew she was right, and let my ego lead the way. "So be it, Mom. I love you."

Those last three words were one more effort at self-righteousness.

I kissed her on the forehead and walked toward the back door where Jimmy and Lupe waited for us.

Carlos went over to Mom right after me, searching for the right words to say. "I'll take care of our boy, Sandy. I promise. He'll make it back, no matter what."

I could see Mom wanted so badly to hug him. To comfort him. To hang onto the man she loved and beg him not to go for the sake of their family.

But all she could do was look away, with her arms folded. She couldn't let him do this with any sort of true peace in his heart.

"Goodbye, Carlos," she said sternly. No emotion registered on her face as she looked away.

Carlos picked up his gun and racked it. He tried in vain to get Mom's eyes back on him. "Alright, Eric. Let's go."

Jimmy cracked the door open. Carlos put the barrel of his gun out first, peeked his head out, and looked around. He followed with his body. He took a knee and scanned the back concrete area of the police station. Carlos's biggest issue here before was the weeds growing out of the concrete that he pulled to pass the time. Now, an assortment of four or five white-and-brown bodies lay motionless between the cracks the weeds grew out of.

He turned his head slightly back and whispered, "Clear. Let's go."

I moved outside. My shotgun at the ready. My heart racing.

The cruiser was about 150 yards away. I could make the run, no problem. But I didn't know how Carlos was planning to do it.

"It's too quiet out here. Something is wrong. Where are they?" Carlos asked.

"I'm going to check out that corner of the wall and see if I can get a better vantage point."

Before Carlos could stop me, I was off and running. I still could run like the wind blew, and I was ready to zigzag. Ready to take action for my family.

Adrenaline is funny. It zoned me out, and I couldn't feel anything. My only goal was the wall. The tunnel vision zeroed in. I felt I was running faster than I ever had in my whole life.

In a singular moment, mid-run, I fell to the ground.

I grabbed my leg. I didn't feel a thing. Just knew I had to grab it, wondering why I had tripped. I felt a sticky liquid in my hand. I knew I was in trouble.

Next thing I saw were the flashes of muzzles going off, and Carlos "slicing the pie," trying to get to me. I dragged myself to a corner, best I could.

Before I knew it, three gun barrels were at my face, held by the three Muerte standing over me, one of which was El León.

"What's going on over there? You guys alright?" a call came in over a walkie.

El León grabbed the walkie from his compadre's hand and smiled at me with a menacing smile. "We good. We just killed Lopez's son as he tried to escape."

They kicked my shotgun away from me and held their guns pointed at my face.

Carlos walked up with his gun trained on El León, knowing if he pulled the trigger, I was dead. "Let my son go. You can have me."

"I don't know, Lopez. I kind of want him to die slow. And I want you to watch it. Maybe we can skin him, and you can see for yourself that the brown is who you are," El León said with a smile on his face.

"I'll kill all of you first before I let that happen. Let him go." Carlos pointed his barrel down. He grabbed the center of his AR and put it on the ground. "You can have me. I'm the one you've always wanted. Let my son go, please."

"I'll make you a deal, Lopez. You give us our boy back. We'll protect him. And we'll let your son go. All you have to do is leave San Eugenio and never come back," El León said with not an ounce of sarcasm and with every bit of centralized power in him.

I looked over at Carlos. "You can't do this. It goes against everything we stand for. I'd rather die than—"

CRACK. The butt of El León's AK hit my mouth.

"Shut the fuck up. Let the men talk, *puta*."

Carlos made a step toward them. Muerte tightened the hold on their guns, ready to shoot him down.

"Why wouldn't you just get what you want and kill us still?" Carlos asked him.

"There's too much death. Even for El León. Too many Muerte have died for the cause. Our *compadres y nos hermanos*. We don't want this anymore."

Carlos looked at me as I held my mouth, blood seeping through gaps of my fingers. For the first time since he had known El León, he agreed with him.

"Deal. We'll release Hinojosa to you. Let my family go."

He loved his son too much.

El León and his Muerte compadres smiled. "I knew you'd see it my way. We Latinos need to stick together. For once, Lopez, you've shown that underneath the blue, the brown still is inside of you. Go get Hinojosa. We'll hold onto the lawyer, and when you're ready, we'll make a trade. You'll all have a way home. And this night will be over."

El León held his gun on me.

Carlos picked up his gun and walked backward slowly to the station with his gun fixed on El León. If for some reason El León chose to be stupid and kill me, that was a shot Carlos wasn't going to miss, no matter how far he was.

Carlos knocked on the door.

Would he let the love for his son take precedent over what he believed so deeply in—his duty to his country and to the Constitution of the United States?

CHAPTER EIGHTEEN

Carlos

"Go get my son!" Sandra yelled at me, visceral pain coursing through her veins. Though we had been apart, I never felt like she hated me. Until now.

"I'm going to. They won't move without me." Yes, it was a failure, but I was in the process of fixing it.

"Sarge, I'll go out there with you. You and I can take them down together," Jimmy jumped in, trying to calm down the situation.

I looked at Roberto with a mixture of shame and disappointment at what I had just done, and what I was about to do. I was confused. There was no excuse for flexing on morals and ethics, except when it came to my family. Family has always been the most important thing to me, whether Sandy and Eric believed that or not. "We have leverage here."

Roberto stared at me. He wiped his eyes, stuck his chin up, and got up from his seat next to the window. If there was one thing Roberto was, it was cognizant of everything around him, resigned to the fact that he knew his role in all of this.

I walked slowly over to Roberto with each step echoing louder than the one before it. "I've agreed to give up Hinojosa to Muerte. In exchange, they're going to let Eric go and provide us a way home."

I had trouble reaching Roberto's eyes. I believed in what I was doing, but my head felt heavy. I'm a man of principle, yet something felt inherently wrong. I believed in every decision I made. If you make the right one, you are able to look someone in the eye, no matter how difficult it may be. It was getting tougher and tougher to maintain eye contact with him. "I'm sorry, Hinojosa. This is how it has to be."

Roberto placed his gun down by the window. "*Yo entiendo*."
He stuck out his chest.

"I can't believe this. You leave my son out there with murderers.
And now, you're going to give up on your morals to make up for
your mistakes?" Sandra stared daggers into my eyes. She picked
up her AR leaned against the remnants of Theresa's desk. "If you
won't care enough about my son, I will."

She racked the gun.

She walked out the door. I ran to her, trying to stop her. "Whoa
whoa. What do you think you're doing? You shoot at them, and
not only is Eric dead, but so is each and every one of us."

I held onto her shoulders with my fat fingers. She didn't try
to remove them, almost like she had missed them there. I felt her
trust in me, and it made me rethink what I was doing. Why, even
with so much anger in her, was she still around me?

I put my hand on her gun, lowering it, trying desperately
to quell her anger. Who was I to stand in the way of a mother
wanting to protect her son? I knew it was my pride and desire to
save face with my son that had put them here.

"Sarge, you know as well as anyone they can't be trusted.
Even if they do give him back, what's to say they won't shoot
you both when they get what they want," Jimmy said with stern
confidence, forcing me to listen.

Jimmy was right. Those guys had spent the evening trying to
kill us all. Why wouldn't they just shoot the people who got in
their way?

I collected my thoughts. I wanted to hold my emotions back,
but try as hard as I could, they came to the surface. I put my
hands on my hips. With my head down, I took a deep breath and
looked at Jimmy. My voice cracked just above a whisper as I tried
to get my words out. "Jimmy, I love my son. If this is the only
option for him to survive, I have to take the shot."

Sandy, Jimmy, Lupe, and Roberto all looked at me. They felt
the truth in this. One definitive truth rang through the night.
No matter how much I wanted to fight it, how little I wanted
to embrace it, and how angry I was at him, I couldn't resist it
anymore.

I loved my son.

Roberto walked up to me with so much courage. He was going to give himself up to save us, to save my son. I feel desperately sad that we failed him. Is this what he had come to America for? He put his hand on my shoulder. "It's time. Señor Lopez. I'm ready. *Vamanos.*"

The room fell silent, a mixture of sadness and acceptance. This was a terrible idea, but it was our one chance at freedom. Too much violence had occurred. Too many people had died. Why couldn't I try something different, no matter how far-fetched it seemed? Both Roberto and I were convinced this is what everyone wanted, what everyone needed.

Roberto led the way to the door. I followed closely behind. Muerte promised Roberto protection. Yet, this felt like an execution. Roberto walked out, as he had always wanted to, with his head held high.

He hugged Lupe. "*Gracias por su fuerza.*"

Lupe held onto him tightly. "*Tu eres amór.*"

Jimmy tapped Roberto on his shoulder and reached out his hand. There was a profound sense of respect in the handshake. "Hell of a fight, Hinojosa. It was an honor." Then, Jimmy looked into my eyes with both disappointment and understanding. He was my partner and knew me better than just about anyone. This was killing me inside, but I had to do it. He knew how much this meant to me. However, no matter how much Jimmy understood, I couldn't continue to look him in the eye. I turned my head away. This wasn't who I was.

Roberto got closer to the door. Sandy gazed at him, in a way only a Latina mother who could see into another's soul could. I imagined Sandy's look reminded Roberto of his mother and grandmother, the look of which he had been on the receiving end so many times before.

Roberto hugged Sandy with her hands by her side. "Your son will live. I am happy to do this. It is *mi tiempo.*"

Roberto just held on. Sandy resisted. And resisted. And resisted, her arms by her side, not returning her hug.

She couldn't hold herself back anymore.

She sobbed in deep anguish, and she held onto Roberto tight in a hug reserved for only her most beloved. "I'm so sorry. I'm sorry we couldn't do better. Thank you. Thank you." She kissed him all over his face, trying to show how much he was loved.

He was a husband and a father. If his child was in the same situation, he would've done the same. He knew what it meant to love someone so much he'd do anything to make sure they had a chance to live. Fuck, we were the same person.

Everyone looked on with sadness in their eyes, all witnessing Roberto's selflessness for someone he barely knew. It was the saddest anyone had been in the evening. Maybe it wasn't sadness, maybe it was an understanding of what was truly taking place this evening inside the police station. That love, as fucked up as it may have been, was motivating this all, and no matter what, there was no right answer. All there was, was love. It was the best any of us could do.

Hard as it was, I separated Sandy and Roberto. "It's time to go."

I looked at Sandy as I moved to open the door. "I love my son, Sandy."

She paid no mind to me, and she took a firing position near the door. Her rifle pointed out toward where Muerte stood around Eric. "Go."

She knew I loved this country and my son. I didn't understand why she didn't have compassion for me. Didn't she understand that this was the hardest decision of my life? To give away everything I stood for and everything I believed in so that my son may live? So that we may live?

I put Roberto in front in the doorway, using him as a human shield. My hand went up slowly—a slight shake to it. It was heavy, like a surrender of everything I had known. Roberto and I walked to Muerte and El León.

El León clapped. He looked down at Eric and put his foot on his chest. Digging in with his boot, he said, "I knew Daddy would come and save you."

A sigh of relief took over Muerte.

I approached Beretta out. It was dangerous territory we were entering. "Pick my son up and hand him over to me."

"Deal is a deal, Lopez," El León said as he reached out his hand to lift Eric up. Muerte raised their guns. Why did they push us to this point? Why did they make us do this? I could've killed them all at that moment. It's what I wanted. I was so angry.

"How do I know you're not going to kill us?" I asked with my left hand on Roberto's shoulder. I held my gun over his right and pointed it at El León's head.

"You've never understood this, Lopez. I love my people. Everything I do is to protect us and to see us thrive in a world that doesn't want us. You're showing me you're one of us. I don't want any more of our blood spilled. Cop or not. I want peace."

I actually believed this asshole. But I didn't trust him enough to take my gunsight off him. "So how are we going to get out?"

"Once you hand Hinojosa over to us, we'll let your boy go, and we'll clear a path. But first, put your gun down."

God, I wanted to trust him. He made sense for once. I held onto everything I knew. El León was lower than me, a bad Latino who perpetuated guns, violence, and drugs into our community. He gave us a bad name in the way he dressed and the way he acted. It was making it hard to let go of Roberto.

Roberto had shown me he was someone to be trusted. El León hadn't earned that yet.

"Carlos, please," Eric begged. "This is our only way."

Goddamn it. He was right. It was the only way. Fuckin' why, though? I just wanted to fight. But we couldn't have any more bloodshed.

"Shit." I put down my gun and gave Roberto a gentle nudge toward El León and Muerte.

El León smiled. "*Vamos*, Hinojosa. *Es tiempo. Ir a casa.*"

Roberto looked back at me as El León shoved Eric forward. Eric stumbled into my chest, almost forcing us into a hug. I put his arm around my neck to prop him up. Eric was in pain from the gunshot wound in his leg. Each step shot the pain harder than the last.

Eric and I looked at each other. This felt different.

"Now what do we do?" I asked.

Muerte and El León hugged Roberto. He did not hug them back. They checked him for wounds, blood. Anything to give them reason to go back on this deal. After they cleared him. They smiled and hugged. They had gotten what they wanted.

"You okay, Son?" I checked Eric. For as much as I wanted Eric to be okay, I also wanted to find something so I could renege on our deal.

"I'm fine. Just a little banged up," Eric said.

"Now what? What do we do from here? How do we get out?" I said, looking at El León.

In the middle of his celebration and with pride in his voice, El León said, "A deal is a deal, Lopez. Get the rest of your familia and—"

A hole pierced through El León's forehead. Blood trickled, then gushed out.

El León went down to his knees and hit the concrete face-first.

One of El León's compadres dropped to cover El León's body with his. The other two raised their guns up. They knew it hadn't come from me.

I covered Eric best that I could.

PFFT.

PFFT.

One by one, they went down. We could barely hear the gunshots as they pierced right through their chests. Down to the ground in rapid succession.

I stood there in shock, not knowing what had just happened.

"Run! We need to get out of here now!" I grabbed Eric by the shoulder and ran him toward the door. I turned back, eyeing El León's dead body.

El León wanted a different life. He tried the same means others before him had. He even found success leading people. It all led to the same result. Maybe he was destined for this ending. No matter how hopeful he was, the cycle could not be broken. It still ended with him on the ground, dead.

As El León's compadre tried in vain to help him, the man fired his gun aimlessly into the night with one last flex of machismo to scare the assailants away.

PFFT.

A bullet went through his chest, and he fell atop El León.

"Move your ass, Eric!" I screamed as he hobbled to the door, doing his best to shake us both out of our shock.

We snapped out of it and realized we were about seventy-five yards from the door. Eric ran as best as he could, ignoring the pain in his leg. The only thing that went through my head amidst every danger around us was, "I never give credit to Eric for his grit." It took him running on a fucked-up, gunshot-wounded leg for me to realize it, but I did. Why did it take that for me to realize this inherent trait? We raised him to have grit.

He showed it on the baseball field when he was seven years old. He was the catcher, and a pop-up went foul and into the net. He popped out of his crouch, ran as fast as he could, dove for the ball, and caught it. I had never seen an effort like that out of a little kid before. I don't think any of the parents had because they gave him a standing ovation for his effort on a foul ball and a catch that didn't even count. How had I forgotten that this was my son? Why did it take a bullet through his leg for me to remember?

Snaps and cracks went off all around us as the bullets flew by.

Sandy and Jimmy knelt in the doorway, furiously returning fire.

"Get out of the way!" I shouted desperately, out of breath.

Ten yards out, I felt the hot bullet enter my right shoulder. Eric took one to his left.

"Fuck! My arm is numb!" Eric shouted as he grabbed it.

Getting shot sucks.

We both made it into the station. The gunfire behind us continued on rapidly as Eric and I tried in futility to recover from our respective wounds.

"Let's go, Hinojosa! Let's go!" Jimmy screamed in between bursts of fire.

Out the door, Roberto kept low cover and zigzagged as best he could.

Fifty yards away.

Forty.

Thirty.

Then a bullet hit his calf, standing him up. Then another through his chest. And another, stopping him in his tracks. He stayed up for a moment, stared off into the distance, and gasped for breath. Muzzle flashes in front of him lit up his face like a strobe light. He slowly lowered himself to the ground, trying to understand what had happened to him.

Roberto put his head down to the ground and closed his eyes.

Eric got up and limped toward the front door.

"Get up, Hinojosa. Get up. Move your ass!" Jimmy screamed hopelessly, hoping against hope somehow he could will Roberto back to life.

As Eric got to the door, Jimmy held him back.

"Let me through. We need to help him!" Eric screamed.

Jimmy shoved Eric to the ground and shut the remnants of the door behind him.

Roberto took his last gasp for breath. I wondered what went through his mind. Was it his daughter? Was it his wife? God, I hope it wasn't the pain. Had he done everything he set out to do? He was a beacon of hope of how things could be different. And now he was gone.

Roberto gave his all to America. Was it worth it? Was this the America I fought my whole life to protect?

Lupe pushed a file cabinet in front of the door. The screeching against the floor sounded louder than before.

She was tired.

We all were.

There was nothing left.

CHAPTER NINETEEEN

Eric

"They're killing them all!" Lupe shouted in abject horror.

Ian looked over at us and smiled.

We watched as the White Patriots killed whatever last Muerte were left standing one by one. All of them executed. Put on their knees and shot slowly and methodically so each one who was killed after would experience the pain of his compadre. Each was meant to watch and suffer.

The last four or five of Muerte fought like hell. They kicked. They punched. They stared into their eyes without saying a word. They screamed a warrior's scream. They cussed at their killers in Spanish. "*¡Coño de puta madre!*" "*¡Soy el diablo!*" And everything in between to intimidate and strike one last bit of fear into the White Patriots.

The White Patriots laughed in their faces. They spit on them. They mocked them and told them to scream out for their Catholic God. They hooted and hollered.

It was a celebration. The white man was all that was right in this world. They tried to trust the "invaders," and the trust had been broken. Now it was time to watch them all die a traitor's death and enjoy the celebration. For this moment, they would not be replaced. They had defended their home, just as they swore they would.

Perhaps the most amazing thing was not one of Muerte … not a single one, begged for his life. They all took their impending deaths, whether they believed they deserved it or not, as a part of life approaching them faster with each passing day. There was no hope for these men. If there was no hope, the best they could do to maintain their sense of masculinity was to battle the Grim Reaper to the bitter end.

A hush fell over the rabid crowd.

Slowly, the crowd began to cheer. It built over about ten seconds, turning into laughter and more celebration.

That was when we reached our lowest point. Not one of us could take in what we would see next without an impending sense of doom. Hope for humanity was gone.

They lifted the body of Roberto overhead with his arms laid out in a T and his legs straight together. They pulsated his body over their heads up and down in a wave pattern.

They screamed. They shouted. Sent shots up into the air. He was a representation of all they hated. They had conquered their fear, and this was worth the party of a lifetime.

"Patriots Protect America. Patriots Protect America. Patriots Protect America." On and on the chant went as they celebrated. They had defended their homeland.

I never felt so sick in my life. As I looked around the room, I couldn't help but think everyone felt the same. Heads were down. Eyes were half watching and half looking away—unable to see this horrid image, but knowing we could not look away.

We needed to see this. We needed to be reminded of what we were fighting for.

We needed to feel the anger. The pain. Otherwise, why were we still living?

Mom just watched. Lupe cried in silence. Jimmy tried to remain stone-faced, but his facade was breaking.

He used his shirt to wipe away tears.

Carlos was perhaps the most attentive. He didn't move for a moment. He sat there and watched, not so much as blinking. He didn't want to miss a second of this. He held his gun at the ready, pointed out toward the front of the station, waiting, anticipating what would come next.

His failure had brought him here. He couldn't hide from that fact anymore.

He didn't want to.

The high-pitched whistle and cackling of the bullhorn began again.

"This is what happens when you betray the White Patriots. This is what happens when the law must be taken into our hands. We are the only ones who can save this nation. All traitors must die." Freedom Frank's words were met with a loud cheer and gunshots into the air. "And now, you must die."

"USA! USA! USA!" rang out in their voices. Their battle cry, filled with so much pride in what they had accomplished.

Freedom Frank calmly handed the bullhorn to Ian, his gaze never breaking from the station. He wanted blood. He wanted justice. Roberto was dead. He had received exactly what he wanted. But it wasn't enough. Now he wanted to hold us accountable for killing his men.

Ian looked over at Frank, smiling a big smile, knowing he had won. His plan was working out exactly as he had wanted it to. He brought the bullhorn up to his mouth. "Partner, you never fail to surprise me with your ways of escaping responsibility. You did it ten years ago, and you just tried to do it again. Where has it gotten you both times, huh?"

Carlos's gaze remained unbroken. He continued to take it all in. I couldn't tell if he wanted to kill Ian or if he felt misery for what he had done or both. He watched as the light continued to shine on his face. His pupils were so dilated, his anger was so palpable that the physical need to look away didn't exist.

"It's about two thirty, partner. As much as I would enjoy seeing you suffer, we have to make this quick," Ian said through the bullhorn. He took a deep breath, emotion overcoming him for a brief second. It seemed the memories of what he and Carlos had experienced together flashed before Ian's eyes—the conversations they had together getting through the academy, the dinners with their wives, watching one another's kids grow up.

All of it was there for Ian.

But most importantly, he remembered their time working at Fort Comanche. They were both cops. They had been brothers. Friends. Partners. And now, it all had to be taken away. It's what Ian wanted when he set out to do this, and now it was about to become reality.

"Partner, there's one last thing I want to tell you before I send you to patrol the streets of heaven," Ian stated.

It felt like Ian wanted Carlos to say something back—an apology, a confession, something that might help him move on with his life.

Nothing ever came.

Ian took a moment. "I just wanted to say, I love you. Brothers in blue."

He released the talking button of the bullhorn. The high-pitched whistle from the bullhorn was overshadowed by the racking of guns and the mindless chatter of the remaining White Patriots.

Carlos stood there, continuing to watch. We waited for his next move. There he stood paralyzed.

He turned around, studying all of us. He looked over to the window where Roberto had held his position for the night. The M21 rested against the windowsill.

Carlos hobbled over to Theresa's body, making sure it remained untouched and had not been further damaged. As he gently adjusted his coat over her head, he leaned over. "I'm sorry."

He pulled himself up, feeling pain with each movement. He walked to Lupe and looked at her bruised eye. "Why?"

We were confused. What the hell was he talking about?

He limped over to me and Mom as she finished patching my leg with a bandage. The crimson filling the white patch. Mom and I looked over at Carlos as he hovered over us and said, "Why?"

Mom got up from the ground. "Carlos, what's going on?"

Carlos pulled out his Berretta from its holster and took one shot out the front door. Then in rapid succession with hardly a moment for the pin to settle on the gun, BAM! BAM! BAM! BAM!

Fifteen consecutive shots. He emptied his clip, screaming a death shrill from the depths of his soul. He held onto the gun tight, moving closer and closer to the door, emptying whatever was left in his clip.

The shots were aimless and directionless. When he was out of ammo, he continued to click the trigger, hoping somehow his gun had reloaded itself.

None of that happened.

His gun was empty.

It wasn't going to reload itself, and he was all but out of ammunition in the station. He threw the gun out the front door. It flew, barrel over handle, cutting the air as it traveled. Maybe it would hit something or someone. Maybe his pain would somehow kill them all. If he screamed loud enough, if he let them know how much he hurt, maybe this would all stop.

The gun landed on the pavement. Carlos stood at the front door and continued to yell. We watched in stunned silence. Ian and the White Patriots didn't react.

There was nothing any of us could do, except sit and watch.

The white and purple of the floodlights shone brightly on Carlos, putting his body and his life into perspective.

When Carlos was all yelled out, he went to the nearest wall. And with the ferocity of his youth he hadn't been able to express properly, he punched. And he punched. And he punched, with more force than a bullet. When the walls had been punched through, and the plaster revealed, he ripped it out. Carlos no longer felt the pain in his shoulder and his leg. The anger overtook him so much, he felt nothing but rage.

He punched and kicked, knocking shards of glass out with his bare hand, slicing his hand. He flipped tables and chairs. Not a soul dared to get in his way. It was the catharsis we all wanted for him.

Carlos picked up what little was left of a lamp and tossed it against a wall. He slipped and fell against it, dropping him to the floor. He started to cry.

He cried, and he cried, and he cried.

With nothing left to hold onto, Carlos was ready to let it go. The time was right because he had nothing left. This was the only way he would have been able to reach this point.

"Why did this have to happen, huh? Tell me! I gave my life to you. To this profession. To this badge. And what did I get? I got my wife and my son killed. I abandoned what I stood for. For what?! For the cop right next to me? For the law nobody cares about? For people to hate me? To throw shit at me and tell me they want me dead? Why did this have to happen?! Why?!"

"You chose this life, Carlos," Mom said with bits of empathy.

"I know I did!" Carlos roared back. "I know I did. All I wanted was to do something good. To be someone who stood up for the people who needed a voice. For those who were wronged. For those who didn't have anyone watching over them."

"So instead, you left us behind?" I chimed in, with not an ounce of anger inside me. It was my reality after all. It was what I had experienced.

Carlos looked up at me as he wiped away a few tears. "I didn't leave you, son. I never left you."

"After the trial, you were gone. You came up here, and you never looked back."

"It wasn't you I was running from, Son." Carlos took a deep breath. "It was me."

I didn't understand what he was saying. Mom was crying. Jimmy's chin quivered as he tried to hold his emotions in.

Carlos had hit upon something.

"I know what I did, Eric. I've always known. Why do you think I'm up here. I couldn't look you or your mom in the face anymore. I wasn't the husband or the father I was supposed to be. I didn't have it in me anymore. Look at your lives since I've been gone. Look at what you've become. Look at how happy your mom is. This world has been better with me exiled here, eating myself to death and hoping someday soon something would bring this to an end. Anything."

"Enough!" Mom glared at Carlos. "Enough of this bullshit, Carlos. I don't care how much you think you deserve to die. Stop playing the victim. You put yourself in this position. You put us here. You'll always want to die until you own up to this."

Carlos looked at Mom. The jig was up. He could convince everyone else in the world his intentions were pure and that the world was responsible for his feelings. But not Mom, not Sandra. In that moment, he was reminded exactly why he married her and why he had missed her so desperately in the five years since he left her.

He took a deep breath. "Ian pulled the trigger that killed the cholo in East LA. I tried to save his life, but I took it long before the night in the alley, before even one round from the AK ever went off. I took it every time someone called me a spic and I laughed. Every time another cop called a Latino gangbanger a 'piece of shit,' not because of what he did but because of the color of his skin. I made it okay for them to say these things because I never spoke up. I sat there and let it happen. I took it because I was scared. I didn't want to be seen as weak. Yet the more I didn't want to seem weak, the weaker I became. Look at me now. Who the fuck am I?"

Carlos turned around and beat the wall harder. He fell face-down on the ground, among the shattered glass and smatterings of blood, with his fists bleeding from punching the broken glass and the wall.

Jimmy walked over to Carlos and placed his hands on his back and shoulder. He lifted him slowly off the ground and hugged him.

Carlos cried in Jimmy's arms.

Jimmy cradled him. "It's okay, Carlos. I'm here for you. I always have been. Not going anywhere. Right here by your side."

Brothers.

I stood there, not knowing how to process anything.

My dad had been honest. He had given all of himself to a different life than what he had ever wanted because he believed it necessary for the greater good. Though I had doubted it, deep down, I knew my father had always loved me. It was in this acceptance of himself, seeing this broken man in the arms of his best friend, that I felt deeply loved.

I had been so angry for so many years. And I didn't understand why. I covered any feeling of missing love with things—money, clothes, public appearances—and all I had ever wanted was this, for me to see my dad, as a person. He was a person doing the best he could with what he had.

As I confronted this, I looked over at Mom, who wore a mixture of sadness and pleasure on her face as she watched her husband. Something inside of me broke. "And you stood by and did nothing."

Mom snapped her head over. "What?"

"You heard me. You and me, Mom. We're just as culpable as he is. We saw him run. We saw him fall into this. We watched him killing himself. And we did nothing."

Mom looked at me with confusion, confusion because she knew.

"You never said a thing to him. You were there for him, you comforted him, you cried with him, but you didn't show him a path out. You followed him here, but you didn't speak up. You didn't say what was in your heart. You didn't fight back. You let him be. And now, you sit there with pride as he breaks himself down like you won something. But you sat and you did nothing."

Sandra started to cry. She looked at me, searching for an answer.

Carlos lifted his head from Jimmy's arms. "Hey, your mom—"

"No, Dad. She needed to hear that," I said. "And I didn't speak up either. Instead of helping him, I got angry. I became a defense attorney to piss him off. I put up a billboard. I said I believed in justice and honor and in the ways he had taught me, but I was petty. I was passive-aggressive. I fought him so hard, and I never once asked him how he was doing. I never cared enough to ask. I was so set up with you guys paying for college, with how hard you worked for me, I never stopped to think of what you gave up for me to be where I am today. Now if we're ever to move forward, we all need to be responsible for what we did and where we fucked up. Otherwise, what the *hell* are we fighting for?!"

I said it. I felt lighter. That weight had rested so hard on my shoulders. I had fought so hard to keep it on me, and suddenly, it vanished. I saw was my mom and dad for all they were—people. People who loved.

"You all need therapy," Lupe chimed in, breaking up the heaviness of the moment.

We all laughed.

Jimmy gave Carlos one last big hug. Carlos and Jimmy held the embrace.

Jimmy stood. He held out his hand and helped Carlos off the floor. "This used to be a lot easier ten years ago, Sarge." Carlos laughed.

Lupe walked toward us. She looked over at a cracked window, the light shining through allowing her to catch a glimpse of her bruises, the purple, black, and blue around her eye. Her puffy lip. Her swollen eyelid. She put her hand to it all and gently touched it. She saw for the first time what had happened to her.

She smiled, staring into the window, and said, "We can continue to lie to ourselves, to say everything is okay and not acknowledge the mistakes of the past. Or we can move forward."

She turned to us. "When I think of the world I want my daughter to grow up in, I look at all of you. When I think of Roberto or of Theresa, I think of the life you all showed me tonight. I think of how life could be different." She pointed to her face. "This didn't need to happen. But it did. All the signs were there from the start, but I ignored them. I ignored them because I was desperate for love. I believed in some fantasy that didn't exist. I wouldn't face reality the way you have here. I don't know, maybe life could have been different. What I do know now is even if we die tonight, I want to fight. I want to have my voice heard. When my daughter hears of this story, whether it's from me," Lupe paused, tearing up, "or someone else, I want her to know that her mommy was brave. That I fought to live a different life for me, but most of all, for her. Our lives don't have to be hers."

We all stood in astonishment at Lupe. This woman who had been so meek, so broken when we first saw her, felt like she was more powerful than any gun, any gang, anybody out there.

She was.

Lupe grabbed the M21 Roberto had used and racked it. "Because you try for the people you love."

"Wait, how did you know how to do that?" Jimmy asked.

"I have no idea. Just a lucky guess," Lupe exhaled and laughed. "I hate guns so much."

We all laughed and collected ourselves. If we were going to die, we were going to die as human beings. Nothing more, nothing less.

We were going to die for a future not yet written.

"Alright, Sarge, what's the plan? What are we doing here?" I asked.

Carlos smiled at me. I smiled back. It felt right.

"Well, we got about an hour to hold them off until help arrives. Jimmy, what do we got?"

Jimmy walked over to the ammo room, turned on the lights, and looked around. As he sifted through the empty shelves and poured empty magazines and ammo cans onto the floor, the sound of it all made it clear we were pretty much on our own.

"We have about fifty 9mm rounds left, two ARs, about five more shells for the shotgun and one breach charge," Jimmy said, trying to maintain a positive attitude.

Jimmy confirmed what we already knew to be true.

We had us.

It was all we needed.

"Well, shit. Guess we'll just have to make do, won't we?" Carlos looked over to me and Mom with a slight smile. He had done the best he could. We stayed alive this long. We were going to have to face the reality of this sooner or later.

"The bus is here! The bus is here!" Lupe shouted in excitement and relief, catching us all by surprise.

We all ran to the windows and watched as the beautiful black bar-windowed and silver steel-plated bus pulled in for our freedom. We celebrated and hugged one another. Salvation was here.

Amid the celebration, I walked over to Carlos with a smile from ear to ear. "You did it. We did it."

Carlos forced a smile. As soon as I saw it, I knew it was bullshit. "We did, Son." He looked back at the window. He was willing to look at the reality of the situation. Those men in the bus were as good as dead.

The bus pulled up to the checkpoint, where the car in the ditch had been stopped. A look of dread came over us all. I understood Carlos's forced smile.

"Come on, they have to see the battered station. They have to see the dead bodies." I said with a false optimism. Trying ardently to rally the troops, best I could.

I smiled through the sadness, just like Carlos.

CHAPTER TWENTY

Officer Carpenter

I'm always on time.

"San Eugenio, this is Twenty-Two Bobcat, coming in for transfer of prisoner 09171810. ETA two minutes. Over," Bill, the driver, spoke into the radio. "San Eugenio, this is Twenty-Two Bobcat, coming in for transfer of prisoner 09171810. ETA two minutes. Please, confirm. Over. I'm not picking up any signals, sir."

"Goddamn them playing grab ass when we got a job to do. Gimme that thing." I shouted into the radio, taking it out of Bill's hand. "San Eugenio, pick up your goddamn radio now, or I will personally celebrate Halloween early and shove a flashlight so far up your ass, you'll turn into a jack-o'-lantern, do you understand me?"

Nothing.

What the fuck was I doing here? I had better shit to do with my time. Lopez of all people was someone who I knew as better than this. No wonder why they have him running the San Eugenio precinct. Takes an ass to watch over shit.

"Now what in the goddamn holy fuckin' hell is this bullshit?" I yelled as the bus rolled to a stop, a cruiser blocking our way. Half cussing at Bill for stopping and half cussing at this idiot in front of us, "I tell you what, I don't care who it is that's responsible for not answering, but when I get back, heads are gonna roll."

Now, what in the Sunny Hell Jesus Christ is this joker doing here? Who didn't tell them I was coming? I'm always on time. Now you're delaying me. Looks like some sort of goddamn trainee didn't get the message.

Bill opened the door. The hiss let out.

"Goooood morning, gentlemen. How can I help you?" the officer said with a pretentious smile that, in my younger days, I would've punched clean off. I don't have time for stuff like that now. He's not worth it.

I walked down the steps. These damn things feel like they get steeper each time. "Cut the shit, boy. You know I'm here to pick up prisoner 09171810."

"Ah yes," he responded. "Looks like you fellas are here a bit earlier than your projected zero four hundred arrival time."

"That's why it's *projected* boy. Your ass is leaving at zero four hundred when you're riding with me. Now, get the goddamn cruiser out of the way, I got a schedule to keep," I commanded. "I thought they knocked the stupid out of these kids at the academy. Shows you how pussified the younger generations have become," I grumbled to Bill.

"Yeah, you would think," he said with a smile. "Jim, what's with all these cars out here? They doing some sort of training or something?" Bill asked.

It was odd. No one told me about this. When does anyone tell me anything? Just expect Carpenter to handle any situation thrown his way. Schedule and security be damned.

I flipped through the pages of the manifest on his clipboard. "Nobody telling me shit. Goddamn these communications." I walked back up the stairs to the front of the bus.

My breathing got heavier. I really gotta cut back on the cigars.

I continued to look through the manifest. If by the Grace of Satan, I somehow made a mistake, which let's be honest, never happens, I'll own up to it. I walked back toward the door. "I don't see any training listed here on this goddamn manifest. Whatever fruity Broadway show you got going on here needs to move along, right this goddamn insta—"

I looked up from the manifest. A brown officer's body fell forward onto the dashboard of the cruiser.

This trainee asshole had his Desert Eagle pointed at Bill. Those weren't department issued. Those were found in a brown paper bag in the back of a busted-up sedan, with the serial number taken off.

I moved my hand to my holster and moved slowly toward the door.

Oh, I wish you would, bitch.

165

"Don't think about it. You make one more move, and I'll kill you both," the white officer said.

"We're dead men anyway, so go ahead and pull the goddamn trigger, you piece of shit," I shouted to him. This son of bitch didn't realize that I didn't care if I lived or died. No one would care. That piece of shit was standing in front of me and my job.

Unless The Virgin Mary herself is giving me a lap dance, no one breaks Officer John Carpenter's schedule.

"Don't get ahead of yourself there. I'm the good guy here. I'm protecting this land from the fucking invader you brought here. You did this. Let me see you tear out the radio, and you'll be home free. We'll be out of your hair in no time," the white officer said. "We're the good guys here. We're doing the job you refused to do."

Bill looked at the radio. "Don't be thinking about doing any hero shit. Just do as I say," the white officer warned.

Does this dipshit not know who he's fucking with?

"I got an idea for you," I said, my heart beating a little quicker.

"What's that?" the white officer responded.

"Go fuck yourself!" I said as I drew my Beretta out of its holster.

Bill shifted the gear into reverse and punched the gas. He grabbed the radio. The officer fired off two shots, hitting both Bill and me. I went down to the ground.

Goddaman, that shit hurt. Right in the chest. He's a good shot. I'll give him that.

It was either the heart attack the doc said I was gonna have or this. Heart attacks are for people in retirement homes, not Jim Carpenter.

I'm glad it was this.

One last bit of service.

"Mayday. Mayday. All available units. Multiple shots fired. Officers down. Ten seventy-nine at San Eugenio. I repeat ten seventy-nine at San Eugenio!" Bill yelled through the radio, hunched over as he bled out.

"Copy. All units. All units. Ten seventy-nine," voices came back over the radio.

Bill collapsed onto the steering wheel.

I felt the bus veer off backward into a ditch.

Maybe the headlights would shine a strong enough light into the sky to signal for help. Maybe it might show the calvary the way to Little Big Horn.

Two shots went off. Bill was gone. Damn.

After twenty-some odd years driving the bus. He loved what he did. And not to sound like too much of a pussy, but I loved him.

This bus bonds you.

I heard this asshole's footsteps approaching. I couldn't wait.

"Why did you make me do that, huh?! Now, all your friends are going to die because of you. You did this. I tried to liberate this country." He shouted as he stepped closer. My God, this guy was a whiny bitch. No wonder why he was here. "And you, all you did was try to hold us back." I heard the hammer pull back.

I smiled. I rolled over and pumped my shotgun.

I saw the fear in his eyes. That made me happy.

"No one makes me late."

CLICK.

BOOM!

The shell went right through the son of a bitch's chest, sending him flying several rows down the aisle.

My shirt was filled with blood from the .357 that had gone through my chest. "Fuck you, you racist fuck."

I dropped the gun.

I did my duty. Though I know these are my last moments, no one can say that Officer John Carpenter didn't live with purpose and service in his heart. That much I know is true. It's probably why I'm so content on going.

My terms. My way.

I hope God forgives me for the thing I said about the Virgin Mary. I just loved this job.

Time to go home.

Right on time.

CHAPTER TWENTY-ONE

Eric

Ian looked over at the remaining White Patriots who tried to help their comrade that Carpenter's chubby butt had taken out, "Well, the backup call is in. We need to finish this. We got thirty minutes tops before the cavalry arrives from Davidson to kill them and get out of here. Lock and load."

"You heard the man. Justice is within our grasp. Take back your freedom, boys." Freedom Frank loaded a clip, racked his gun, and shot rounds into the air. The White Patriots cheered. They reloaded their weapons and formed into squads.

"Jimmy, set the breach charge at the front door of the ammo room," Carlos said.

Jimmy smiled. "I like where your head's at, Sarge. White Patriots go boom."

He ran to the front of the ammo room and set the small breach charge. If we got lucky, it might send some shrapnel through an artery. Nothing more. It was a shitty last stand, but hey, at least none of us were named Custer.

We held tightly to our guns and started to take our positions. We all looked at each other, not sure if we'd see any of us alive again. Even if we didn't, we were different people. Each one of us.

Change was something to be grateful for.

"If they overrun the station, whoever is left, get into the ammo room. The breach charge will buy you some time. Me and Jimmy will hold them off as long as we can. When we go down, whatever you have left, just keep shooting until you hear sirens."

"Carlos, we can't leave you alone," Mom stepped in.

Carlos looked over at Mom with a slight smirk, looking at her the way he used to when I was a kid. "Sandy. You knew why I called you, and you still showed up. Let me have this one for old times' sake."

A tear rolled down Mom's face, and her voice cracked. "In another lifetime, Carlos."

Carlos gently grabbed Mom by both of her arms and held her. He looked into her eyes longingly, just as he had done in the twenty-two years before things fell apart. He wanted to, but he knew what the right answer was. He leaned in and kissed her on the forehead. "I fucked this one up pretty good. And now, I'm dealing with it." Carlos and Mom laughed together. And they meant it.

Regardless of what was coming next, life was going to be okay.

Things were happening just as they were supposed to.

I looked out the window. The White Patriots moved toward us in crouched positions. "As much as I want you guys to have makeup sex, we got much bigger issues on our hand." I paused. "God that was such a fucked-up statement on so many levels."

I watched as each small squad of three or four took a different angle of the building.

"What do we do, Carlos?" I yelled, starting to assume the position.

"We fight for those we love," Lupe said as she took a prone position near the back door. She pointed Roberto's M21 at the door, waiting for anyone who dared to come through it.

"I think I love you," Jimmy shouted with his back turned toward Lupe as he finished setting the breach charge on the ammo room door.

Carlos smiled. "You heard her. Take your positions."

This was it.

Fight for the ones you love.

Or die trying.

CHAPTER TWENTY-TWO

Carlos

For as long as I could remember, I always wanted to be a cop. I just did.

But I suppose that's what Sandy and Eric wanted me to understand. That's what I think that whole night was about. That night was about acceptance, understanding the "why" behind what I was doing. So in an attempt to be more open and understanding, here it goes.

I didn't have much growing up. We moved a lot. My parents were always struggling to make ends meet. My dad was a loving man. He wanted to give us so much, but he battled so many demons. And he fought those demons with alcohol. Every single day.

He was so much fun. But the fun never seemed to end. It was always one wild idea after another. He was never home. He traveled a bunch. He was a salesman, but not a very good one. And after every trip, he came home with a story, somehow less money, and the smell of alcohol on his breath. Each new idea he had, whether it was moving to another state or buying dozens of popular Christmas toys in a bid to resell them for profit, "This was going to be it."

"It for what?" I would often ask myself. We still had a life to live.

My mom was as stoic as they come. She didn't say, "I love you." She just did what needed to be done. She cooked. She cleaned. She made sure we were where we needed to be when we needed to be there. I always wanted more from her. I wanted what the other kids had. I wanted my mom to look at me the way their moms did. To hug me as much as their moms did. To throw me birthday parties. Anything to make me feel like I was loved and appreciated.

I was lost when I got out of high school, so I joined the Marines, just in time for Saddam to invade Kuwait.

Imagine me. Taking US history one minute and becoming a part of it the next. Eighteen-year-olds aren't ready for war, even a war lasting only a few months.

I loved it. It was my chance to fight for something I believed in. To be an extension of the American Dream and protect liberty and democracy all across the world. I felt like I had purpose. I felt like I was something more. For the first time in my life, I felt like I was a part of something bigger than me. My life meant something to the greater good. Maybe, if I offered to fight, I'd find the love I was missing.

I felt like I belonged.

I never fired a shot in Iraq. Not many of us did.

In the Marines, we were bred to fight. We wanted to fight. Oorah!

After a few months in the desert, I was left with a GI Bill and nowhere to go.

As Marines, we were "sheep dogs," watching over the herds, protecting them from the wolves. But without the Marines, I was back to being nothing again, left wondering who or what I was. At that point, I knew how to party with the best of them—a trait I learned from my dad. I improved those skills in the many late nights in and around Coronado with my fellow Devil Dogs.

I knew how to handle a weapon. Yet here I was with the desire to fight the evil in this world and no war to fight. No good to defend. Just years of junior college ahead of me with no finish line in mind.

I fucked around for a few years, working odd jobs. I did anything and everything you can think of, short of becoming a gigolo. I spent a couple of semesters in junior college. I might as well have earned my doctorate. I didn't really care about school. I did it because I figured, "What the hell else am I supposed to do? This is what everyone does."

For the sixth day in the row, I was stuffing my mouth with pizza in my shitty apartment, littered with trash and dirty dishes as far as the eye could see. In between commercial breaks of a *The Price is Right* rerun, it came on.

I saw the uniforms. The cars. The purpose in the people's faces. The taglines of "Integrity" and "Serving with honor." It was like God called directly to me.

A recruiting commercial for the police department.

I didn't find my calling. My calling found me. The next day, I put in my application. Six months later, I was at the academy.

The day before I went into the academy, looking to have one last good time, I walked into a liquor store with some of my Marine Corp buddies to pick up a rack of beer—what was intended to be our first run of the night—and a bottle of Jack. We were laughing and shooting the shit, probably being loud and obnoxious.

I placed a rack of Budweiser on the counter, still laughing from a joke one of my buddies told me.

Then I heard a voice say to me, "Twenty-four dollars and thirty-eight cents."

Because I didn't react, the voice raised a few decibels. "Twenty-four, thirty-eight!"

We shut up. I turned to look up at the register and I saw her.

My world came to a standstill. I had never seen anything so beautiful. It was Sandy, with her dark-brown hair, piercing brown eyes, and never-ending calm demeanor that made me feel so loved. It was a love I had never experienced before. Everything I was searching for suddenly didn't matter.

As I looked at Sandy, for the first time in my life I felt like everything would be okay.

A couple years later, I was married to Sandra and the department, and Eric showed up.

The day he was born, the moment I saw him, I promised myself he wouldn't feel the pain I experienced growing up. He was going to know what it was like to have stability in his life. And he was going to have every opportunity I never had. He was going to know no matter what, I would always be in his life.

There were Little League games and plays. And I was there for all of them. But I worked. And I worked. And I worked.

I don't know how we balanced Sandy attending med school, me working at the jails in the evenings, and raising a kid, but we did.

When you're a parent, you figure it out. You just do. And we did.

Sandy and I had a fair share of arguments about whose career was taking precedence. It was all ego, until we would look at Eric and remember the reason why we were doing it all.

Honestly, I don't know if we could have done it without Uncle Jimmy watching Eric on his off days. I would come home every so often to find Uncle Jimmy had lost twenty bucks or so to six-year-old Eric, the price he paid for teaching the kid Texas Hold 'Em.

Our house got nicer. Our vacations got bigger and to more exotic locales. Eric never suffered. I got assigned to East LA and Fort Comanche. I had gotten everything I ever wanted and so much more. This was my dream. In the early 2000s, East LA was the place to be if you *really* wanted to be a cop.

We were truly sheep dogs. You had to be the best of the best. If you proved yourself to be a weak link, you endangered the rest of the team, and you were gone.

I was a Latino taking on Latino gang members in one of the most dangerous areas of the country, seeing the darkest sides of humanity night after night. We were the guardians of the light, or so I thought.

I got called in more frequently. Ten-hour shifts turned into thirty-six hours with OT. OT meant more money and more stability. One missed game turned into two. Two turned into half a season.

But my department needed me. My brothers needed me. My community needed me. If I wasn't protecting and serving, who was I? Providing the safety for others that I never felt made me both happy and empty. I was neglecting Eric and Sandy, but I also was living my life's calling.

Shouldn't they have been okay with it?

About a year or two into my tenure at Fort Comanche, I met Ian and Bishop. Ian had just transferred over from TSB, and Bishop was his new trainee. Ian and I formed a quick bond. We believed in the law. We believed in policing. We believed we were sheep dogs, put on this Earth to protect and serve.

Bishop showed his true colors quickly. One time, we pulled over a car of suspected Mexican Mafia gang members. I think it was about 0130. We couldn't see much into the car or even who was in it. But the car was registered under Ramon Castillo, who had a warrant out for skipping bail on a weapons charge.

As I approached the car from the rear passenger's side to ask questions, Bishop approached on the driver's side. I shined my flashlight, and the reflection of the light off an Uzi caught Bishop's eye. He put his hand through the cracked window and grabbed the Uzi from the gang member's lap, saving us all.

Clearly, Bishop was going to make lieutenant, and he did.

"L-T," the guy who told us we were to watch over Hinojosa for the night, who told us there was a no-fly zone, and who told us we'd have to hold a high-profile prisoner with little protection was Ian's ex-trainee. Make of it what you will.

Brothers in blue … bullshit.

Look, I always believed in the law because I believed in what it means and what it stands for. American freedom, liberty, and democracy are some of the greatest gifts this world has ever known. To see people, especially Latinos, who had an opportunity in this country abuse and take advantage of it drove me nuts. I had made a good life for myself. Why couldn't they?

It infuriated me.

Then to have defense attorneys try to free those people I put in jail made no sense to me. They were scum. They didn't believe in America.

Don't get me started on the politicians who allowed all of this.

But then again, it's the balance of justice. Everyone, and I do mean everyone, regardless of what type of scumbag they are, deserves a shot at a fair trial. And no matter how I felt about the person, it was the American justice system. I believed in it. I would fight and give my life if necessary to defend it. That's why making sure Hinojosa had a shot was so important to me.

I digress.

I wanted to give Eric and Sandy more than enough to make sure they never had to worry about anything. With Sandy running her own medical practice, I wanted to be an equal contributor. My family was not going to fail because of me. No matter what happened.

I dove further in. Hoping somehow this pain would leave me. But it wouldn't. No matter how hard I worked, I never felt like I was giving enough, protecting enough, or doing enough. I wanted to be enough. But I couldn't.

I was so proud of Eric when he got into Columbia. My kid, an Ivy League student. Wow.

I didn't hear from him much when he was away. And I didn't want to bother him. That seemed to drive a wedge between us. Every time he came home, he had some liberal college ideal on his mind that I thought would fade away as he got older, but it never did.

He was against the wars in Iraq and Afghanistan, saying shit about the "military industrial complex" he knew dug at me and insulted my beloved Corps, the very institution that had given me direction and built the foundation for the opportunities he would get.

And then he found himself at law school, and Black Lives Matter and all that shit came to be. Policing was put under a spotlight, and Eric felt the need to shine the light the brightest. He protested and walked against policing.

I couldn't believe it. My own son. Protesting against police. Didn't he understand how much I loved it. How much I had sacrificed for him? That all of it had been made possible by my dream of being a police officer?

The phone calls from Eric became even less frequent and shorter. I became angrier. How did my kid end up so spoiled? To top it all off, he had aspirations of becoming a defense attorney.

I was stunned. Hurt. I didn't know how to react. Bob Shapiro, Johnnie Cochran, these were the people he wanted to align himself with, people who made fortunes getting criminals free and didn't feel an ounce of shame about it. They wore "justice" in their Armani suits and Gucci shoes.

Sandy pushed harder for me to accept Eric's choices. But I felt my son had turned his back on me.

After all I had sacrificed and fought for.

He didn't see the murdered bodies, the dead teenagers thrown through windshields after a drunk driver hit them head-on. He didn't have to talk to the parents of the dead kids, knowing the pain would weigh on their heart and the inevitable tears would follow. He wasn't there for the gun fights and the drug deals. He didn't see the hungry kids sleeping on floors. He wasn't there for any of it.

Instead, he wanted to free the drunk driver. He wanted to liberate the murderer. He wanted to allow the drug dealers recruiting kids to be their mules to walk the streets. He spit on everything I had sacrificed for.

This was my son.

If he was going to do that, I was going to dig further into my work and continue to stand for true justice.

Someone had to.

I saw Sandy less. She fought for me, but I didn't want to fight for her. I wanted to show that none of this bothered me, that I could be man enough to continue to provide. I wanted to prove that despite Eric, I could still hold our family together.

Then the night with the AK happened.

I testified in court and told the jury what I saw Ian do. He had executed that gang member.

But somehow, I was the bad guy.

The entire department turned their back on me. I became a pariah because I spoke out against a bad cop. As much as I loved Ian, he broke the law. And he had to pay the price for it. But they sent *me* to San Eugenio.

I got angry at Sandy. I got angrier at Eric.

Sandy and my relationship faltered. I was less present, even if I lied to myself saying I gave her more. The disdain I had for my son, his values, and who he wanted to be drove a wedge between all of us. I hated myself so much for putting my trust, my life, in what I believed to be a calling, and yet it let me down. The people who were supposed to watch me and care for me, my "brothers in blue," had turned their backs on me for standing up for what I believed in.

Somehow, I blamed my son. I blamed my wife.

All the stability I had cultivated was gone. And it was my fault, not necessarily how things unfolded, but how I handled them.

Eric and Sandy had wanted to be there for me, but I drove them away.

This night has shown me that.

I didn't want to. I just didn't know what else to do. For so long, I received everything I needed from what I got. My value was tied to who I was and the *things* I pursued. Not who I am.

For what? For these so-called cops to protect each other. I didn't know how to forgive myself for how I turned my back on my own child. I was so busy making up for what I didn't have that I forgot to give him what I did have—me.

All of me.

I thought things—bigger, better, and more—would resolve this for me. I felt being a man of hard-line principles and self-righteousness would help me heal. How could I stand for something if what I stood for was built on fear? Fear of losing what I had. Fear of living a different life. Fear of being rejected. Fear of not being seen.

Fear that I wasn't enough and would never be enough.

What if I loved so much and my family left me? What if I loved them so fully and completely for exactly who they were and not who I wanted them to be?

For the longest time, San Eugenio felt like a prison sentence. Worse, a death sentence.

Not a single night passed that I didn't think ending it all with my department-issued Berretta was the best route for everyone. Getting rid of the thoughts in my head by any means necessary felt like the best way to go. Maybe I would finally be understood.

I started to hate people who I swore to protect in San Eugenio. The Latino farm workers who looked like me, the people I felt were responsible for my pain. The reality was that something terrible had happened to me, but they weren't responsible.

Were they breaking the law? Yes, they were, but they were here to give themselves an opportunity, to fight for the values of the American Dream they were sold on.

Not all of them were great. El León proved that time and again.

Most of them were like Hinojosa, good people who wanted to thrive, give their families a life, and push the American experiment forward. I didn't know that when I met Hinojosa. But I found that was who he was.

Now as my fate awaits me, I feel I can let go of this pain that I have held onto for all these years. I'm ready to be the man I set out to be. It might be too late, but better late than never, or so I've heard. Yes, I want to protect and serve.

I want to protect my family and American values. But most of all, I want to protect people's right to dream. That's what this country was built on.

Everyone has the right to dream. To believe.

That's why I became a cop.

For as long as I can remember, I always wanted to be a cop.

Now, I understand why.

I did it to love.

CHAPTER TWENTY-THREE

Eric

Hands and body parts of White Patriots pushed through the cracks of the door, trying everything they could to break through. The hinges of the door clung to last bits of life. Lupe's makeshift barricade was breaking down. First the chair went flying, the metal legs of the desk scraping against the laminate flooring.

"They're breaking through the doors!" Lupe shouted in between shots she fired into the back door, not knowing if the bullets were hitting anyone or anything.

Jimmy and Carlos shot ferociously out the front doors with their ARs on full automatic. The flashes of the guns lit up their faces. They moved the barrel of the guns side to side as they fired, trying to keep the White Patriots as far back as they could.

I pumped and shot. Pumped and shot. I wasn't hitting anything. The White Patriots' approaches were more tactical and cautious than their Muerte counterparts. They weren't out here to prove a point.

They were out here to kill.

One climbed up and over the windowsill. He grabbed the barrel of my gun and pushed it down. He looked like he could have been an accountant next door, wearing a striped, blue-collared shirt. His blond hair was a flat comb over, and he was clean shaven. This wasn't the backwoods hick I expected.

His grip was strong, and he pushed the gun into my chest. The fear, anger, and death all around us made him stronger. He grabbed the shotgun sideways with both hands and stuck it up to my neck, strangling me. "You're going to fucking die. You hear me?"

I pushed the shotgun forward, knowing if I let go, we were all dead.

The shotgun started to slip from my fingers. The metal crushing my throat, I gasped for air. Another White Patriot climbed through the window. The blond-haired Patriot pressed harder, trying to squeeze the life out of me. "You betrayed this country, you fuckin' spic. You deserve to—"

My vision faded.

Suddenly, his blond head snapped left to right, and his blood splattered against the wall. He violently dropped to the ground. I looked to my left to see Carlos with his Beretta pointed, still smoking from the shot he sent through the White Patriot's head.

As soon as the other White Patriot landed on the floor, I caught my breath and pulled the trigger of the shotgun. The impact through his chest sent him out the window and back outside. I continued to pull the trigger out of both fear and anger.

CLICK!

CLICK!

CLICK!

"You're out, Son," Carlos said, clearing the clip from the Beretta. He reloaded it and handed it to me. "Take this, grab your mom, and get to the ammo room. Now."

It was his way of saying goodbye.

I stared at the gun. "No, Carlos. I'm not doing it. I'm not leaving you out here to die."

He shoved the Beretta into my chest and pulled his AR back to his shoulder. "Son, let me be your dad, please."

"But, Carlos," I said. More White Patriots climbed through the window. Carlos fired bursts toward the window, and they dropped.

"Now!" he shouted. "Go, please!"

I grabbed the gun. I had wanted him to be my father for so long. And now, when he was showing me the ultimate sign of love, I didn't want it.

I wanted my dad for one more moment.

I couldn't bring myself to say goodbye. I took the gun and ran over to Mom.

Mom shot out of Roberto's window. She shot and she shot and she shot. Mom had always been a fighter. It was in her blood. And when she needed to fight the most, she was the warrior only a mother could be. I don't know a single soldier in their right mind who would have crossed her.

I tapped her on the shoulder. "Mom, we gotta go. We gotta go!"

Her gun clicked empty.

We ran across the station with shots flying off all around us. With each step, it felt like the room filled with more bullets. The walls closed in as more White Patriots got further into the station before they were gunned down.

"I'm out!" Lupe shouted as the door broke completely off the hinges. She threw the gun as hard as she could at the door, hitting a White Patriot in the face and sending him back into the crowd, holding them back in their place for a brief second, so Jimmy could look back.

"Get to the ammo room, Lupe!" Jimmy shouted.

"Don't tell me what to do!" Lupe joked back as Jimmy got to her position.

Jimmy got into a kneeling position and fired into the crowd of White Patriots. Lupe hugged him.

"You're messing up my shot!" Jimmy quipped.

"Thank you, Jimmy." Lupe kissed him on the top of his head.

"Ah man, did I just get friend zoned with a dopey kiss?" Jimmy shouted with a big smile on his face.

"Thank you, Jimmy. For everything," Lupe said as Jimmy regarded her lovingly. He couldn't believe he could love someone like this. As he looked into Lupe's eyes, he couldn't believe how loved he felt. It was a deep sense of love and affection he had never encountered before. What they had was special. After all, it was the first time in his life he had truly been seen in this way.

They smiled at each other one more time. Jimmy motioned with his head. "Get out of here, kid. You're bothering me. Jimmy got him some fresh ass to kick."

Lupe smiled and ran, and Jimmy's burst of fire rang out behind her.

She caught up to us and grabbed Mom's hand as we got to the front of the room.

POP.

POP.

"Ah come on, seriously!" Jimmy lay on the ground with one shot through his chest and another through his leg. He sat up, blood coming out of his mouth. He picked up his gun and started shooting again.

He looked over at us in the ammo room, one more time. "Don't worry about me. I got 'em right where I want 'em." He smiled. He turned back as the White Patriots closed in on him. "Suck it, Fort Comanche. Welcome to Jimmy Choi's House of Pain, you punk bitches!" He shot off a burst of fire.

Then two loud pops.

Jimmy was gone.

Carlos looked over and saw White Patriots closing the gap behind him. He shot three of them down, clearing the room. He saw Jimmy's dead body.

Carlos was all alone.

He paused and loudly proclaimed. "Love you, Partner."

It was silent, except the sound of boots scraping the cement. The boots sounded like they were coming from every which way, echoing throughout the station and through our souls.

"Hold your positions. Eagle four to the right. Eagle seven to the left. The rest of you, hold with me up the front. They got nothing left!" Freedom Frank shouted.

Carlos looked back at us, desperation in his eyes. "Get inside. I'll set the charge."

Mom and Lupe walked into the room, looking for anything they could use to fight. "Mom, the AR in there?"

She looked around and saw it up against the wall. She picked it up. "Yes."

I stood at the front of the ammo room door. I looked back at Carlos. His gun at the ready as he checked where the next one may come from. His breathing remained steady. His motion fluid. All of this like he had envisioned it before.

This was his moment.

"Is there ammo on the top shelf?" I asked.

"Get in! Now!" Carlos shouted.

Mom turned her back toward me as she looked on the top shelf. "Yes," Mom said, grabbing it.

"Good." I shut the door. The door lock lit up. The breach charge was armed.

I heard pounding on the door from the inside. Mom yelled hysterically, "Eric! Get in here. Eric, not you! Get in here. Eric! You can't do this to me. Eric!"

I stood in front of the door and put my hand on it, hoping her hand might be there too.

"I love you, Mom."

Mom's shouts of anguish rang out through the night sky.

"Everybody in?" Carlos said, not wanting to look back.

I looked at the door one last time, pulled the slide back on the Berretta, and limped over to Carlos. "Did you miss me?" I stood next to him, barrel of the Beretta pointed out toward the front door.

"No! Why?! Get out of here!" Dad shouted in a mix of disappointment, sadness, and disgust, the pain of my decision cutting him to his core.

"If I wasn't a pain in your ass, would I really be your son?" I said, not breaking my focus on the front door.

Carlos shook his head and smiled, resigned to the fact I was with him now and I wasn't going anywhere.

He reached over to the Berretta. "You got the safety on, dingus." He reached over and clicked it off.

I smiled at him. "Alright, I'll give you that one."

We laughed together.

We stood side by side, each with more bullet holes than hearts in our bodies.

"You could have just made fun of me. You didn't actually need to get shot in the leg to hobble," Carlos said, as he looked at my wounds through his peripheral vision.

"I figured if I'm going to do it, might as well do it right. No half-assin'."

"Who taught you that?"

"Some asshole," I said with a smirk.

"You've put up a nice fight, Partner! Come on out, and fight us like men. Clock is ticking. I want to see you die with my own eyes!" Ian shouted.

"This guy ever stop with the speeches?" I joked.

"Gotta say he's better than you. I've seen you on TV. I have some notes."

I laughed. "Fair enough."

The boots got closer and closer. White Patriots were coming in through the windows and back door, slowly and calmly with their guns up. We were surrounded.

"Well, the only way out is through, isn't it?" Carlos said, as the lights shone brightly on our faces, causing us each to squint and look away. Carlos looked back up. "Well, shall we?"

I shrugged. "Hm, why not?"

The White Patriots moved slowly and methodically to our rear and sides. They knew it was close to the end, and they didn't want to lose any more of their men.

As they approached, we walked slowly out the front door with our guns pointed at the abyss of high beams and silhouetted gunmen. Hoping if we needed to, we could hit some shadows and gain a few more seconds together.

We were going to fight for each other no matter what.

And that's exactly the way I would have wanted it to end.

CHAPTER TWENTY-FOUR

Carlos

What felt like a thousand blazing suns blinded us in the early morning hours. The purple-and-white light from the headlights cast heavy shadows over our faces. We walked out of a place, which in its destruction, had brought us back together stronger. It would always be a part of us, but it no longer dictated who we were going to be. As those white-and-purple head beams cut through the night sky, we were able to see one another clearly.

We surrendered to forces greater than ourselves.

I was at peace, at least as at peace as a man with about twenty-five guns of all shapes and sizes pointed at him could be. I was proud of who I was and what we had done.

"Well, Brother, looks like this is the end of the road for you. What can I say? You and your boy fought valiantly. You really have always been a tenacious son of a bitch," Ian snickered as he walked closer to us. The sound of his boots rang out a reminder of the fate we approached. The only sound in an eternal night. In his hand, Ian held a pistol—the department-issued Beretta 9mm 92 FS.

"Ian, I always knew we would go down together, receiving the honor a police officer deserves," I responded.

The remaining White Patriots, bruised and battered, sweat and exhaustion proliferating through their bodies. Their eyes were baggy, and the energy had been visibly taken from their souls. Their shoulders were hunched. Their posture, not as mighty. They mocked me with laughter.

The laughter was missing something. It lacked a spark. The night had defeated them. Ian laughed almost uncontrollably.

I looked over at Eric. What was I supposed to say if these were going to be our last moments together? What fatherly advice could I give him to make up for all the time I missed, and all the ill will?

"Leave the world laughing, Son. Really, what else can you do?"

"What's our plan now, Dad?"

"There is no plan. We need to let what's going to happen, happen."

"Come on. There's got to be something we can do."

I looked at Eric. As the light hit his face just right, I really saw my son for the first time. His face was marred by sweat and fear.

It's going to sound strange, but my heart lit up. I don't remember the last time I felt this much love for my son. I didn't want to miss another moment, even if those moments were rapidly dwindling. I wanted my son to know how much I loved him.

I was so proud of him and the man he had become, not because of his fighting or his career accolades, disagree with them as I might, but for exactly who he was. He was a good son, loyal, courageous, and faithful to the person he wanted to be.

Ian fired rounds from the Beretta in his hand up into the air.

"Enough of this Hallmark-movie bullshit. It's time to die, partner. We're giving you the Butch and Sundance, heroes exit you've always wanted with you staring down the barrel of a gun."

I thought about that for a second. I recognized what I had cultivated.

Everything in my life had brought me to this point. I found solace this night was now coming to an end. I thought about the Medal of Valor, the citations, the distinguished police service awards, and most of all, the honor of my brothers in blue once news reached of what happened. This would give me everything I wanted and felt I was owed.

"I don't need this anymore. I don't want this anymore."

"A little late, don't you think, Dad?" Eric asked with a shit-eating grin on his face.

"Thanks for being here with me, Son. And I'm sorry."

"Don't be. I wanted to be here. I'm glad I'm here. Thank you for tonight."

A tear rolled down my face, a tear that held back hundreds of others. I wasn't keeping the emotion from my family anymore.

Rather, I held it back because Ian and these men didn't deserve to see it.

"Let my son go, Ian. Let my family go. They had nothing to do with this!"

"Not how I see it, Partner. Your boy is just as liable as you are in all this. He killed, just like you did."

"He didn't do this, Ian. We did. We did this to ourselves."

Ian thought about that. He had such a strong desire to prove his actions were just.

After all, we all thought we were just. We all think we do. That's the funny thing about truth. It is subjective. But it is something that we all believe we're correct in, no matter how many angles there might be.

We have to believe in something.

The need for vengeance, the need to be right can overtake the truth. And that's what Ian decided. He was too far gone to see anything different, and he wasn't going to let us see anything different. The pain ran too deep.

"Partner, he's going to talk. If I let him leave, it's a life sentence for me and everyone here." That was the singular truth in this.

Someone had to be held responsible for this night.

"Dad, there's only one way this ends. And it's okay. I'm glad I'm here with you. I'm glad we did this together."

I didn't respond. I surveyed the cars lined in front of the police station. I turned around and looked at the remnants of the place where I had felt imprisoned for so long. A bittersweet feeling came over me. I was glad to break free as I took accountability for my life. However, this place was where I got the thing I wanted most—my family.

The bullet-riddled sides of the building, and the shattered glass were remnants of what once was and never had to be again. All of it was my doing.

"I'm free," I whispered to myself under my breath.

I turned back toward Ian, who laughed a bit nervously. My calm made Ian skittish. He had never seen that side of me before. Honestly, I was glad to see him turn back into the insecure child he was.

"Brothers in blue. What a load of horseshit, Ian," I said as he took a few steps toward those who wanted to end my life, or at least, at one time vowed they would. They raised their weapons toward me.

"Easy, boys. It's one against a thousand. I got nothing to harm you with."

As I took steps toward Ian, a wave of voices yelled at me. "Get down on the ground! Get down. Take another step, and I'll fucking kill you!" all phrases I had yelled night after night to all sorts of criminals over the years. Now, as an unarmed man, these words took on a different meaning.

I dropped to my knees with my hands behind my head. I wasn't going to resist. I had no need to. I was powerless. But man, I was satisfied.

Eric knelt next to me. His energy had shifted. I felt comfortable around him again, like he was my son.

There was a release of everything.

A trust in whatever fate would reveal was meant for me, at this time.

Ian put up his hand to calm down the White Patriots. Their roars of expletives and threats faded into the darkness.

Ian, the White Patriots, each of them had been heard. Ian seemed to feel he'd done what he'd come to do.

Had everything I'd done in my years on the force been just? No. Was I as righteous as I thought I was? Not likely.

What had once been black and white was now gray. The thin blue line between good and evil grew so narrow that the line up and disappeared.

The dissolution of the blue line allowed me to see the world for all it was.

I saw reality. A reality he had sewn and now lived in.

There was no longer time for saying sorry or for making amends. There were only last moments of a life to be lived.

I was no longer Sergeant Carlos Lopez. Medal of Valor recipient. Cop.

I was just Carlos. Husband. Father. For the first time in my life, I was exactly who I wanted to be. It was all I ever needed. It took staring down the barrel of fifteen guns to see it. But I saw it.

"What becomes of all this, Ian? You kill me. You kill my son. And then what?"

Ian considered that for a moment. "I'm leaving the country until the heat dies down. Gone but not forgotten. I'll have gotten what was mine. I'll have served these people."

"Served them what?"

"Justice. It's all these people want. It's what I want."

"And then what?"

Ian couldn't give me an answer. He didn't have one.

"You'll never be satisfied, no matter what. You can have me. Just please, let my son go."

Ian walked toward me. He hit me with the butt of his gun. Blood gushed from the ridge of my nose.

"I think we got 'em right where we want 'em," I said to Eric. Ian's once intimidating presence was completely gone. I was looking at a broken man, someone who reminded me of the man I once was and the man he no longer wanted to be.

"I don't give a fuck if I'll ever be satisfied. I need you dead. I need him to suffer. That's fucking it," his voice shook and broke as each word fell out of his mouth.

"I can live with that," I said.

He cocked the Beretta and held it to my forehead. I felt the pressure of the barrel on the front of my skull. For all Ian and I had been through, I never expected for it to come to this—face to face, looking each other in the eyes.

The headlights reflected off the blood on my face. I loved it. I felt alive.

"Dad," Eric whimpered.

With all the passion and fire in my gut, I said, "I love you, Son,"

"You're getting soft, old-timer."

I laughed.

BOOM. My head snapped back as the 9mm left Ian's chamber. I fell to the asphalt.

"Dad," Eric whispered.

CRACK. The butt of a rifle hit the side of Eric's head. He fell atop my body. As I laid there, fading in and out of consciousness, I felt his final breath. The American flag waved in the distance.

America the Beautiful.

My eyes shut.

Darkness.

CHAPTER TWENTY-FIVE

Eric

"U-S-A! U-S-A! U-S-A!" jarred me back to consciousness. For a moment, in between the blur of consciousness and unconsciousness, I had forgotten what had happened.

As I picked myself up off the asphalt, looking for my dad, I felt cold steel against my temple.

"Don't fucking move," a White Patriot muttered, unenthusiastically. His voice shook so much I could care less if a bullet entered my head. He was doing his job with due diligence. It was ingrained in him from a young age after Sunday School when he was a teenager and taken into the deserted flat lands behind the Chosen Ones Christ Church. As I started to understand, he had done exactly what he was supposed to do, and he didn't understand why he felt this push and pull within himself. He knew it wasn't a way to live, but all he knew was anger. All he knew were the beliefs he was brought up with. This was his only way out. His future was uncertain. The bravado of the night made him feel he had nothing but control.

At least, that's how I understood it. How could I know? I never walked in the man's shoes. How could anyone really understand anyone? How could we even make assumptions like that? Yet I know I'm guilty of it. Those assumptions, that thought of knowing what the other person is thinking, is essentially what brought us all here.

"I'm not going anywhere. I'm good," I said. I looked up at my captor's face. He couldn't have been more than twenty-four. He looked scared shitless, facing the reckoning of what he had played a role in. By this time, he just wanted to go home.

I turned my head toward the station. I felt the last bit of hopelessness I would feel for the night. Raised above the White Patriots' heads were Dad's and Roberto's bodies, being pulsated in celebratory jest.

That was the worst bit of humanity I had ever seen. So much hate. So much hurt, all to the chants of "U-S-A! U-S-A! U-S-A!" and American flags waving through the crowd. What had we become? What had we caused?

At the moment, I understood Dad's last words—no matter what, none of this would be enough. No revenge or celebration of victory were going to make these people feel fulfilled. The pain was in their hearts. This was the expression of their pain.

Even more oddly, I empathized with them, recognizing how lost and fearful these people were. They had received everything they ever wanted with the death of these two men. Now what? What had this "victory" brought them? They had won, but their spirits were fundamentally broken. They were more disconnected from who they truly were more than ever. More than anything, I wanted them to feel love again. To feel they didn't have to go down this path anymore, so we collectively didn't have to go down this path anymore. But I didn't know what to do.

Military-grade and consumer-brand boots of all shapes and sizes shuffled through shards of glass and broken plaster. The movements were slow and deliberate. The guns hanging by their sides might as well have been toys with plastic orange tips covering their barrels.

They were searching for any sign of life, finding nothing.

About five White Patriots who hadn't hoisted the bodies searched the remnants of the police station for anything that might give them pause and one more reason to kill.

A swarm of cop cars wasn't too far out. The patriots would soon be surrounded, tried, and taken to prison for life. This was their one last bit of cleanup before they left and spent the next few years fleeing and fading into the background of society once again.

The background was somewhere they said they didn't want to be. They had fought so hard to get out of it, but it was where they belonged. They were never going to shed that feeling of unworthiness. Try as they might through violence or other means, nothing outside of them could make them feel whole. They couldn't understand that.

Their world views, that much hate wasn't sustainable. It felt good for a moment, but as they walked around the police station with what remained, they knew how much this had taken out of them. They had shouted and shot to be heard, and they were. Yet now that they had everyone's attention, they'd reached the final breaking point. What was left for them to do?

Ian looked around the station with an emptiness inside of him he tried to cover up with his chest puffed out and an awkwardly tall, slow gait. He was projecting confidence.

But he had none of it left.

He looked down and saw Jimmy's body near the exit. If there was one way Ian had expected Jimmy to die, this was it. A gun in his hand, his body riddled with bullets, standing by his friend. Say what you want about Jimmy, but no one could ever say Jimmy wasn't a dedicated, loyal friend to the end. It's who he was and who he had been. Even in death, Jimmy looked peaceful. That was perhaps the hardest thing of the evening for Ian to swallow.

Jimmy lived his life with such a dedication to service of his fellow human being. He died a most violent death, yet to those he loved, he seemed at peace. And Jimmy loved pretty much everyone. Jimmy had always given people a second chance. He wanted to see people for who they really were. Ian hadn't given Jimmy the same basic respect.

Ian had killed a good cop.

He looked down and saw Theresa's dead body. Ian squatted next to her and pulled the jacket off her face. He saw her closed eyes and the restful look on her face. He looked over and saw the photo of Theresa with her daughter making goofy faces. So much had been broken and destroyed. That photo was one thing among all the destruction, which had been untouched, almost as if preserved by God for Ian to see. Any way he tried to spin it, he had killed a mother. He had killed a cop, someone he said he dedicated his life to and would die for, with his brothers and sisters beside him. He had killed his brother and sister. And for what? For doing their duty?

He placed Carlos's jacket back over Theresa's face.

He grabbed an AR out of a fellow White Patriot's hand and held it vertical toward his shoulder. "Gentlemen, congratulations on a hard-fought victory!" He looked to them for acceptance and community. They were lost in thought, as they surveyed the damage.

But as is almost always the case with men, the hubris and need for acceptance of their fellow man was priority. "Hell ya! Mission complete!" They sputtered as they continued their search through the wreckage. The life and spirit behind their once robust and sickly spirited chants had started to dissipate. It was all being forced now. Most of them were distant and off on another planet, as they had to contemplate and digest the decision they had made, with the bodies of their two selected enemies for the moment resting above their shoulders.

This was the reality of what they had done. It was a reality they would have to live with the rest of their lives.

THUMP! THUMP! THUMP!

A hush fell over the frenzied. The frantic thumps grew louder. Their guns went up.

Freedom Frank held his gun to his shoulder. Searching rooms willfully still standing, looking to see if he could find any survivors. Clearing rooms is what he had been trained to do in the Army, and it was coming into use here, or so he thought. Of all the White Patriots remaining, Freedom Frank, genuinely seemed to be unaffected by what happened. As he continued to go room by room, yelling, "Clear," his process was surgical and emotionless. To leave any "evidence" behind would be asinine and lazy. He wasn't going to risk being either one of those things. He followed through this night with purpose and, in his mind, honor. He had received his just rewards. He had protected his people and the need for white supremacy in the US. He had done his part for the country, with the hopes his bravery and his message would be received by the brothers-in-arms throughout a white man's nation.

He stood for Don Watts. He honored his memory. He stood against tyranny. He held the law in his hands and utilized his version of justice. He got everything he wanted. What more was left for him to do?

That question allowed him to clear these rooms so effectively, and so quickly. To address that question would lead to answers Frank didn't want. He avenged. Revenged. And killed. He had done everything he wanted. What was left for him?

"I got something here, Ian. I'm not sure what it is," a White Patriot in his fifties said flatly and without much power in his voice. He was clean shaven and dorky looking. He could have been an insurance adjuster for all I knew—a fucked-up Jake from State Farm. Freedom Frank's opposite in every way. In another life, he would be on the brink of retirement, ready to head down to Sarasota, Florida, to play shuffleboard. He looked exhausted. The man didn't understand why he was so tired. Yes, he was in his fifties, it was almost four in the morning, and he had been up all night, but this was a different kind of tired. The mystery was something only his version of God could solve, or so he believed.

Freedom Frank walked over to the door where the White Patriot in his fifties knelt. He saw the device on the door. "It's a breach charge. Get back, or you're liable to get some shrapnel through your neck. You don't want to be closer than three feet."

The White Patriot backed away and moved behind a wall. It was the chance to not look like a coward. The company man had received permission from his superior to stand back. It felt like the pressure had been lifted, and he felt like, even for a moment, he could be an old man.

"Frank, you think you can disarm it? See what we got behind door number one," Ian said, trying to illicit a laugh out of the guys around him. A few forced smiles and smirks followed.

Frank knelt and put his AR-15 behind his back. He held the wires in his hand and looked it over cautiously. "Whatever idiot put this on here forgot to actually set the charge. It's not live. Get me a sledgehammer. I'll break this down, and we'll see what they were hiding behind here."

THUMP! THUMP! THUMP!

"Eric! Carlos! Let me out of here!" Mom yelled, muffled behind the door.

Ian did a quick body count in his mind. Carlos, Eric, Hinojosa, Theresa, he had seen all their bodies. They had the building surrounded. They would have seen if Sandra and Lupe would have left.

Ian realized the charge was set for a reason. The explosion would have killed anything behind the door or in front of it. Ian's head dropped.

He had thought this was all over. When would there be enough killing?

A White Patriot handed Frank a sledgehammer. He handed his AR-15 to the patriot. Ian watched in silence, hoping he was wrong.

"Make it quick. We gotta get out of here."

BAM.

Freedom Frank swung with ferocity. The door started to give.

BAM.

His sheer brute strength took it off the hinges quicker than most would be able to.

BAM.

The door really started to give.

Freedom Frank wound the sledgehammer back to give it everything he could. He was going to break through it one way or another. He swung the hammer back and swung it forward with as much power as he could. He made contact with the door. It broke through.

BOOM. BOOM.

Frank fell forward to the floor as two shots went through his stomach and his chest, respectively.

The White Patriots' guns went up. They approached the entryway. Whatever was behind the door scared them. It had taken down Freedom Frank. While they normally would have shot back, whatever had killed Freedom Frank kept them in a state of terror.

Maybe it was exhaustion. Maybe it was fear. I like to think it was fear.

They didn't know what they had just woken up.

"Don't shoot!" Ian yelled.

"She killed Freedom Frank."

"It's what's coming for us all, sooner or later."

If they wanted to, they would have killed Mom, but the truth was, everyone was done killing. No one wanted any more to do with it. It gave them nothing.

Ian walked over to the doorway slowly.

Mom was sitting against the wall with her AR-15 in one hand, still smoking from the shots she had fired. Lupe was nestled into her chest with her hands over her ears, crying and sniffling lightly. Mom was tired. Her eyes were puffy from all the tears. She had had enough of everything. She wanted nothing more to do with this.

As Ian walked in, he put his hands up. He actually meant it. He didn't know what to expect. Maybe, some mercy might be held on him.

"Sandy, still looking as gorgeous as ever. Shame on Carlos for letting you go."

Mom sat there with a look of sheer ferocity on her face.

"Look, I'm sorry about this mishap, but you understand why it had to happen, yes?"

Mom squeezed Lupe tightly and kissed her on the top of her head. She stood up and then lifted Lupe with her, the sight of her gun never leaving Ian's body.

Mom saw Dad's and Roberto's bodies above the patriots' shoulders outside. Unadulterated rage burned inside of her. In her eternal grace, Mom didn't let it show. Instead, she looked the men directly in the eyes and commanded, "Put their bodies down, now."

The boys had been caught with their hand in the cookie jar. These big, hulking men became the uncared for children they always believed themselves to be.

Mom didn't need to yell. She didn't need to scream. She just needed to tell them this ended now.

The White Patriots lowered Dad's and Roberto's bodies to the ground, and they stepped away from them.

Mom stepped over Freedom Frank's body.

She saw Jimmy. She saw Theresa.

All of it was a harsh reminder of what this night had given to and taken from her, none of which she asked for, yet all of which she felt responsible for. As she walked through the station, White Patriots continued to hold their guns on her, albeit with little gusto or effort. Her power spoke volumes. She and Lupe may have been small in stature, but their presence was massive. There was nothing the patriots would do to get in their way. When they looked at Mom, they saw a mother. Their mother. They saw their wives. But most of all, they saw a woman who loved. Her love was so visceral and palpable. She was furious. But there was a calm inside of her none of them would ever break through. They hadn't been able to the whole night, even with guns and bravado. How were they going to now?

Each White Patriot she passed cleared the way for her in a parting of the White Sea.

As Mom walked toward their bodies, a deep wave of overwhelming sadness took control of her. She realized what she had to confront. Lupe needed to start to hold Mom up. They were in this together.

Roberto and Dad laid there among the carnage.

Mom fell to her knees in anguish. There was no other option. When she saw them, despair overcame her heart. Roberto was a man with a family who had stood up for his right to live and to make a life his own.

If we couldn't do that, what did we really have? Why were we all here?

She and Dad didn't love each other the way they once did, but she still loved him deeply. It was a new type of love she felt. A different type of respect. And with this new type of love, came pain so bad she couldn't even cry. All she could do was stare.

Stare and love.

She picked Dad up and held him in her lap. She brushed through his hair one last time. She wiped down his gold-plated name tag. She wanted people to read his name, Sgt. Lopez, clearly. She hugged him and kissed him on the cheek one last time. She laid his body down among the rubble of what remained, of what he used to be. As she looked around, an undeniable pride came over her. A tear rolled down her cheek. She looked into his closed eyes and whispered to him, "Thank you."

Mom got up. "Where's my son?" she asked softly.

Nobody responded. No one had the courage to look her in the eye.

She raised her AR in the air and shot a burst of rounds into what remained of the ceiling.

"Where's my son?!" Mom screamed. Everyone in the room felt it. It was like their own mother was there with them. A deep sense of shame took over them all. Their heads dropped to the floor. Ian tried with futility to hold his up.

With his hands in the air, Ian pointed out toward the front door, uncertain, if I was still alive or not. "Look, Sandy. You have to understand Little Eric volunteered to go out there with his father."

Mom dropped the gun to the floor. She held Lupe tight by her side, and together they walked out of the room methodically, Mom not wanting to face what she was about to, but knowing she must. As they exited the doorway, Mom looked around and saw the embers with small bits of life to them. The walls reduced to bits of plaster. The shattered glass.

Mom always lived by the credo, "You take care of business first, then you fall apart later." There was no other business to take care of, and yet she still didn't fall apart. She didn't understand why. Her husband lay dead, and her son was sure to follow, if he hadn't already died. She didn't feel the need to fall apart. How could she fall apart when everything else inside of her had already been shattered?

"Mom," I said with as much energy as I could.

Somehow Mom heard me. I remember coming home during high school, late at night from hanging out with my friends and being impossibly quiet. And somehow, some way, Mom was always at the front door ready to answer it. She somehow felt I was home, regardless of what wayward hour of the evening, or morning, I walked in. It was like she lived with one eye and one ear always open, waiting for any sign of her child's safety. I never knew how to explain it. Right then was no different. How she heard my faint call was beyond me. Mom and Lupe ran over toward me.

The young White Patriot held the gun toward her. Shaking, he said, "Get back. Please. Don't make me shoot you. Please"

Mom walked up to his gun and gently pushed it down. "I want you to hand the gun to me, go home, and never look back. This is not your life. This is not who you are. Go."

The young White Patriot started to cry. He looked up at Ian, still trying to see if this was a good idea. He looked back at Mom. Her love was too strong for hate. Her love was too strong for fear. He dropped the gun in an act he believed to be cowardice, but would realize years later was the greatest decision he had ever made.

Mom dropped her gun, knelt, and grabbed me. She tried to grab more of my body and hold on tighter, as if there was no limit to how much she could hold me.

"Why?! Why? Just make this make sense to me. Please. What was ever going to come of this? Just tell me, why you needed to do this!"

The faint sound of sirens rose in the distance. Blue-and-red lights broke the distant predawn sky. Help was arriving at last. Better late than never.

The racking of a gun.

Mom stopped crying and wiped her eyes. She felt Lupe's breath quicken on her neck. Mom's heartbeat didn't change.

"I can't let you go, Sandy. You know this is how it has to end," Ian said.

Mom sat tall. She pulled my head up to her with her arms and kissed me on the forehead. She looked at me just as she had done the day I was born, and she put me down.

"Go ahead, Ian. Do it already," Mom said with no emotion in her tone, as she looked off into the distance. Any ounce of life had been taken out of her.

"You're all loose ends. You know this is how it has to end."

Mom got up from her knees and turned around slowly.

She stared Ian right in his eyes. "Then do it. There is nothing more you can do to me. I know the emptiness you feel. Whatever you decide to do next to us won't be enough."

Mom walked closer to Ian's gun. Ian shook. She looked over his shoulder and saw the White Patriots all standing outside in front of the police station with their weapons unenthusiastically pointed toward Mom. Not a single one of them was willing to even fake it anymore.

"When does this end? When does this end?!" she screamed, her voice echoing through the night, her lip quivering from the pent-up fury. The patriots had no idea what was inside of her and, no one was willing to find out.

She walked even closer to the barrel of Ian's gun. Ian gripped it tighter. "I can't let you leave. You know Bishop has my back. So, what if the cops show? I'll be fine. All of us will be fine."

She knocked the barrel away from herself. Ian didn't have the strength to bring it back up. He couldn't. He didn't want to.

The sirens grew louder. The red-and-blue lights shined brighter.

"That meant something once, the power you thought you had, the hate you had in your heart. But it means nothing now. And all of this means nothing. Yes, Bishop might be able to save you, but you'll live in a lie. You'll want to resist the truth of what happened here, and you will. You'll continue to ignore it, and you'll convince yourself no matter what people say you will never buy into the truth residing in your heart. You'll continue to cover it up. But you'll live out your days with an uneasiness in your soul, knowing you ignore the truth. So go ahead. Shoot us. I don't care. It'll never feed you. None of this ever has, and none of it ever will."

The hums of the engines turned into a hornet's nest bearing down on Ian.

"Hurry up, Ian. You don't have long. We're here, waiting for you." Mom walked closer to Ian's face and shouted, "Kill me!"

Ian didn't know what to say. He looked back at the group of White Patriots and hoped one of them could do something he couldn't—shoot these women. They all started to put their weapons down. One by one. The power of a mother in anguish spoke to those men. Everything she said was the truth. Once and for all, those men decided to listen. But their time had come and gone. They wanted forgiveness. They wanted redemption.

Mom was not going to offer it. As much as it was in her heart to want to, she couldn't. Too much had happened. Many years later, she would forgive each and every one of them for what they did.

Now was not the time.

"I want to hate you so badly. All of you. But I can't. I want to see you all as people. But I can't do that either. So, you're going to do what you need to do."

Mom picked me up off the floor. She hugged Lupe and me as we awaited our fate. Whatever it might be.

They walked slowly out toward the road into an uncertain future. The police cars got closer, the sirens got louder, and the red-and-blue lights cut a little crisper through the air. Ian resigned himself, for all intents and purposes, to the fact his life as a cop had come to an end.

Mom and Lupe walked by Ian. He asked in one last moment to try to save his false power, "Where do you think you're going?"

Mom looked to Ian. She looked at Lupe with stern resolve. This was a different woman than whom she had first met, and she was different because she chose differently. Mom realized what it was she had to do. She looked at Ian, and with an emerging hope in her eyes, said, "I'm going to continue to live. To hope someday there will be a time when our hearts can be open again to being there for one another. I'm going to grieve the rest of my life. I'm going to continue to give everything I have to this life. Whatever it is; however it will happen, will be my new path forward."

Ian for once didn't know what to say.

Tires screeched one after another. White lights hit Ian squarely and lit up the rest of the White Patriots. A different sound of uniformed boots hit the pavement. Car doors opened. Guns racked.

Ian lifted his gun up.

"Put it down, McGinnis! Drop it, McGinnis!"

Ian put the butt of his gun to his shoulder with tears in his eyes and said, "Brothers in blue."

A burst of gunfire.

White lights flashed.

It was over.

CHAPTER TWENTY-SIX

Eric

I stopped speaking for a moment, trying to gather my thoughts, wondering where I was going with this. I stood in the hot sun and took a deep breath, searching for my words, trying as hard as I could one more time in front of my dad not to be overcome with emotion.

I couldn't do it. I stared at the four caskets with a mixture of deep sadness and gratitude.

This heat, the same one Roberto had worked in so many times before had a different meaning to me. It made me feel like my dad was there.

And Theresa. And Roberto. And Jimmy.

All of them now watched over us as we all looked over them. Their caskets were lined one right next to another in the strawberry field. They were San Eugenio now and forever, a place they all fought so hard to be free of, yet was so deeply a part of them.

I lifted my head and wiped away a few tears. The lump in my throat was beginning to pass, and I was regaining my ability to speak. How could I express my gratitude to them? How could I express my sorrow? I didn't know. I had written out words, as I had done so many times before in previous statements when I went in front of the media. But I didn't want to read what I had written. It all felt so false.

I looked up again over the crowd of people who attended. The family of San Eugenio, white, brown, old, young, citizen, undocumented, and everyone in between had gathered here to honor these heroes.

Then it hit me.

In death, these people had brought us together.

Jimmy's grandma and grandpa sat next to each other. They held a folded flag in their hands. A stoic expression was set on his grandma's face, and a tear barely escaped through her forlorn pride. They had given so much to ensure their grandson had opportunity in America. He had put his head down and worked, just like they had raised him to. In the process of doing so, he had given back to his community in a way even they couldn't have imagined. It was exactly what they wanted for him. And it was what Jimmy wanted for himself. Jimmy had fulfilled the American Dream. To give, to protect and serve, it was all Jimmy ever wanted.

Next to Jimmy's grandparents sat Lupe, holding Brava in her arms. Although faded remnants of purple and black around her eye and lip remained, her face looked refreshed. She held her chin high. As I gazed at her, she looked into her daughter's eyes. She smiled at her, knowing the greatest gift she could give her daughter was showing her what it meant to live a life of bravery, courage, and acceptance of who she was. Lupe epitomized all those things. I witnessed her vow to herself that no one would take away her soul again.

She had found power in peace.

In that moment, I knew Brava would be okay.

I didn't see Roberto's wife cry a single tear. I thought perhaps the sadness was too much for her to bear. The anguish was so deep she was unable to feel anything. But that was totally inaccurate.

That man who worked the fields and had the courage to stand for his humanity had changed us all. He changed the country, if only for a moment. Social media posts, tweets, and blogs remembered him and his sacrifice. For a moment, his life meant more than just fodder for debate for television pundits.

He had changed his family forever. He had changed this community forever. His approach of starting small, of being who he was, of doing the work, simply because it was the right thing to do, made us all look at each other differently. His daughter would grow up knowing he stood for something. He took the biggest risk of all to give her the chance at living a life that called exactly to who she was and who she wanted herself to be.

His wife might or might not remarry and move on. But that was the beauty of Roberto's heart. His sacrifice, his will to live, and most of all his courage to dream would open the door for her to do whatever she wanted for herself in a foreign land. In a land that promised so much to them, Roberto had bet, and he had won.

Theresa's daughter, Isabella, sat nestled into Mom. Her little head pushed in between Mom's side and her arm, her feet swung from her chair, trying to seek comfort any way she could and feel the motherly presence she would never feel from Theresa again. But Mom would be there for her as long as she needed. Mom consoled her and took care of her. She was going to fulfill Dad's promise to Theresa to always look over her. It was an extension of family that existed between Carlos and Theresa and was now passed on to his wife and her daughter. This bond would hold them together as a new mother and daughter.

As Mom held onto Isabella's hand, Mom's wedding ring rested on her left ring finger once again. She found acceptance in what had split her and Dad up. She understood why they never signed the divorce papers. Their bond was too deep, their love for each other was too strong. No matter how much they resisted each other, the only way she knew she would find peace in her life was to accept it, just as Carlos had.

They were there for each other forever and always. Mom recognized in Dad, and Dad recognized in Mom, that what they had done for each other was to bring their deepest insecurities to the surface. The more they each tried to run away from them, the less they felt like themselves. In each other, they had found the person in this lifetime who would help them to navigate it all. It might have taken them too long to realize it, or maybe it happened at exactly the right time.

Regardless of timing, they had found peace in each other.

Mom rubbed Isabella's hand as she looked at me. Although she did it for Isabella and for her own comfort, something about it soothed me. Mom's motherly instinct made me realize no matter what I did she would always find a way to comfort me and give me courage.

The task in front of me was proving hardest of all. How was I going to be able to say goodbye to my dad? How was I ever going to thank him?

I had tried for so long to show him I didn't need him. I had done everything to spite him, yet now I felt like I needed him more than ever. I had never been afraid of public speaking or crowds. But I was nervous. My mind was blank. The crowd seemed too big. The weight of it all felt daunting. For such a large part of my life, I was so keen on proving Carlos wrong that I lost sight of who my father was.

Searching for courage and for my voice, I looked away from Mom and saw Dad's casket.

As I looked at it, I caught a reflection of myself.

I was my father's son.

That's what I needed to express to these people. That realization gave me the courage to speak to my father, to speak to this crowd, to honor my father's memory, and to honor his life.

I looked up from the casket and out at the crowd who mourned their community. They had painted over my billboard. Truth is, I was glad to see it go. I didn't want to be that man anymore.

The crowd stood arm in arm, shoulder to shoulder of all colors, ages, and beliefs. I realized what my dad had helped to do.

I took a deep breath and spoke. "Carlos Lopez wanted death. It was a death he resisted, though he knew he needed it. In death, he brought us hope. So did he want death? I think he did. He did because he wanted to see life anew. I can say in those final hours with my dad, he saw the world differently. We all did. Because he saw me. And I saw him. My dad was a cop. He was far from perfect. But he was a man who loved. And it was his love that made me believe truthfully in myself for the first time. He showed me that if there's one thing worth fighting for, it's love. His love made me confront my deepest fears, and his life made me feel safe while I did. I hid my fear so well with anger and self-righteousness, but I knew it was something I didn't have to be afraid of anymore. Carlos Lopez, Dad, showed me that when I love more than I fear, I'm never really alone."

THE END

Acknowledgments

I have to start with my Dad, Mario Estrada. When I first told him about this project, as a former cop, he said, "Son, I may not agree with everything you write in it, but I trust you to write a story that's honest and fair. So write it." On top of the encouragement, my Dad also allowed me to pester him with endless technical policing and legal questions. The stories he shared were invaluable. Most of all, in the way that he loved us and continues to do so, served as the primary driver for this story and its themes.

Next, and of equal importance, is my mom, Martha Estrada. Where Dad was the inspiration and guiding light, Mom was the heartbeat. Her endless encouragement throughout the writing process, willingness to read countless drafts, honest feedback and willingness to share her philosophies had a big impact on making this better. Most of all, she always showed most everyone in our life that the answer to every difficult thing in life is more love for ourselves and one another, served as a primary motivator for this story.

Grandma Dell & Grandma Connie whose endless strength and respective outlooks on the world helped me to understand that real power was in the peace that I live in my heart.

Grandpa Fred & Grandpa Alex I miss them both dearly and am so grateful for all the ways they showed me how to be a perfect combo of leadership, goofiness, strength, and tenderness.

Paul & Cristina, Steph & Johnny, who constantly show me the best time and help me to stay focused on the bigger picture of life. You are all hilarious and I count myself so fortunate to have you as siblings.

Daniella, Ari, Adrian, and Damien who always keep me grounded and remind me that so much of the joy in life is the time I spend with them.

Lauren, Lawrence, Lawrence of Arabia, who was not only the first beta reader, but was also a consistent sounding board for everything between thematics of the book, to character, marketing, and always, and I mean, always there with a swift verbal kick in the ass to get me right. I don't know how I get to the deeper truths of this book without our hundreds of hours of talks about growth and reflection of our respective lives.

Michael Nicklin was, is, and continues to be the greatest friendtor, I could ask for. His willingness to always give me unvarnished truth, focus on my growth, and show me different tools to get to deeper, capital T, truths in myself served as probably one of the biggest themes of this book. You have forever changed my life.

Uncle Gilbert, Chris Plaushin and Jean Jean the Dancing Machine for serving as early beta readers. Your excellent notes and encouragement made this book infinitely better.

My main bros Nick Quincey, Andrew Bencomo, Jona Ward, Drew Fosgard, Brett Smith, Anthony Schiro, Jeff Diamond and super food, super friend, Cale DeTevis. Their consistent ability to speak up, tell me exactly how they see it, and most of all, for all being hysterical human beings, consistently keep me on a balanced path.

My Nino and Nina for taking me to lunch, letting me hang out at their house, calling me to check in, making me laugh, and delivering a verbal kick to the ass when I need it (there's a lot of that going around).

Jennifer Bright, I would not be here without her. Her encouragement to continue down the path to tell the story in a way that wasn't watered down pushed this book to further heights. Her energy, positivity, and "get it done" approach is everything I could have wanted in an editor, publisher, and now, friend.

Long Beach Women's Shelter, my day with them forever changed my life. Thank you to those who shared their stories of survival. Your strength, resilience, and acceptance helped me to understand so much about what it means to be a human being. My time with you made me a fundamentally better man, and a better person.

Ladiarius Williams, whose teachings on the physical embodiment of yin yang through martial arts, consistently kept me centered while writing this book, and helped me to stay focused on the heart and soul of the book.

Lee Toland Krieger who about once a year asked if I'd ever thought about writing a book inspired by my dad's time as a police officer. That nugget catalyzed everything.

Tiffany Boyle whose simple note on the original screenplay of, "can everyone not die at the end?" fundamentally changed the heart and theme of the book for the better.

Nicole Resciniti and Marisa Cleveland thank you for helping to guide the initial process and encouragement along the way.

Brené Brown and Arthur C. Brooks whose work has been instrumental to my understanding of internal peace.

Marcus Aurelius and Lao Tzu, whose words coarse through my veins and the work that I do every day.

Call to Action

This book was independently published. As you may know, independently published books don't have the marketing engine that traditional publishers have. We lean on our readers a bit more than normal to help get the word out about our work.

If the message of the story, resonated with you, I ask that you please share this book with friends, loved ones, and others you think this may be a good read for. A big goal of mine with this book is to encourage all those that read to embrace pain, overcome our personal fears to take deeper accountability for our lives, in order to see one another more fully and with more love. Me personally, I think we can all use it in the world a bit more right now.

To spread the word and dip more into some of the insights behind the book, it's thematics, and it's story, I'd ask that you follow me on Tik Tok (@atestrada22), or Instagram (@anthonyestrada22). Sign up for my newsletter (www. thosewhofearus.com) where I share essays about personal development and growth, information about the book, and stories from people that inspired the characters of this book.

Thank you for taking the time to read and I hope that you enjoyed this book. And whether you choose to sign up & share or not, I hope that you join me in doing our best every day in living with a love first mindset.

About the Author

Anthony Estrada is a Los Angeles-based producer and writer. A native of Southern California, and a third generation Latino, he has been working in the entertainment industry for the past ten years. Most recently, Anthony worked for Nicki Minaj, as part of her growth development team as she expanded her entrepreneurial and creative endeavors across multiple sectors. Prior to his work with Ms. Minaj, Anthony worked as part of the management team for Jennifer Lopez, under media entrepreneur, Benny Medina.

Currently, Estrada is developing the stage musical, *Labor of Love*. He is also dual tracking The Revolutionary Kids as a multi-series set of young adult graphic novels, and a television show, based on a short film he produced and directed.

Estrada continues to pursue projects and opportunities that help develop the influence of Latinos in front of and behind the camera, in the film, television, and non-scripted genres.

Milton Keynes UK
Ingram Content Group UK Ltd.
UKHW010252130324
439347UK00006B/112